# MIRAGE

# MIRAGE

*a novel*

## NAHID RACHLIN

🐓 Red Hen Press | *Pasadena, CA*

Book design by Mark E. Cull.

Library of Congress Cataloging-in-Publication Data

Names: Rachlin, Nahid, author.
Title: Mirage: a novel / Nahid Rachlin.
Description: First edition. | Pasadena, CA: Red Hen Press, 2024.
Identifiers: LCCN 2024006055 (print) | LCCN 2024006056 (ebook) |
ISBN 9781636281148 (paperback) | ISBN 9781636281155 (ebook)
Subjects: LCGFT: Novels.
Classification: LCC PS3568.A244 M57 2024 (print) | LCC PS3568.
A244 (ebook) | DDC 813/.54—dc23/eng/20240213
LC record available at https://lccn.loc.gov/2024006055
LC ebook record available at https://lccn.loc.gov/2024006056

The National Endowment for the Arts, the Los Angeles County Arts Commission, the Ahmanson Foundation, the Dwight Stuart Youth Fund, the Max Factor Family Foundation, the Pasadena Tournament of Roses Foundation, the Pasadena Arts & Culture Commission and the City of Pasadena Cultural Affairs Division, the City of Los Angeles Department of Cultural Affairs, the Audrey & Sydney Irmas Charitable Foundation, the Meta & George Rosenberg Foundation, the Albert and Elaine Borchard Foundation, the Adams Family Foundation, Amazon Literary Partnership, the Sam Francis Foundation, and the Mara W. Breech Foundation partially support Red Hen Press.

   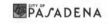 

First Edition
Published by Red Hen Press
www.redhen.org

Printed in Canada

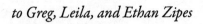

*to Greg, Leila, and Ethan Zipes*

# MIRAGE

"Why are Tala and I identical?" I asked Grandmother.

"God must have made you alike for a reason."

"What reason could it be?"

"Roya joon, don't worry, God is beneficent," she said. After a moment, she added, "So that one could rescue the other in time of trouble or carry on for her if she becomes disabled or dies. Being alike makes all that possible."

# Chapter 1

It was a cool spring day when my identical twin sister Tala and I took the trip that changed the course of our relationship irrevocably.

After periods of ups and downs between us, being pregnant at the same time brought us close to each other again. Though I was the firstborn, coming out of our mother's womb ten minutes earlier than Tala, the milestones of our development were identical. We began to crawl, walk, and talk at the same age, only Tala was a little quieter, shyer, and had periods of unpredictable tantrums and sleeplessness. We got our first and last teeth at the same time.

When we got married, we hoped to get pregnant at the same time, and that happened easily, even though she married a year before me. During the pregnancies, we took daily walks together, compared what our doctors advised us to do, and much else.

On that day, we were taking the one-and-a-half-hour train ride from Tehran to Rey against our husbands' objections. They both thought it was risky to take the rickety train while we were only three weeks from our due dates. Tala, interested in art, wanted us to visit Rey Castle, which was having an exhibition of ancient tapestries for a short time. She didn't want to miss it.

The ride from Tehran to Rey was bumpy and uncomfortable. Our advanced pregnancies didn't help. But Tala did not regret taking the trip. It was important to her to see the exhibition.

After we exited the train, we began to walk toward the castle, keeping to shady spots beside sycamore and acacia trees and tamarisk bushes lining the narrow streets. The passersby clogging the streets were a combination of old-fashioned and modern, women covering their hair with scarves as Tala and I did or wearing dark chadors, and men in jeans and sneakers or suits. Most of the women in chadors were going toward the shrine of Shah Abdol-Azim, a revered Shiite Muslim figure. The shrine's golden dome and blue minarets glittered in the sunlight. Vendors had heaps of merchandise, mainly religious items—*Mohr*, a clay stone to put foreheads on when praying, prayer rugs, rosaries, and some locally made pottery and garments.

We passed a little park where children were running and holding pinwheels up in the air. Scents of flowers—lilac, roses, gardenias—blew toward us.

"Just think, soon, we'll be mothers," Tala said. She sank into herself for a moment and then said, "Anton keeps saying he wants a son."

"You aren't in control of what you're going to have."

"He's unreasonable. It's one thing to favor a son, it's another to demand it."

"You know my problems with Reza are of a different kind. I wish he would stop writing those articles. Sooner or later, he'll be arrested."

"I understand," Tala said in a sympathetic tone.

We had, of course, always talked about our husbands, but since the pregnancies, everything had more significance.

We stopped by a stall, ordered pomegranate juice with crushed ice, and drank it before going on to the castle.

At the booth next to the castle, we bought passes, then went in. The castle was a tall cylindrical stone structure with several levels and a cavernous basement that once was used for storage.

The exhibition was on the fourth level, but we were determined to see it, so we walked up the steep stairways and entered the room. It was filled with visitors, some with their children. A crystal chandelier hung from the ornate ceiling. Tiny bits of cut mirror covered the walls, refracting light in hundreds of directions. A green carpet with bird designs lay on the floor. We paused in front of one tapestry after another, all preserved and restored from years ago. Some of them illustrated the poetry of revered ancient poet Omar Khayyam, the poem written at the bottom—depictions of men and women embracing by a stream or of a man holding a goblet of wine and sipping from it were common themes, all off limits in the present culture.

We paused by one of a deer standing alone in a green pasture, looking back with alert eyes. Below was a poem we recognized:

*To wisely live your life, you don't need to know much*
*Just remember two main rules for the beginning:*
*You better starve than eat whatever*

*And better be alone, than with whoever.*

Tala said in a half-joking tone, "I certainly didn't follow this advice," which I knew was a reference to her marrying Anton.

We were interrupted by the floor shaking and a loud rumble sounding throughout the room. People started screaming.

"Oh, sister, I'm falling," Tala said, grasping my hand. We leaned against the wall, both of us screaming for help. But we were thrust forcefully down into a cavity. It was dark and hard to see others there, but I could hear cries for help, and then Tala's voice, "Roya . . . Roya . . ."

"Yes, Tala, I'm here."

She said something that I couldn't hear.

Sharp pain stabbed at my belly, and I felt liquid trickling down my thighs. Everything around me faded and then went blank. I don't know how much later, I was roused by the shrieking of an ambulance, then I blacked out again.

Where am I, I wondered, opening my eyes to an unfamiliar room—small with white walls, lit by soft fluorescent lights on the ceiling. I felt as if I had been asleep for years and had awoken to a reality I didn't recognize. I was weak and ached all over my body. I closed my eyes, hoping I would wake up in my own bedroom with Reza lying next to me. I drifted back to sleep but was awoken by a voice saying, "Time for your medicine, dear."

A nurse in her white uniform was standing next to me. She raised the bed and put the medicine she was holding on a tray in front of me.

"I am Fereshteh. This is Mohammadi Maternity Hospital," she said. She was young, but her posture was bent as if under a heavy weight.

"The Red Crescent rescue team brought you here three days ago. You slept most of the time. One of us nurses woke you to make sure you ate something."

I didn't remember anyone waking or feeding me.

But I suddenly remembered the shaking, the rumbling, the dark cavity, and the debris covering me. I put my hand on my belly. It was more flat, and there were no feelings of movement inside of it. "Where is my baby?" I asked.

Suddenly, I saw images of a baby lying beside me in a ray of sunlight skipping into the darkness of the cavity and Tala lying a little further away with a baby next to her.

"Where is my baby?" I asked again, alarmed.

"Take the pills first, I'll explain," the nurse said in a gentle tone, her soft brown eyes reflecting sympathy. She gave me four pills with water. "The yellow pills are painkillers, the orange ones, sedatives."

I took the pills with the water and looked at her, waiting anxiously for her to say more.

"Your baby boy was taken away by God. His soul rests in heaven," she said.

"Taken away?" I stammered.

"The rescue workers informed us and your husband that your baby was lying next to you with his umbilical cord severed," she said in a sad, slow way. "He wasn't breathing. It's lucky you had only minor injuries, nothing serious."

"My baby, dead," I lamented, choking on my words. After a moment I managed to ask, "Is my sister here?"

"We sent her home earlier this morning, but her baby is in Julia Clinic. It has better facilities for children than we do here."

I had to concentrate hard to absorb what she was saying.

She went on, "Your sister's baby, a boy too, isn't seriously hurt. He had some minor injuries. He just needs protection for a week or two. You and your sister look so alike, it's amazing. I'll get your breakfast."

She pointed to a button on the headboard. "Ring that bell if you need anything," she said and left the room.

A window across from the bed was covered by a thick black curtain, letting in no light. Another overlooked a courtyard, and I could see the top of some trees. I was hurting and closed my eyes. Was this real? Had I miscarried? Lost the baby? Tala's baby had survived. The burden of my feelings, jumbled and contradictory, was too heavy, and it pushed me to sleep. But I fell into nightmares that I forgot upon awakening. Except for one.

In that nightmare, I was holding my baby in my arms and cooing to him, "Oh, my baby, my sweet baby?" He slipped out of my arms and fell on hard ground. He began to cry, his wrinkled skin going red, then he became still. Silent. I screamed, help, help, but no one heard me, or maybe worse, no one wanted to come to my aid.

After the nightmare, I couldn't go back to sleep. I lay there, my mind drifting to other moments, days.

I thought of that night, not long ago, when I lay next to Reza in bed and he touched my belly and said, "I feel our baby." In the moonlight coming through the small window of our bedroom, I could see bumps on my stomach created by the baby's hands and feet.

After we found out I was pregnant, Reza started spending much more time than usual at home. He brought me flowers, took me to my favorite restaurants—whenever we could afford it. How devastated he must be now, how angry that I went to Rey against his advice.

Fereshteh returned, holding a tray with my breakfast, which she put down on the side table.

"I'm not hungry," I said.

"You can eat later."

"Has my husband been here?"

"Yes, a few times, but you were sleeping, and we didn't want to wake you. I am going to take you to Dr. Akbari's office for examination," she said and helped me get up.

"Do you have any numbness in your legs or arms?" she asked as she led me to the door.

"My arms and the sides of my body hurt."

"That is due to the impact of the fall, but luckily nothing is broken."

We went through a corridor with white walls and pale fluorescent lights and then to another corridor with its lights off, except one that glowed at the top of the exit door. A woman was talking on the black telephone that hung on the wall next to the nurses' station. Another woman prowled around, wailing, "Oh, my baby girl, my baby girl. Oh Allah, the Merciful and Beneficent, help me die too." Her sad voice echoed and then faded.

Dr. Akbari, a gray-haired, middle-aged man, was standing in his office, holding a stethoscope. "How do you feel?" he asked.

"Not good."

"Of course, this is very difficult to take. They should have closed the castle until they had it repaired. Very irresponsible. It was damaged years ago when war was going on and they never did anything to make it safe."

"We didn't know," I mumbled.

With Fereshteh's help, I lay on the examination table. Dr. Akbari began to tap me here and there, listening with the stethoscope.

"Can you walk a little for me? I'll help you off the table."

I did what he asked.

"No sign of nerve damage," he said. "Most likely, you'll be going home tomorrow. You and your sister are among the lucky ones."

Lucky ones? I lost my baby, I thought bitterly. Only Tala was lucky.

Fereshteh took me to my room and helped me to bed. "Try to eat your breakfast."

"I can't eat now."

"Okay, dear, eat it when you feel like it. Ring and I'll bring it back. Your husband will be here tomorrow to take you home."

She picked up the tray and left.

## Chapter 2

The following day, Reza came into my hospital room, holding a canvas bag. He put it down on the floor, leaned over, and kissed me.

"How do you feel?" he asked, obviously controlling his sadness and maybe his anger at me for going to the castle.

I just could get out the words, "I'm sorry."

"I brought your clothes. I'm taking you home."

He helped me get out of bed and dress.

I wanted to ask, "Will you forgive me?" but the words got caught in my throat and I could not articulate them.

On the way out of the hospital, we stopped by the nurses' station and found Fereshteh sitting behind a desk. In a kind voice she said to Reza, "Replace the bandages once a day." Then, turning to me, she said, "Come back here in a week. Dr. Akbari will be in all day. You don't need an appointment." We both thanked her and left.

Outside, I realized this was the clinic that Tala and I didn't want to give birth in because it hadn't yet caught up with more recently built hospitals with better equipment and doctors. Its facade was gloomy—the brick walls were covered by soot, and the windows overlooked dark alleys and dismal courtyards. Part of it was closed off for repairs, as so many places still were years after the war with Iraq. Due to neglect in repairing the old castle, I had lost my baby. I couldn't stop my next thought: I had given in to Tala's pressure to go to the castle.

Reza took my arm and led me into a taxi. Soon we were in the midst of the hectic Tehran traffic. Drivers with old Paykans or Mercedes diesel trucks, many of them with dented sides, raced through the streets, not pausing at red lights, shouting curses at each other, honking their horns impatiently. Motorcycles and bicycles zigzagged through the cars. Pedestrians rushed to their destinations, scurrying through the moving traffic, slowing it down.

The taxi driver turned on his car radio. A male voice came on, saying, *There is only one God, Allah, and his prophet is Mohammad,* an introduction often used before an announcement. Then the announcer said, *The number of deaths at Rey Castle's collapse is inconclusive . . .*

The driver turned off the radio. "More bad news every day," he mumbled.

We were approaching Goo Alley, where our apartment was. We got out by the pharmacy on the wide Jamaly Avenue, and Reza filled the prescriptions Dr. Akbari had given—a painkiller, antibiotics, and a tranquilizer.

As we entered our alley, the smell of tobacco from water pipes, mingling with mint and cinnamon tea, came out of the Ramadan Teahouse. Khasem, the owner, was standing by the door, watching the customers coming and going, their footsteps sounding loud on the cobblestone ground.

"Everything Allah has created is for the good of humanity. There's a purpose for what is ugly and what may appear disastrous," Khasem said to no one in particular. The gold covering his front teeth, a display of prosperity, gleamed in the sunlight. Was losing my baby good for me? I thought, outraged at what he said.

The outside door to the two-story house where we were renting an apartment was open, and we walked in. The courtyard was quiet except for the stray cat mewing yearningly as it sat by the pool and stared at the goldfish floating in it. Reza held my hand, and we climbed up the stone steps, chipped at their edges, and entered the corridor on the second floor. With relief, I noticed that the door of the only other apartment on the floor was shut. Its tenants, a middle-aged man and his much younger wife, were conservative Shiite Muslims. They would perhaps report Reza if they knew he wrote under a pseudonym for an underground newspaper critical of many beliefs and practices in our culture. Hossein, the publisher of Reza's newspaper, had inherited a sum of money from his grandfather; instead of spending it on himself, he founded a newspaper. Aware of social injustice and superstitions of all kinds, he made it his mission to awaken people. He kept the entire production hidden; otherwise, he would be arrested. The paper was distributed by members of the staff, including Reza, who left piles of them in the hallways of university buildings so that they could reach young people. The secrecy made it necessary for Reza and me to keep a distance from the tenants. The husband, Payman, had a lithography business, mainly making posters of ayatollahs. Rumor was that he was among the young students who stormed the American Embassy in 1979, taking the American staff hostage. Before the Revolution, he made posters of the shah.

In our apartment, Reza tucked me in bed like a child. He gave me two of the pills he got from the pharmacy with a glass of water. Then he left the room to make lunch. I looked at my face in the mirror on the wall across from the bed. Four gauze pads covered wounds on my forehead and cheeks. Oddly, I liked seeing the external reflection of the psychological pain I was feeling.

When I was pregnant, Reza had divided the room with a large wooden screen so that the baby would have its own space. Then he painted the apartment, making the baby's area pistachio, ours linen white, and the living room pale blue. The kitchenette's and bathroom' walls and floors were covered by blue tiles.

His four sisters, three of whom had several children, were able to provide us with baby furniture—a crib, a chest—that their children outgrew. The freshness of the apartment and the baby moving around in my belly had filled Reza and me with gaiety and excited anticipation. We thought of names. We settled on Shadi for a girl, and Salim for a boy, both meaning happy and safe.

Our part of the room had enough space for the brass bed, the wooden wardrobe, and the small rug with a pattern of flowers and cypress trees that once belonged to my grandmother.

On the mantel stood our wedding photograph. Reza was wearing a navy suit with a red geranium in its lapel. I had on a white dress with blue, green, lavender, and red sequins around its neckline that my Uncle Ahmad, who owned a sequin shop, made for me. I was wearing gold filigree earrings and a matching bracelet and necklace, presents from Reza's sisters. Reza had his arm around my waist, and we were looking into each other's eyes, him with the same thoughtful expression he still possessed.

Next to the wedding picture was a photograph of Tala and me together when we were five years old. Our hair was the same length, to the napes of our necks, and parted in the middle. We were wearing blue dresses with belts tied in front, one of the belts white, the other dark blue—what Mum had wanted so that she could distinguish which one of us was Tala and which Roya. There were very minor differences, barely noticeable, between us. Looking closely in bright light, you might have seen a few green pigmentations in Tala's brown eyes, whereas mine were just brown. We had the same shade of light brown hair, but again, you might notice a few strands of gold in hers. Those small differences weren't visible in the photograph, and it was impossible to tell us apart except for the different colors of the belts. I only knew I was the one with the white belt because, on the back of the photograph, Mum had written our names and identified us by the colors of our belts. I thought about how Tala and I used to look in the mirror and ask each other, "Who is me, and who is you?"

As soon as Mum found out she was pregnant with twin girls, she, with Baba's help, had to quickly shop for an extra crib and more clothes and select another name for the second baby. They called the unexpected child Tala (gold), because of the few strands of gold in her hair. They chose the name Roya (dream) for me because Mum saw something dreamy in the expression on my face. She herself had been a dreamer. Growing up in Olivera, a small town in Argentina, Mum dreamt of a future different from that of girls around her. In the evenings while the girls went out to bars and clubs and hung out with boys, she stayed home and studied. While most of her friends married before finishing college, she went to the US on a scholarship, finished college, and got a master's degree in linguistics. She met Baba, who had also gone to the US to study, in one of their classes. Mum told us that when we were babies, she and Baba did tandem feeding; Baba would hold one baby while the other sucked on one breast. Then Baba would take that baby away and put the other one at the other breast.

Mum's pleasure with us was captured in the photographs of her holding us in each arm and looking at us with an expression of delight on her face. In spite of all the pressure from the old-fashioned family members about the importance of having a son, she and Baba decided against more children. They wanted to devote themselves to us, provide us with the best.

Alas, we lost her when we were ten years old and then lost Baba when we were nineteen. Grandmother, who moved in with us after Mum died, passed away a few months before I got married. They weren't here now to comfort me.

Under the burden of pain in both my body and mind, I drifted to sleep, though it was still daytime and light was pouring into the room from the window facing the courtyard.

# Chapter 3

Days went by, and other than a follow-up visit to the doctor at Mohammadi Maternity Hospital, I mostly rested in bed. My mind kept going to Tala. Why hadn't she called me?

One afternoon, I got out of bed with difficulty, went to the phone in the living room, and dialed her number.

"Can I speak to Tala?" I asked Batul, their maid, who answered the phone.

"I'm sorry, she's resting," she said.

"How is the baby?"

"Doing well. We'll be bringing him home tomorrow."

"Please tell my sister to call me when she gets up."

"I will, *khanoom*."

I went back to bed and kept thinking of Tala not calling. We had been best friends and confidants since childhood. This was a deviation from that, and it threw me into an abyss. Finally, I drifted to sleep. I was awoken by the murmur of conversation, a baby crying, cats fighting, and a scratchy record playing a song full of expressions of lamentation and loss coming through the window that opened into the courtyard.

The sound of our phone ringing rose above all the rest. I thought it must be Tala. But then I heard Reza talking on the phone, seemingly with his best friend, Abbas, judging by their complaints—among them, the city mayor having left many monuments, including Rey Castle, unrepaired, leading to the tragic injuries and losses.

After he got off the phone, he came to the bedroom to check on me. I burst out with what was upsetting me. "Tala hasn't called since the accident. She had her baby and I lost mine. She should at least try to comfort me."

"She's probably resting. Needs to recover. I know how you feel about losing our baby. I feel the same loss. But we have to be strong and hope for you to get pregnant again."

"It doesn't take much to talk for a few minutes on the phone. I get the feeling she's avoiding me."

"Roya, you're a grown woman now. Behave the way your sister wants you to behave."

"How is that?" I asked.

"She wants you to leave her alone, at least for now."

To soften this blunt remark, he said, "She's the darker side of you, not easy to understand."

I thought of Grandmother saying to me, "Your sister has a sly side, keeps things to herself. When you were infants, she would lie quietly in her crib, staring for long stretches at the ceiling, while you kicked and babbled." But then she added affectionately, "I love both of you."

She understood the range of emotions that connected me to Tala. Because of that, her remark about Tala being sly didn't upset me the way Reza's criticism of her did, even now that I was feeling hurt by her.

I tried to change the subject. "I shouldn't have gone to Rey."

"You let Tala influence you," he said. Then, to lighten our conversation, he went on in a joking tone, "If Tala and I were in danger of drowning, who would you try to save first?"

"I'm not a good enough swimmer or strong enough to save either of you," I said in the same light tone. "I'd scream for help."

"Who would you tell the lifeguard to save first?"

"Don't ask silly questions," I said. Then I thought maybe the questions were valid. Saving Tala would be like saving myself from drowning, we were so deeply connected. I love Reza, but he isn't me; his image doesn't reflect my image. But would I save her or Reza? In my hazy state of mind, I couldn't possibly answer that question.

Reza left the room and I lay in bed, feeling bitter and upset. My eyes went to the oil painting on the wall that Tala had made for me. It was of two young girls sitting under a wild sumac tree by a stream. The girls looked identical but had no resemblance to Tala and me. One of them was leaning over the water, her long hair flowing down. "That woman is trying to fall in and drown," Tala had told me, something that saddened me but also made me want the painting, as if by possessing it, I could somehow prevent the drowning.

I drifted back to sleep. But I was plagued by nightmares.

*. . . I was just born, and the polluted air of the city had seeped into my hospital crib, making me cough. Another baby in a crib adjacent to mine started talking to me in a language I didn't understand. Everything around me was white. A large nipple dangled from the ceiling above the crib, but it kept moving higher when I tried to suck on it. Then I was no longer a baby in a crib but a grown woman looking out of a window overlooking an alley. Tala was standing under the streetlight, looking up at the window.*

*I picked up the pot of flowers sitting on the windowsill and threw it at her head. She fell down, and blood flowed out of her mouth and head. I screamed, I killed her, I killed my twin . . .*

I woke, my heart pounding painfully. I couldn't go back to sleep. My mind kept going around and around to Tala's withdrawal from me. During our pregnancies, we had talked so much about giving birth and being mothers; now, it was just days of no talking, no contact.

I went through a list of reasons she could have for her avoiding me. She feels such intense pity for me that she can't bear being with me; she believes I'm envious of her and wants to separate herself from me so that she can feel the joy of having her son without guilt; Anton has told her not to see me.

I thought of that spring day, not long before the collapse of Rey Castle, when Tala and I went to Mellat Park, where we thought we would bring our babies in strollers. On the way, we looked at children's clothing stores, occasionally going inside.

In the park, we sat on a bench shaded by a row of acacia trees.

Children were trying to float paper boats on the lake at the center of the park. Mothers went by with their babies in strollers.

Tala sank into herself for a moment and then said, "Anton is so jealous of my closeness to you. Sometimes I don't tell him I'm with you."

"Reza has moments of jealousy too, but I can reason with him."

"It's not easy to do that with Anton."

"Dr. Pishva says when I feel labor pains, I should breathe deeply, close my eyes, and count," I told Tala. We went to different obstetricians. Anton wanted Tala to go to one his friends had recommended. Reza wanted me to go to the one his sisters used.

"We have to try not to look graceless like so many pregnant women," Tala said.

So far, we had managed not to gain too much weight and to keep up with our appearances.

In quiet tones, we began to talk in detail about the times we could have conceived, which type of lovemaking it had been. She guessed it was when Anton had been gentle, otherwise, she would have withdrawn from him before his semen flowed inside her. I said that Reza was always gentle, so it could have been at any time.

Talking so intimately took me back to our childhood when we often moved to one of our beds and talked in our exclusive language.

More people, mainly mothers with their children, began to arrive at the park, some sitting on benches near us, so we stopped talking. Mothers watched their children play. Two little boys rushed to the lawn in the center of the park and began to do somersaults, laughing gaily.

"I chose the name Tavoos and Anton went along with it," Tala said.

I understood why Tala liked the name—it meant peacock. The beautiful colors of the peacock's feathers were representative of the kaleidoscopic arts of Iran.

"What if you have a girl?"

"Anton doesn't want to think about it."

"Reza and I picked names for a girl or a boy."

"I only saw Anton alone a few times before we were married. Not enough to get to know him." In a near whisper, she went on, "Once when we were having sex, Anton said, 'You'd better not waste this. I want you to produce a boy. I could have just as much fun with a prostitute.'"

"You can't just will yourself to have a boy!" I said, cringing at Anton's language.

"He's already thinking of our son becoming prime minister. Amniocentesis is available now at the Russian hospital, but it isn't easy to set up an appointment. Anyway, it's supposed to be somewhat risky, and Anton decided against it. Good thing, or I'm afraid he'd have forced me to get an abortion if I was pregnant with a girl."

"Maybe he'll learn to love her if you have a girl."

"I don't know. I can't predict him."

At the beginning of her marriage, she had been amazed and delighted by the change from the life we had been raised in. "I can't believe I have been transitioned to a house, a neighborhood I never believed was within my reach."

But that feeling, and the perceived romance between her and Anton, was quickly unraveling. It took a short time of living with him for the change to happen. "I was thoughtless, misguided," she said.

Two women, one of them holding a large notebook, came over to us.

"We're collecting signatures for a petition to equalize the law for men and women," the one with the notebook said. "Don't worry, we aren't doing anything against the government."

Tala and I signed. The woman looked back and forth at Tala and then at me.

"Two signatures for one person," I said jokingly. She smiled and walked away.

A group of young girls came and sat on a bench next to ours, talking among themselves, oblivious to us. They were concerned that something was going to explode any day now. The black market offering liquor and foreign videos and satellite TV showing foreign channels could all be discovered by government spies and stopped.

On that day, I was still feeling totally connected to Tala. After leaving the park, we walked to her house so she could show me the room she and Anton had set up for the baby. Her neighborhood was like a different city from the one I lived in. The late shah had once resided in this area in a palace complex, and some of the luxury was still apparent in the glitzy shops and restaurants and large, well-kept houses. Being at the foot of the Alborz Mountains, the air was free from smog and was much cooler than in my neighborhood. Late-model European cars went by, rather than the old Paykans that clogged the streets of my neighborhood. Women wore colorful silk scarves and tight-fitting pants and jackets instead of the standard dark *rupushes* and scarves or the alternative, chadors. Tala blended in with them in her way of dressing since she got married, buying her clothes at the Palladium Mall, which carried items far more expensive than what the average family, including mine, could afford. She barely covered her hair, wearing a colorful scarf halfway over her head, something she could get away with in her neighborhood but I couldn't in the old neighborhood that I lived in, not by choice, but because the low rent was all we could afford. We entered the tucked away Fadai Street, where her house was located. Her house combined traditional and European features. Trees showed above the walls of its courtyard. Two large stone lions kneeled on each side of the massive wooden filigreed entrance door. We went into the courtyard with its flowerbeds, shady trees, benches to sit on, and paths to walk on. Then we went up the marble stairway, flanked with potted plants, leading to the living room. She took me to the second floor, where the baby's room and her and Anton's bedroom were. Even though she told me Anton wanted a boy, I was still surprised that the baby's room was decorated and furnished to be appropriate for a boy. Everything was in shades of blue—the crib, the rug, the walls. A lion and a tiger were painted on the sides of the crib.

We went back to the living room with the floor-to-ceiling window revealing a vast view of the Alborz Mountains. Since the last time I was in her house, she had redecorated the room with light Scandinavian furniture, duplicating Mum's taste, replacing the dark, ornate Italian items that were there before. The new pale green color of the walls matched one of the rug's rectangular patterns with striking effect. The color also enhanced Tala's own two landscape paintings that were hanging on the wall. After she took her manteau off, I noticed she had on a blue dress with white polka dots I had seen on display in the boutique recently opened on Vali Asr Avenue, which carried clothes by American and European designers.

Noticing my gaze on her dress, she said, "Let me buy you one."

I shook my head no. She had offered a few times to buy me dresses or handbags and other items. I always said no. I knew Reza wouldn't approve of it. He had said already, "She's trying to buy your love." As an afterthought, he added, "It's her way of feeling superior to you."

I came out of my thoughts to Tala's voice saying, "Anton frightens me. He gets into a rage over nothing. He accuses me of being unfeeling, 'a piece of wood.'"

"Are you that way with him?"

"Sometimes I freeze up when he touches me." In a barely audible voice, as if talking to herself, she added, "He got me out of . . ." She stopped. I knew she meant out of our neighborhood, out of the deprivation we felt.

Our father's income as a professor and Mum's work translating Spanish into Farsi didn't allow for a luxurious life.

It was getting dark, and I got up to leave. We made a date to go to the park again in a few days. Outside, when I reached the main avenue, a bus was coming, and I got in. Looking out of the window as the bus approached the neighborhood where Reza and I lived, I was keenly aware of how the streets became more run-down, the air more smog-ridden. On Khanat Abad Avenue, most of the women were wearing dark chadors. I pulled up my scarf so that all my hair was covered.

I couldn't help feeling a twinge of envy for Tala.

# Chapter 4

Still preoccupied with Tala's withdrawal from me since the fall in the cavity, I wondered if she was trying to separate herself from me so that she could have Tavoos to herself and avoid sharing him with me. As we were growing up, she had attempted to separate herself from me at different times, for different reasons.

No matter what was happening in the present, our past, so interwoven, couldn't fade, be forgotten. Some memories were obscured by the passage of time, others were nearly dead, and a few were glaringly bright as if sunlight was shining on them.

Our interdependency was apparent as soon as we came into this world. We cried when one of us was taken out of the room. We babbled to each other, with me initiating the sounds and then the words and her imitating them or forming some in response. Until we were six years old, we slept in the same room, first in cribs, and then in beds next to each other. We distorted the Farsi language so that others could not enter our sphere. Sometimes we communicated silently by just looking at each other without uttering a word.

We were miracles of creation, Mum said, as people in her hometown in Argentina said about identical twins. She took many photographs of us, keeping them in albums or framing them and putting them on side tables. In some of these photos we were intertwined, one of us sitting on the top of the other, or our legs and arms tangled together. It was as if we thought we were still connected to each other in Mum's womb. She dressed us alike with some small differences, one having a fuller skirt than the other or wearing a different color belt so that she could quickly tell us apart. She loved us but was also fascinated by us. Everything we did drew praise from her or amazed her. She told us that when we were just a month or so old, as we lay in our separate cribs, we communicated with each other silently. If one of us raised a hand and waved it in the air, so did the other. We cried, one after another. When we were a little older, we spoke to each other, using words that seemed private to us.

Baba, with his mind occupied by his philosophical thoughts and theories, still lavished attention on us.

As much as Baba, Mum, and Grandma focused on us, Tala and I still stayed in our own world. But as we grew older, at times that closeness was burdensome to Tala; she rebelled against being indistinguishable from me to others. Once, when we were playing in the hollow of the ancient tree in our house's courtyard, she said, "I'm going to get my new doll," and dashed out. After waiting for what seemed like an eternity but was probably only a few minutes, I went looking for her. I finally found her hiding in the living room's closet. She came out and said, "I was playing hide-and-seek." There was a glint of something like hate in her eyes before it gave way to playfulness. Then she started to run from room to room, and I chased her.

Another time, when we were older, we went to the public bath for relaxation.

"I want to get my ears pierced and wear earrings so that people can tell us apart," she said. We were sitting in the steamy room, at a distance from the grown women, some of whom were being washed and massaged by *dalaks*. "Don't you hate it that someone looking like you is always following you, that people call you Tala by mistake? I hate it when they call me Roya."

"No," I said, "I like that I have someone just like me. We're each stronger that way."

"But we're two," Tala said. "The egg split."

"Maybe we can be put back together, like when Baba glued the broken pieces of the ceramic bowl," I said in a jesting tone, but that only made her sink into silence.

The *dalak* who pierced ears was still on the premises. She took Tala to a special room. When they came out, Tala's ears were pierced and had temporary gold in them, put there by the *dalak*.

"Now people will be able to tell us apart," Tala said. But a few moments later, she was regretful. "You should get your ears pierced too."

So the same *dalak* pierced my ears and put in temporary gold, identical to Tala's.

When we returned home, we showed our ears to Baba and Mum.

"You can get an infection, you know," Baba said. "Those public baths aren't sanitary."

Mum agreed.

"We won't go there anymore," I said, and Tala repeated it.

Not long after that, Tala felt oppressed by our similarity again. "Let me cut your hair short, and I'll keep mine long," she said.

I gave in to her and she took the sharp scissors from a drawer in the kitchen, and we went into the bathroom. She began to cut the locks at the bottom of my hair. The brown curls lay on the tiled floor like feathers. Then we stood in front of the tall mirror on the back of the door and studied ourselves.

"It's so strange to see you with short hair," Tala lamented as if that hadn't been her idea. "Here, cut my hair." She gave me the scissors.

I cut her hair so that it was the same length as mine. Our hair, fallen on the floor, mingled together. She picked it up and put it in the garbage can.

Then she began to hum something she seemed to have made up and practiced to herself, *There is no such a thing as mirror image, when one is looking at oneself in the mirror . . . the only way to separate is to hide.*

She made other attempts to be able to stand on her own, separate from me. After Mum died, she stopped talking to me in Spanish as we occasionally did. Her lack of interest in the language and in the written word, instead appreciating art, was perhaps another way for her to build her own character, different from mine.

Before her wedding, after the brief time she spent with Anton in the living room, she came over to me and we talked. What stayed with me from that conversation is her telling me, "Love doesn't survive without keeping a part of yourself hidden."

"What are you hiding from him?"

She shrugged. "Oh, just general things."

I wondered now, is she hiding things from me too so that I wouldn't condemn her and would continue loving her? It seemed she had disappeared behind a dark curtain, where her reflection was blank to me.

Then, as if the curtain were pushed aside, I recalled in vivid detail one of her betrayals and her attempt to hide it until she felt burdened by the secrecy.

We were in the second semester of our freshman year at Al Zahra University for Women. Entering through the forbidding iron gate of Al Zahra, we felt apprehensive that something terrible had happened or was about to happen inside, as it often did. Teachers were fired for not observing classroom protocol—neglecting to preface their lecture with *In the name of Allah* or using texts that had words like *navel* or *naked* in them. Students, too, had been expelled because they were caught meeting boys secretly or for wearing lipstick and nail polish in public. The *Basij*, appointed by the government to spy on people and catch them if they violated the "moral rules of conduct," were more visible in this conservative university. They didn't wear uniforms, but the male *basiji* wore beards and loose-fitting shirts that fell untucked over their pants. Women members of the *Basij* were usually covered in head-to-toe black chadors.

There were private universities that weren't so conservative, but our father couldn't afford tuition for two children, and we had scholarships at Al Zahra that we weren't awarded at the other universities we applied to. So that was our only choice.

But something different was awaiting us on that day, something far more interesting and enlivening, that pushed us toward disobeying the rules. Our biology professor was late, and as we waited in the classroom, with its cinderblock walls, I glanced out of the window at the lemon-colored April sunlight and wished we could get out of the room. When would someone come in and dismiss us? Then, another professor who taught history walked in with a young foreign-looking man. She introduced him as Henry Wallace and told us he'd be giving us a special lecture, that he was a floating substitute.

Henry Wallace was obviously foreign, judging not just by his name, but also by his coloring, blue eyes, curly blond hair, and the way he spoke Farsi with an accent.

He seemed to be only four or five years older than us. His voice was lively, without the dogmatic drawl of most of our professors. He talked a little about himself—startling since our professors were dry and distant and rarely ever revealed anything personal. His father was English, he said, and his mother Iranian; he was interested in studying film and was going to the School of Dramatic Arts.

He began his lecture by talking about the extinction of many animals, often due to climate change. Then he went on to talk about how plants and animals benefit each other. For instance, flowering plants rely on bees and hummingbirds to pollinate them, while animals eat plants and sometimes make homes in them. When animals die and decompose, they enrich the soil with nitrates that stimulate plant growth.

After his lecture was over, he said, "I'm happy to answer questions."

But no one asked any. We'd rarely been asked for questions before.

When the session ended, as Tala and I were passing him, he looked at us intently and said, "I thought it was an illusion. You're so alike, it's amazing. Identical flowers."

Tala and I smiled and walked out of the room.

The following week, to our delight, again Henry substituted for our usual professor. The focus of his lecture was more or less the same as the previous one.

At the end of the session when Tala and I left the classroom, Henry caught up with us in the middle of the yard. "I'm enchanted by your alikeness. You're so cinematic," he said with a smile. "I want to invite you to Gina Café one day."

Tala and I looked at each other. What did this invitation mean? I could tell from Tala's expression that she wanted to accept. I felt the same way.

"We'll come," I said.

"How about next Wednesday after your classes? In case you haven't been to Gina Café, it is on Gholestan Alley, branching out from the main street. I will be waiting for you," he said, looking surprised at our easy acceptance of his invitation.

The truth was, Tala and I were craving any stimulation. As we walked to our next class, she said, "He is a refreshing change from the other professors."

"Yes. If someone sees us with him at the café, we'll say we had questions to ask Henry about what he lectured," I said, set on carrying out the plan.

Tala and I kept talking about the date we had set with Henry, wondering what he really was like, what he wanted from us, and if we were taking a chance meeting him. But still, we were determined to meet him. Coming home an hour or so late didn't raise questions from Baba and Grandmother. Sometimes we stayed to participate in special lectures after the last class ended.

## Chapter 5

My thoughts were interrupted by the phone ringing again, but it stopped before I picked it up. On Wednesday, before leaving for school, we paid extra attention to our appearances, wearing the lightest color *rupushes* and headscarves we had. We practiced letting our scarves slip down a little, just enough to get away with it.

After our last classes, we immediately left for the café, which was about ten blocks away. As we walked, we kept wondering if it was a bad idea to meet him; what if one of the students or teachers happened to be there? But almost as if we were out of control, we continued walking.

When we arrived at the café, we looked at people sitting at different tables, trying to see if we could identify anyone from school. But we didn't see anyone we knew. Then we saw Henry sitting in the café's garden under the shade of a large sycamore tree, looking at a notebook. He was the only one in the garden, and we went there to join him. He got up and pulled out two chairs for us at his table.

A waiter came over and Henry ordered their specialty pastries, zoolbia and bamieh, and a pot of black tea for the three of us. The waiter brought them promptly and arranged them on the table.

"How do you like your school?" he asked.

Tala and I exchanged a glance. "We don't like it," I said. "So many restrictions, so many dull lectures."

"Of course, I understand." He told us more about himself. He worked part-time at the Ministry of Culture and studied part-time at the School of Dramatic Arts. "Imagination is everything to me," he said. Looking from one of us to another, he asked, "What are you interested in?"

"I like art," Tala said.

"I like languages and writing," I said.

Then he asked us about our family life. I told him we lost our mother but had our father and our grandmother who moved in with us after Mum passed away.

"Oh, I'm so sorry about your mum passing. It must be very difficult."

"Yes," I said, and Tala nodded in agreement.

He told us his father was English and his mother Iranian. They lived separately now, his father living in London and his mother in Tehran. His mother didn't want to get a divorce because she was a Catholic.

We talked a little longer until it began to get dark. "We have to leave now," I said.

Tala nodded in agreement.

I got up and Tala did the same.

We offered to pay our shares, but Henry said it was nothing, and he put down cash on the table.

He followed us outside and said, "Will I see you two again?"

"You know how difficult that is," I said.

"I understand," he said.

We said goodbye without making another date.

"It's flattering that he likes us," Tala said as we walked home.

"I think he likes you more," I said, without proof, only to flatter Tala.

"No, he was more interested in you, but he was covering it up."

I laughed. "I don't think he'd go through the trouble to cover up. He hardly knows us. It doesn't matter anyway. We aren't going to see him again. We shouldn't."

My thoughts were interrupted by the phone ringing. Reza had left the apartment, it seemed. I got up and picked up the phone. There was no caller ID; it could be Tala calling. Anton didn't want a caller ID on their landline, he had told her, because sometimes he wanted to be anonymous when he called a certain place or person. She didn't have a cell phone, though now all the young people who could afford it had one. He didn't want her to have a phone independent of his.

I said to the silence, "Tala, is that you?"

Whoever it was hung up the phone, leaving my heart pounding even harder than from the tension the memory of Henry evoked.

As soon as I lay down again, my mind traveled back to Henry.

The following week after we met him in the café, I was walking across the campus with Tala, and there was Henry coming in our direction. "I'm showing a documentary to a group of your professors today," he said.

"Tala." It was Miss Nezami, the art professor, calling. "Will you come to my office for a moment? I want you to help me carry some paintings to the classroom." Tala reluctantly walked away to Miss Nezami's office.

"Will you meet me in the park one day? Park-e Jamshidiyeh?" Henry asked when I was alone with him.

I blushed and said nothing.

"I'll wait for you in Park-e Jamshidiyeh on Thursday at 12:30, during your lunch recess. I hope you'll come."

His smile was so alluring that my resistance was melted. "I'll try to come," I said, still hesitant. As I walked to class, I thought about how I would meet him. Our lunch recess started at twelve and ended at two thirty. I could go and see him without cutting classes. And I knew the park, at the foot of Alborz Mountains, wasn't carefully patrolled.

"I knew he liked you more than me," Tala said later in the day when I told her about the invitation.

"I don't know . . . it just happened that I was the one alone with him."

"Meet him and then tell me all about it,"

Tala encouraging me to meet him made me more daring, and Henry didn't appear to be a flame that would burn me—which was what we were warned against all our lives. He was from another world; his coloring, and his accent, made him different from most men around us.

On Thursday, just before lunch recess, I went into the school's bathroom and studied myself in the mirror. Tala followed me in. "Don't worry," she said. "You look good."

Sima and Zizi, more daring than the other girls, were in the bathroom, too, talking about where to buy the sexiest lingerie, the best makeup and perfume. I knew they indulged in secret dates, had kissed boys. I had heard them say in whispers, but audibly enough, "His lips on mine sent a thrill through me," and, "He tasted my lips like candies."

Sima suddenly focused on Tala and me. "You two can pretend you're each other. You're standing in front of me, and I can't tell you apart."

I laughed, but her comment made me wonder if I was right to assume Henry asked me because I was the one alone with him in the yard after Tala went to Miss Nezami's office—that Tala and I were indistinguishable to him. The thought pained me, made me hesitant to meet him.

A little later when Tala and I were alone together, she said, "Don't be afraid. It's good to break the rules once in a while, not to be enslaved to them."

Always influenced by Tala, I found the courage to go and meet Henry. The park was uncrowded and serene. A shallow pool stood in its center with a fountain splashing water into the air and a cluster of smaller fountains gurgling around it. I spotted Henry on a bench; he was writing in a notebook and smoking a cigarette.

"You're here!" he said, getting up. "I was hoping you'd come. Why don't we walk to Pascalu Café; it is practically hidden in an alley. We can walk there separately. You just follow me."

I followed him at a distance until he reached the burgundy door of Pascalu Café, on a street otherwise lined by empty lots. The café's main area was oblong and had a high ceiling. It was furnished with sleek dark wood and leather upholstery against stark white walls. The lighting was low, and Turkish music played in the background. Young couples were sitting at different tables.

"I'll order cocktails for us, and their famous Turkish yogurt dumplings, would you like that?"

I hesitated. He leaned over the table toward me. "Don't worry, they call them cocktails, but they don't have alcohol in them."

The drink tasted of red berries, honey, and mint. What does Henry want from me, I wondered. Romance? Quick sex? And why was I here? The same reasons? Confused, I was tempted to jump up and leave. *Take a chance for a change, don't be afraid, break the chains* . . . I said to myself.

After we finished eating, he paid the bill and we left. Outside, he said, "Do you want to see my apartment?"

*No, I can't go that far. I hardly know this man. And what if someone sees me going into his apartment?*

But struck by an irresistible force, I said yes. He gave me his address, saying, "Take the back door—it's always open—and go to the second floor. Number twenty-nine." I watched as he got on a motor scooter he must have parked earlier on the sidewalk near the restaurant and rode away.

In less than twenty minutes, I was walking up the stairs to the second floor, to his apartment. He opened the door quickly and led me inside.

In the living room, I sat on the sofa, letting my eyes cling to different objects—a world map on one wall, a globe on a desk, a CD player.

"Would you like a drink?" he asked. "*Doogh*, cola?"

"Cola." Though Baba kept wine in the house, he didn't encourage Tala and me to have it.

Henry went to the small refrigerator and came back with glasses of an Iranian version of Coca-Cola and put them on the low wooden table in front of the sofa. He sat down next to me and said, "Won't you take off your scarf and *rupush*? What a shame you have to cover up."

I removed my scarf, leaving the *rupush* on.

"Would you want me to play my guitar for you?"

I nodded, unable to let go of my stiffness.

He went to the corner of the room and picked up the guitar on a table. As he walked back, I noticed he had a slight limp. In my insecurity, this flaw made me feel more comfortable with him.

Noticing my gaze, he said, "I fell once when I was playing basketball and hurt my hip and knees. One knee never quite recovered."

"I hope it doesn't hurt."

"Not anymore." He sat on the armchair across from the sofa, holding the guitar, and began to play and sing a song I knew by heart.

> *We are the lost generation. The confused generation.*
> *The present is enveloped in dark melancholy that obscures our vision.*
> *We live for the future.*

After he put his guitar down, he said, "I've always been an outsider in Iran. My blond hair, blue eyes. My father being English."

"I feel the same way and I don't have blue eyes and blond hair. Our mother was foreign too, from Argentina."

He got up, came to the sofa, and sat next to me. He put his arms around me and kissed me. This was the first time that a boy kissed me, and it filled me with a thrill, tinged with awe and apprehension. He took my blouse off, then my bra; I was wearing one with a floral pattern on lace that Tala and I had selected in the shopping court. He looked at my naked breasts.

"They're so beautiful, like pears," he said. He took his own shirt off and embraced me.

As his hand moved from my breasts to underpants, panic took over me. "I can't!" I said, and moved away from him and began to put my clothes back on.

He didn't pressure me. He didn't seem angry, only disappointed.

We were silent for a moment. I was afraid of more happening between us and got up to leave.

He saw me to the door, and not seeming discouraged, he said, "I'll wait for you in the park next Thursday, in the same spot. I hope you'll come."

"I'll try."

Later, when I was alone with Tala at home, I told her about meeting Henry and what went on between us.

She asked me to tell her all the details, how I felt about taking my clothes off, the kisses. After I told her everything, she said, "You let all that happen? When you get married your husband expects you to be pure."

"I didn't let him go that far."

"If you see him again, you may give in," she warned.

"You're right. I won't meet him again."

But by Thursday, I weakened, and at lunch recess, I started to go to the park to meet Henry. When I got there, I found the bench empty. I sat and waited, but he never came. I got up and left.

On the sidewalk outside of the park, I looked up and down, hoping to see him coming, stopping by me, and explaining his delay. But there was no sign of him.

Disappointed and hurt, I went back to school.

Tala wasn't at school; I couldn't find her anywhere. Later, at home, as I walked to my room, I saw her standing in front of the bathroom mirror. It was as if I was seeing two reflections of her—one smiling, the other one weeping, tears rolling down her face. Then I realized I had split from reality for a moment. Tala, the real one, not the reflection, was smiling enigmatically. It was as if I were looking at a version of her at the end of a long, dim tunnel.

"Tala," I called. "Tala."

"Roya, I have a headache. My art project wore me out. I'm going to bed."

But she was smiling just a moment ago. "Can I get you an aspirin?"

"No, I'll do without it."

The next morning, as we walked to school, I told her about Henry not turning up at the park.

"Does he have our phone number?" she asked.

"No."

"Did you try to call him?"

"He didn't give me a number, Tala."

"You could have tried information."

"You know how inadequate information is."

Tala only shrugged.

Days went by, and Henry didn't come to our school again, nor did I go to the park to see if he was there. One afternoon, I was sitting in my room, trying to concentrate on my essay for my literature course. I had pulled the shade over the window to shut out the light so that I could concentrate better. There was a knock on my door, and Tala walked in. She looked disheveled, her hair uncombed, her eyes red. It was as if she had been crying, or as if she had been asleep and had just awakened. Then she burst out, "Roya, I've been seeing Henry."

Her words set off an avalanche inside me. "Seeing Henry?"

"I went to the park on that Thursday . . . the Thursday you said he wasn't there. I only wanted to watch. But you were late, and then Henry noticed me. He thought I was you. I corrected his mistake but that didn't stop him from asking me to follow him to his apartment."

It seemed that I should have known what was happening, and I blinded myself to it. Visible changes had come over Tala ever since we met Henry, a range of new gestures and expressions—a slight sway in her hips, an enigmatic smile.

"We saw each other two more times but . . . I won't see him again, I promise. I just wanted to experience what you did with him. How he kissed you . . ."

Stunned by what she said, I was silent. Her next words hit me even harder.

"Roya. I let him . . . it broke so easily . . . blood just flowed . . ."

"You let him? You warned me not to let that happen . . ."

"It was a force stronger than me."

I couldn't believe that Tala, the shyer, quieter one of us, was so daring, took the risk of losing what was cherished in us girls more than anything, what was pounded into us that we needed to preserve for our husbands-to-be on the wedding night. I couldn't bear hearing another word.

"Tala, leave my room," I burst out. "Go, go."

She just stood there, silent.

"Tala, leave my room or I'll throw you out."

She left and I lay down on my bed and began to cry. I'm never going to talk to Tala, I thought, will never confide in her, tell her anything. I will go to school separately instead of walking with her. I will not eat my meals with her.

But how lonely it was to be disconnected from her in our household, with Grandmother spending hours praying or reading the Qur'an, Baba away at his work or, when he got home, going to his study and shutting the door. Tala had always been my companion. At school, we were each other's best friends. No one else could substitute for her—our endless conversations, sharing our impressions, laughing, and being sad at the same things. The rhythms of our hearts were as magically close as they must have been when we were in our mother's womb.

It was impossible to stay with the resolution. It made me feel like I was cut in half, a part of me dead. The only way I could revive was to forgive her. One evening, feeling intensely lonely and isolated, I went to her room and started talking to her again. "It was Henry's fault," I said. "He's older than us, more experienced."

Not long after Tala and I made up, one afternoon as I was looking at the bulletin board in Panah Bookstore, I came across a Farsi-English magazine, *Persian Accomplishments*, on a stand among other magazines. I picked it up and looked through it. I gave a start as I saw a photo of Henry accompanying a brief article. *Henry Wallace, from an English father and Iranian mother, won a scholarship for studying at the prestigious Carl Johnson Film School in London.*

I bought the magazine, and at home, I showed it to Tala.

"I'm glad he left," she said.

Still, for a long time after that, I was watchful of anything Tala said and did, not sure if I could trust her. She eventually regained my trust by keeping herself by my side as much as possible, not going too far from the vicinity of my vision.

Now, contemplating those memories, I realized a part of the reason I forgave her was because, in a way, I was the one who had betrayed her. Up to the time of my going and meeting Henry, Tala and I stayed in a world of our own—not mingling with our classmates or neighborhood girls our own age. We didn't go to their parties or set up getting together in any form. I stepped out of the capsule by going to meet Henry, and perhaps she just retaliated.

Still, the memory of this betrayal made me wonder now what she was hiding from me, or if I was somehow guilty of something that made her withdraw instead of confronting me.

## Chapter 6

The phone ringing again interrupted my thoughts, and again, by the time I reached it, whoever it was had hung up. If the caller was Tala, it could be that she wanted to confess or confront me about something, but then she changed her mind. I called her, and as usual, Batul answered and said Tala was resting. I asked her to tell her to call me.

Then, speculations filled my mind. Did her avoidance of me have anything to do with Anton? Perhaps he forbade her to talk to me because she had her baby and I didn't and he was afraid I would be demanding of her, perhaps wanting to share her baby daily. The marriage had been full of problems and conflicts from the beginning, and Anton had never liked my closeness to Tala.

I remembered the day Tala met Anton. From then on, the differences between us that we were not quite aware of began to manifest themselves more frequently.

We were juniors at Al Zahra. Looking out of the classroom's window, we could see snow covering the trees and the ground. The snow was untouched by footsteps and still solid in spite of the bright sunlight shining on it. Snow shovelers began to prowl the street, shouting their services. Tala and I whispered to each other that we should cut classes and go to the Dizin Ski Resort. We didn't have ski equipment and we wouldn't be able to afford to rent any, but we decided we would still enjoy the day.

At the next recess, we left for the bus station. The wide avenue just beyond Al Zahra was maddeningly crowded and packed with taxis, buses, cars, and pedestrians. In Safar terminal, buses and minivans were idling, waiting for passengers. Since it was a weekday, not many people were there to make use of them. The words, *O Hossein, O Mohammad, O Ali, Remember God, Good travels, Allah be with you,* were scribbled on the buses' sides. The drivers shouted out destinations: Shiraz, Tabriz, Qom, Dizin. The driver of a minivan, noticing us looking for transportation, said, "Get in. I have the most comfortable seats. I will take just the two of you, won't charge you more."

We got in, and he began to drive speedily. As we passed Capital, a gigantic shopping center with stores selling imported electronic equipment, Tala said, "I wish I had a video camera. I'd make videos of us. You would be the star." A moment later, she pointed to a twelve-story building and said, "If I were rich, I'd live in this area, maybe in a building like that." The building's lobby was visible through its glass door—brick walls, cedar ceiling, pale green tile, black steel, and walnut slats that were accented with linear lighting. Again, she changed her mind. "No, this looks like a hotel."

At the Dizin station, we paid the driver and got out. We walked to the outdoor café at the bottom of the slopes and sat at a table. *Ya Hussein* was written in electric bulbs on one of the hillsides. The slopes were dotted with boys and girls. A bulky ski suit and a wool cap met the dress code, substituting for a *manteau* and a scarf. A waiter came over and we ordered Olivier salad, cola, spinach, and yogurt salad, to share.

Four girls were sitting at the large table next to ours and eating.

"I don't mind the *hijab*," one of them said. "When I wear it, I don't have to worry about how I look every time I leave the house."

The other three laughed.

"You obviously do care about your appearance. Your headscarf is of the highest quality silk and has such a beautiful shimmer," the girl sitting across from her said. "You've highlighted your hair and let patches of it fall on your forehead in a most attractive way."

In a few moments, they paid their check and got up to leave. A man came and sat alone at the vacated table. "Salaam," he said to us. We ignored him. He looked to be thirty, was very handsome, tall, with high cheekbones, blue eyes, and sleek blond hair. He was dressed in a business suit—a dark jacket, white shirt, and cufflinks.

The waiter came over to take his order. The man asked for their lunch special—white fish, cherry rice, and *doogh*. After the waiter left, he turned to us and said, "How can anyone tell the two of you apart? I feel like I am seeing an illusion."

He introduced himself as Anton Alexandrov and then kept talking. He worked for the National Iranian Petrochemical Company, he said.

"We do important work. We provide much of the electricity for the country from the nuclear facility just outside Natanz. We collaborate with a Russian company. My parents were Russian; I was born there."

As Tala and I listened silently, he went on to say that he and his parents came to Iran when he was twelve years old. They were unhappy in Russia, being Muslims, discriminated against. "Tragically, I lost both of them; they died in a plane crash on the way to to Russia, where they went yearly to visit family members." Not discouraged by us ignoring him, he went on, "I moved in with my aunt and uncle after they died. My cousin Maxim is like a brother to me." He looked at Tala and then at me and said, "You must have had a father or mother from another country. You don't look all-Iranian."

Tala said nothing.

"Our mother was from Argentina," I said. "Sadly, she died when we were ten years old . . ."

He gave a start, "Is your father Dr. Arjomandi?"

I nodded, surprised by his remark.

"My aunt, who used to work at the University of Tehran, told me Professor Arjomandi was married to an Argentinian woman and had identical twin daughters."

Two girls covered up with conservative dark scarves and *rupushes* came and sat at a table near ours. Tala and I, apprehensive that the girls could be *Basij*, turned away from the man.

He got up. "I'm sure I'll be seeing you again," he said, keeping his eyes fixed on Tala.

After he left, Tala said, "Handsome and rich," with an emphasis on rich.

At that moment, I was aware that we were going in different directions in our reactions and values. Had that desire for wealth always been with her and I missed it? I didn't feel that being rich made the man enticing.

When we returned home, Tala went to her room and I to mine. What drew Anton more to Tala, I wondered? Maybe he liked her being quiet, just listening to him.

In bed that night, I was kept up by all sorts of questions. Was Anton going to come over and ask Baba permission to marry Tala? He had said, "I'm sure I will be seeing you," his eyes on Tala.

Suitors, some even older than Anton, had started to come for us since we were in the last year of high school. Once two cousins indicated they didn't care which one went to which of them. Then there was a businessman who also didn't care.

In our neighborhood, most girls married as soon as they finished high school or even before. But Tala and I, against all the prohibitions, had woven a tapestry of romance. We wanted to use Baba and Mum as examples. They met at the University of Kansas, when they were students, at a holiday party given by one of their classmates. Baba had immediately fallen for Mum, her looks, a mass of curly light brown hair and green-blue eyes, and her friendly manner. It had been a mellow evening with a pleasant breeze blowing, and they left the party and took a walk outside. After that they continued taking walks, going to restaurants, and soon he proposed to her. They were married by a justice of the peace, neither of them practicing their religions; her born to a Catholic family, and he to a Muslim family. Baba was attached to his home in Iran, but Mum had no desire to return to Argentina, a home tinged with pain for her. When she was still in high school, her sister died, falling from the window of the second floor of their house, and the tragedy lingered with her. Her parents died not long after she went to the US. Before moving to Tehran, Baba and Mum married again at a mosque in Kansas in a Muslim ceremony so that their marriage would be accepted in Iran.

Mum was aware of the limitations here for women, but she liked many things about the country. When Baba brought her here, she was pleasantly surprised by people's warm reception of her, which she had been uncertain about, as anyone would be moving to a new country. As it turned out, whatever she did that wouldn't be acceptable for a true native was excused in her case. "In her country, people do things differently," relatives and neighbors said in her defense. They liked the fact that she had learned Farsi and cooked some traditional Iranian meals. If she made mistakes when cooking them, Grandmother helped her do it the right way, and at the same time praised her for trying. She was able to get jobs as an interpreter and translator for foreign companies and institutes.

She was gregarious, whereas Baba was more solitary, but that didn't take away from their closeness. Baba, teaching philosophy at the University of Tehran, stayed in his study for long hours, preparing his lectures and then reading for pleasure—books on Western and Eastern philosophy, history.

During our childhood, Tala and I would go to the square near our house on Fridays, when a group set up a platform to dramatically tell the feverish love story of *Layla and Majnun,* written by an ancient Persian poet. Mum said it was the same as *Romeo and Juliet* of the Western world. As we grew older, we learned more from "forbidden books" and foreign movies. In those books and movies, people openly showed their interest in the opposite sex and finally fulfilled their desires, usually with happy endings. These were all different from Iranian movies, novels, and songs, where such fulfillment always ended in disaster.

If Anton came over and proposed, was Tala going to accept it even though her knowledge of him was confined to a short interaction? I wondered. Finally, I fell into the oblivion of a dreamless sleep.

Tala and I didn't talk about Anton again, and he receded from our minds, or at least from mine. Then, several weeks after we met him at Dizin, one morning at breakfast, Baba put down *Bostan,* a reformist paper that had escaped being banned and turned to Tala. "You have a suitor—Anton Alexandrov," he said. "He sent his aunt over to my office at the university. She said Anton met you in Dizin." Baba, usually mild-mannered, now was emphatic as he said, "I'm inclined to dismiss him unless he's willing to wait until you finish college. If he's really interested, he'll wait."

If Mum were alive, she would combine her voice with Baba's, I was sure.

Tala just nodded and I said nothing. As soon as we finished breakfast, Baba went to his home office.

Alone with Tala, I said, "Tala, he was smitten by you."

"Maybe it was you he liked," she said. "How could he tell us apart?"

"He must have. His eyes were on you even when I was doing the talking. Are you going to accept if Baba goes along with it?"

She shrugged. "I don't know."

Later that day, she said what she had already told me at one time. "I'm ashamed of our house, neighborhood. I don't feel comfortable with him coming here."

"The house could use some repairs, but it's still beautiful," I said. "And the neighborhood has its charm—the interwoven alleys, the little bazaar, the teahouses..."

I went on to point out the features of the house that I liked—the intricate mirrors on some of the walls, the five rooms in a row, the French doors with stained-glass windows at their tops, the decorated columns on the porch, cupulas at the edges of roof. Our grandfather, an architect, had designed the house himself, left it to Baba, and gave cash to his other son, Ahmad, to start a business. The main changes our parents made from the original were modernizing the kitchen and adding two Western-style bathrooms.

Tala sank into herself, and the subject was dropped.

# Chapter 7

The past was occupying a larger part of my mind than the present. I recalled that a week later, when I was in Tala's room, Baba came in and told us Anton was coming to the house to talk to him.

As soon as he left the room, the outside doorbell rang, and Baba went to get it. I stayed with Tala in her room, trying to imagine what they would talk about, what Baba would think of him. They were so different from each other, at least in their manners—Baba mild-mannered, thoughtful, Anton boisterous, unreflective, judging from the brief interaction we had with him.

In an hour, we heard footsteps going into the courtyard and then the outside door clanging shut. Shortly, Baba came into Tala's room, and with his eyes on her, he said, "I'm not sure what to think of him."

Tala blushed and said nothing. After Baba left the room, Tala said, "I sense he's right for me."

"You met him only once," I said.

She shrugged and I wasn't sure if I could express my opinion strongly without sounding jealous. Then I thought, maybe I'm jealous and that colors my impression of Anton negatively.

A few days passed by, and Baba came over to Tala and me in her room again and said, "I tried to do some background checks on Anton, but I couldn't find anyone who knows him. It is up to you, Tala," he said in a resigned tone. Since Mum died, he had coiled up inside himself, never showing interest in remarrying. His health had declined, and he was often tired. He didn't invite friends over as he used to. Our main visitor was Uncle Ahmad.

Had it not been for his declining health, he might have been more firm in his own belief that Tala should wait until she graduated from college before considering marriage.

"You can meet him in the living room and talk to him," he said to her. "I will set up a time for next week."

The following week, soon after we returned from school, Anton came to our house, holding a small box wrapped with gold-colored paper and ribbon. With Baba's permission, he and Tala went into the living room, shut the door, and stayed there for an hour or so. After he left, she came into my room and showed me what was in the box. A gold necklace with a cluster of rubies on it.

"It's beautiful," I said, but my heart was sinking at the thought that she was being bought by this stranger. "You have already accepted his proposal?"

Instead of answering, she said, "He'll provide me with a good home, in a nice neighborhood."

As it turned out, the wedding didn't happen immediately. Anton called our house and told Tala that he had to go on a business trip and would be back in a month, then they would set a date for their wedding. Tala was disappointed and upset that he didn't give her a phone number to reach him. He had said he wasn't in a particular location and his cell phone didn't work properly in Russia. Anyway, he would be immersed in meetings and there was no point in them communicating during that period.

Baba was not focused on the idea of Tala accepting the marriage proposal or the wedding date. He was growing more tired and sick and spent a lot of time in bed. Grandmother rarely interfered in such matters, and though her set of beliefs was different from Baba's, her being an observant Muslim and Baba a nonpracticing one, she went along with his decisions.

On the following days, while waiting for Anton to return, Tala, perhaps thinking he would show up sooner than he said, spent most of her allowance buying clothes from a department store that had recently opened. Their clothes were of better quality than those sold by the shops near us, but not as expensive as some in more luxurious neighborhoods. She borrowed money from me, which I had saved from the allowance Baba gave to each of us.

Anton didn't return in one month as he had said. He called our house and told Baba he wasn't finished with what he needed to do. Despondent, Tala said, "I'm not sure I can trust him." While in that negative state of mind toward him, she decided to sell the necklace he gave her. "I want to buy more clothes, throw out all the old ones." A jewelry store that advertised they would buy gold jewelry gave her good money for it and she went on a spending spree and insisted on buying some clothes for me too. Once again, we resumed our intimacy.

One morning, Baba did not join us for breakfast. Grandmother had set the table but then left the house to go to the butcher to get the best cuts of lamb. I knocked on his bedroom door, but there was no answer. "Baba, Baba, are you all right?"

Still no answer. I slowly opened the door and looked in. He was lying motionless with the sheet pulled up to his chin. I tiptoed over to him. He was breathing in a strange, guttural way. "Baba, Baba," I called again. He didn't answer. I shook him gently, but he kept breathing in the same way and didn't respond.

"Help, help," I screamed, and Tala rushed in.

"We have to call an ambulance," Tala said, and went to the phone. She got off and said, "They'll be here in a few moments."

As we waited, we kept trying to wake up Baba, but he was fixed in his position and making odd, rasping noises. We heard the doorbell, and I ran to open it. I accompanied the two young men who were standing there to Baba's room.

"How long has he been like this?" the younger of the medics asked as the other began to examine Baba.

"I found him in this state when I went to his room, just before we called," I said.

"We have to take him to the hospital," the older medic said.

They lifted him up, put him on a stretcher, carried him outside, and laid him in the ambulance parked on the avenue at the front of our alley. We got in too. At the emergency room of Motajedi Hospital, they took Baba inside, and Tala and I stayed in the waiting area. In an hour, a doctor came out and said, "I'm so sorry . . . I'm sad to say, your dear father left this world."

"Can we go in and see him?" I asked, my voice quivering.

"I'm afraid we had to take him to the morgue while help was available. He died peacefully in his sleep; you can be sure of that. His heart had failed. Do you have someone to sign the necessary forms?"

"We can sign them."

"Is there a man in the family who can attend to the burial?"

"Yes, our uncle," I said, referring to Uncle Ahmad, who was a frequent visitor to our house, often having dinner with us. According to Islam and the rule in the country, the body had to be buried within twenty-four hours of the time of death. So we needed to reach Uncle quickly. The doctor said we could use the phone at the reception desk and call him.

I used the phone, and Uncle answered. I told him what had happened. Instantly, he began to sob. After he calmed down a little, he said, "You can count on me, I will arrange everything." He would take Baba from the morgue to the cemetery in Qazvin, where Baba had told him long ago he wanted to be buried. Baba and Uncle Ahmad grew up in Qazvin and lived there until their father moved his architecture firm to Tehran.

Uncle was very different from Baba, but that didn't stop them from being close to each other. As was the case with Grandmother, his and Baba's differences didn't cause friction between them. Their brotherly love won out over any other considerations. He started working right after high school, did not go on to higher education as Baba did. He followed Grandmother in observing Islam's rules. He never married. He had many friends, some of them married, and they often invited him over for dinner. He and Baba also looked different. Uncle was heavier and had bolder features. He shared some of Baba's interest in ancient Iranian poets and knew a lot of poems by heart. He liked to recite one to make a point. His presence in our household was comforting.

When Tala and I returned home, Grandmother was back, and we told her about Baba's death. She burst into tears and kept repeating, "My son, I wasn't with you when you took your last breaths. You were a good man and will be sent to heaven . . ."

Tala and I sat with her, mingling our tears with hers, while still trying to say some comforting words.

## Chapter 8

Uncle requested that Baba's body to be transported to Qazvin and they agreed they would send him to the morgue there. Uncle drove us—Tala and me and Grandmother—in his work truck to Qazvin, five hours away from Tehran. Tala and I lay on blankets spread in the back of the truck while Grandmother sat in front with her son. Stretched around us were rugged hills, continuations of the Alborz Mountains capped with snow at their highest peaks and masses of bright wild-flowers on their lower levels. Villagers in colorful clothes stood by the roadside selling shawls or tea cozies. We came upon vast, barren vistas, pastures with goats and sheep grazing. Finally, we were in the cemetery at the outskirts of Qazvin. It was small and well-kept. Trees, a few in bloom, were scattered among the graves. Swallows darted in the sky.

Baba had no relatives or friends left in Qazvin; most of them had relocated to other cities. But a few of them came to the burial from far away. A blank stone had been put on Baba's grave by the local cemetery attendant, to be engraved as soon as possible. The starkness of the gray stone was softened by a large willow tree standing next to it, as if protecting it with its long, drooping branches. An *aghound* Uncle hired said the prayer for the dead as everyone cried.

"Nothing is worse than outliving your own child," Grandmother wailed. Looking heavenward, she said, "God, please take me away too, let me unite with my son."

A bird appeared on the side of the grave and then flew away, going up and up until it was swallowed by the sunny sky. "That was the good man's soul," one of the men said. "He's destined to go to paradise."

After the *aghound* said the prayers for the dead, a man from the funeral home came over and served halva and tea that Uncle had ordered from the local shop.

After we said goodbye to the friends, Uncle drove us to the city center to check into a hotel. We went through a high, arched, ornate gate and soon we were in the midst of the ancient city that had once been the capital of the Persian Empire. It was full of grand architectural sites— mosques, castles, fortresses with cupolas and cornices and mosaic tiles. A small, blue-domed mosque stood at the top of a hill, surrounded by tall, thick trees.

After we checked into the hotel, we left to go to a restaurant nearby. We ordered *Gheimeh* (minced lamb and lentils) and *polo albaloo* (rice and fresh cherries), dishes often served in mourning ceremonies.

After dinner, Uncle took Grandmother to Jame Mosque so that they could pray more for Baba's soul.

The rest of us withdrew into our hotel rooms, Tala and I sharing one. The room had green walls, green drapery, a dark, busy Persian rug on the floor, and two single beds. We moved the beds together so that we could talk easily above the murmur of a stream and the sound of tree leaves thrashing against each other.

"How can a person just disappear?" Tala said as we lay in bed.

Then we began to reminisce on what we recalled about Mum dying when we were ten years old.

Mum had begun to lose weight; her skin looked flushed from a low-grade fever that wouldn't leave her. The atmosphere of our household became heavy, somber. Baba stayed with Mum in their bedroom, doing his work there while she slept.

One afternoon when Baba wasn't in the room, Tala and I went in and sat on chairs by Mum. She was wan and thin with her illness, but a gleam of a smile came to her face as she said, "Will you promise to always help each other, to be best friends?"

Tala and I each promised. "Of course, Mum."

Later that day, Baba told us that doctors didn't have a diagnosis for our mother yet. He was going to try to take her to Argentina so that she could see her family members who were still there and consult other doctors. He arranged for Grandmother to stay with us while they were gone.

In two weeks, Baba returned from Argentina without Mum. With tears in his eyes, he said, "Doctors there couldn't do anything for her. I had her buried in her family's plot in the cemetery there." Then, in a voice he tried to keep reassuring, he said, "She died peacefully." With Pedro's help, he had buried her in the village her parents were from.

Cousin Pedro was the only relative of Mum's we had met; he came to visit us once. He was muscular, had green-blue eyes, brown hair, and a thin mustache. We had learned some basic Spanish from Mum, me more than Tala, and Pedro had learned a few phrases in Farsi in preparation for the trip. He entertained us by making shadow pictures on the wall with his hands and doing magic tricks. One was putting a silver coin in one hand and then letting us find it in his other hand. He put on a record of tango music that he had brought for Mum, and they danced. Sometimes, he danced with Tala and me, holding one of us in each arm.

On that tragic day, our grandmother's promise to move into our house was the only thing that comforted us.

Her own house was only five blocks away, and she had always been a part of our lives anyway, but now it would be more so. When Grandmother moved in with us, we became immersed in her stories, which reflected her religious beliefs. "Angels" was our favorite. They were light-based creatures, and incorporeal, but could manifest themselves at times in a form comprehensible to human eyes. There were four Archangels. Gabriel was responsible for revealing the Qur'an to Muhammad *surah* by *surah*. Michael was the Archangel who brought down thunder and lightning onto Earth. He was also responsible for the rewards doled out to good people in this life. Azrael was the Angel of Death, responsible for parting the soul of the human from the body. The actual process of separating the soul from the body depended on the person's history of good or bad deeds. If the human was a bad person in this life, the soul was ripped out very painfully. But if the human was a righteous person, the soul was separated like water dripping from glass. Raphael was the angel who blew the horn and signaled the coming of Judgment Day. Archangels had thousands of wings. Then there were other angels, some of them created solely for the purpose of praising Allah; they had seventy thousand heads, each with seventy thousand mouths that spoke seventy thousand languages. Angels were free from any defect in body and mind, did not have any gender; God did not create them divided by gender since they did not reproduce. We went over those details with excitement, immersed in what was beautiful and mysterious at once.

We took turns being one angel or another. Neither of us wanted to be the Angel of Death.

Tala drifted to sleep. But I stayed awake for a long time. I remembered one morning when Tala was still sleeping and I was alone with Grandmother in the courtyard, I became focused on the two identical-looking stray cats with yellow fur who had wandered in, then on the identical mourning doves that she kept in a cage in the corner of the yard, and then on identical maple leaves fallen on the ground.

"Why are Tala and I identical?" I asked Grandmother.

"God must have made you alike for a reason."

"What reason could it be?"

"Roya *joon*, don't worry, God is beneficent," she said. After a moment she added, "So that one could rescue the other in time of trouble or carry on for her if she becomes disabled or dies. Being alike makes all that possible."

Now, in the hotel room, remembering what Grandmother said, I wondered if it was my responsibility to rescue Tala from Anton, help her in the journey ahead. But again, the thought that I might be biased against Anton because he chose Tala over me, that jealousy was a part of my not liking him, kept me silent.

# Chapter 9

Soon after we returned from Qazvin, Anton reappeared. On a Friday afternoon, three months after Baba died, Tala and I were sitting in the courtyard, talking about what we hoped for our future. Neither of us could come up with concrete answers.

Our conversation was interrupted by the sound of a knock on the outside door. Grandmother was out visiting a friend. Tala went to get it, and in a moment, she came back, accompanied by Anton. Anton greeted me, and then Tala led him to the living room. I went to my room, feeling apprehension at his presence. But then again, I questioned the negative feelings I had toward him. Not just the jealousy of him choosing her over me, but also my fear that Tala's and my ongoing exchanges and dialogue would be interrupted.

I wished I could look inside the room. But the door didn't have a keyhole. They stayed in the room with the door shut for an hour, and then I heard footsteps going toward the outside door.

In a few moments, Tala came to my room. She started talking rapidly, her words jumbled, "I'm going to marry him. He's so worldly . . . generous. It isn't just money . . . he's interesting, with his stories of travel, his worldliness." She paused and then added, "You and I both need to get out of the situation we're in. We are orphans, our income is low. I know someone will come for you once I am married." After another pause, she said, "Roya, I'm actually attracted to him. He's dynamic."

*Dynamic.* She had never used that word before. Was that a word she had heard from him?

She went on to more praise. "He has magnetism, doesn't he?"

I nodded. Yes, he did have a vibrant manner.

"I feel comfortable with him," she went on. "In some ways, he fits our family well. Like Mum, he grew up in a different country, knows another language. Like Mum and Baba, he doesn't observe religion."

"Have you set a date?" I asked.

"He wants it as soon as possible, June 1. He is going away again for a month to Moscow to finish what he left of his work."

But in the middle of that night, I woke to her making strange sounds. I rushed to her room. She was in the midst of having a nightmare, talking to herself in an incoherent way.

"Tala, Tala," I said. She opened her eyes and sat up.

"Oh, I was climbing a winding stairway that kept going higher and higher," she said.

"I'm here now. Don't be afraid." I kissed her on her cheeks and waited until she seemed calm. Then I went back to my room.

Would Tala have married Anton if Baba had not died, leaving us grief-stricken and vulnerable? If Mum were alive, would she have insisted, more firmly than Baba did, that Tala continue with her education before thinking of marriage?

But we were filled with a sickening anxiety—what could we expect of our future now, with both Mum and Baba dead and Grandmother sunk into irremediable grief, repeating, "God, why didn't you take me first before my dear son?"

Grandmother, who married at age thirteen to a much older man, had been lucky. She learned to love her husband. But she couldn't really be a role model for Tala, or me. She said, "Girls who don't marry have no status . . . they're old maids."

Now with Anton back in Tala's life, she dressed in clothes that outlined her figure in flattering ways. Before he would arrive, she tried one after another on for me to comment on.

Grandmother, always agreeable and in favor of early marriage, still expressed concern about Anton. "A man's character counts for more than anything. We have to make sure he's a good person," she said. She would have liked to ask neighborhood people about him, but no one knew him. She did stop Tala from going out with him; she insisted that they continue meeting in the living room, or else we would get a bad reputation with neighbors who saw them together outside.

Tala reasoned, "He's educated, approves of my art. He is offering a large *mehrieh* but wants nothing for a dowry. He admires that I am a painter. I will have the luxury to paint as much as I would like."

Then, for a few days, Tala seemed uncertain about Anton. The confusion manifested itself in strange behavior. It was one of those periods when she became opaque to me. One morning, she wasn't at breakfast. I searched for her in every room and then went to Grandmother's room. She was leaning against a green velvet cushion, reading the Qur'an.

"Have you seen Tala?" I asked.

Grandmother lifted her head and said, "No, she didn't come here."

I went back to Tala's room, and this time I heard a faint noise from under her bed. I leaned down, and there was Tala, lying under the bed, curved, her arms tight around herself as if she were a fetus. "Tala, what are you doing? Come out."

She was silent.

"You're worrying me. Come out of there." I fell to my knees and reached for her, but she pulled away. I reached in again, this time I managed to take her hand, and gently pulled her out.

"I know you don't want me to marry Anton," she said in a strange voice.

"I wouldn't stop you," I said. "I couldn't, even if I wanted to."

Her face softened, she took a deep breath and said, "I'm sorry. I'm so torn, so miserable. How can I go through with the wedding?"

I said nothing. I helped her get off the floor, then led her to her room. She said she wanted to be alone. I left and went to mine, still shaken by her strange behavior.

On one midafternoon when Tala and I were sitting with Grandmother in the courtyard, having tea, there was a knock on the door. Tala went to open it and returned with Anton by her side. "Look who is here," she said.

He barely acknowledged me with just a nod, but he greeted Grandmother with respect. He said to her, "With your permission," and followed Tala to the living room.

By the end of that visit, Tala said to me, "He explained he wasn't allowed to be in communication with anyone outside of the country. That was why I didn't hear from him,"

"Why is that?"

"His work is very important, of a sensitive nature."

At that point, we didn't assume that his job might have a criminal nature.

"We will always be best friends and confidants. I would never tell him what we confide in each other. He is aware of our closeness and that's why he ignores you, out of jealousy."

Though Anton said he didn't want a dowry since he had already set up everything in the house for his bride, Grandmother, as a token, still began to make a patchwork quilt for her from scraps of fabric she collected over the years. She paid great attention to detail as if she were weaving the course of Tala's future into it. Alas, later, after her marriage, on one of my visits to her, she took me from room to room, but I didn't see the quilt. She explained that Anton thought it didn't go with the decor of the house. That saddened me, made me think she hadn't resisted his idea, indicating to me that she didn't want any reminders of her past way of life.

# Chapter 10

A few days before the date of Tala's wedding, I accompanied her to see Madam Karimian, an Armenian dressmaker praised for her good taste. People said that the high prices she asked for were justified. Most well-to-do Tehrani girls had their wedding dresses made by her. Anton was paying for all the expenses of the wedding.

The shop was on the second floor of a building in a north Tehran street lined by luxury shops. Inside, clothes were displayed on mannequins, shielded from the *Basij*'s scrutiny by a thick, dark curtain over the window facing the street. The low necklines would certainly be objectionable to them. Two large tables held cutting material; another had a Singer sewing machine on it.

"I've seen so many brides-to-be in my life, but never an identical twin," Madam Karimian exclaimed when we walked in. "Is only one of you getting married?"

I pointed to Tala. "She is the one."

"I hope I'll be making a dress for you too soon," she said to me. Then she showed us patterns and photographs of dresses.

Tala pointed to one of a bride in a white satin dress with crystal beads at its neckline and a veil with thin strands of silver woven into it. "I like this," she said listlessly. I could tell she was excited and at the same time still hesitant to go forward with the marriage.

"Good choice," Madam Karimian said.

In a few days, we went back to the shop and Tala tried on the dress. "I like it," I said.

"Yes, I like it too," Tala agreed.

Madam Karimian packed it for us, Tala paid her, and we left.

On the day of the wedding, I accompanied Tala to a beauty salon to have her hair set, her eyebrows trimmed, and her makeup applied.

At home, Grandmother prepared the *sofreh aghd,* spreading the *termeh* cloth that she had used for her own wedding, saying, "They don't make such good things these days." At its center, she put symbolic objects—a mirror, crystal candleholders with white candles in them, and a copy of the Qur'an. She used the rest of the cloth for platters of sweets and fruit.

Uncle Ahmad, our guardian in all matters since Baba died, came in, followed by Anton and his cousin, Maxim.

An *aghound* came in to perform the wedding ceremony that would legally bind the bride and the groom. While Tala and Anton sat on chairs, the *aghound* read the appropriate *surah* from the Qur'an. Then he asked the bride and groom if they consented to the marriage. After they both said yes, Anton put a large diamond-encrusted wedding ring on her finger. Tala put a gold ring, which Anton had paid for, on his finger. She was wearing the necklace with diamonds strung along it, one among many presents Anton gave her during their courtship. Anton and Uncle Ahmad signed the contracts the *aghound* had drawn.

Throughout the ceremony, I kept thinking, who will I be apart from Tala? Now she would be sharing Anton's bed, perhaps she would talk about me to him, telling him her reactions to things, her thoughts.

Before leaving for the reception, which was in Anton's Russian Club, Tala stepped out of the room and signaled to me to join her. We went to her room, and she shut the door. "I'm going to miss you . . . all our nightly conversations."

"You know I will miss all that too."

Anton called from behind the door, "Tala, we're leaving." Tala and I locked eyes for a moment. "Tala!" Anton shouted so irritably that it gave us a start. She broke away and slipped out the door.

The Russian Club was located in Darband. Grandmother and Uncle Ahmad didn't attend this part of the wedding. They felt uncomfortable in such places where men and women mingled freely, hidden from the *Basij* who would be bribed by the managers or the person in charge of the party. Maxim and some of Anton's friends came. Maxim, I noticed, was wearing a custom-made suit that could only be from Bijan, an exclusive shop with branches all over the world. He looked at the guests with his heavy-lidded eyes like a cat stalking prey. He reminded me of

Anton, with something troubled and wounded beneath his veneer of arrogance and self-confidence.

As male guests scrutinized single women, waiters in dark navy uniforms walked around serving appetizers, soft drinks, and illegal alcoholic drinks. After dinner, the waiters brought out a large, multilayered wedding cake. Anton led Tala to the table and cut two slices from the cake and they fed each other. Some of the guests began singing a loud Russian wedding song, words I didn't understand.

A waiter finished cutting the rest of the cake and other waiters joined him to serve it, along with tea, coffee, soft drinks, and champagne. Anton had hired a band of Russian musicians as a tribute to the country he had grown up in was still connected to through his work. Standing on a platform set up in the middle of the garden, three musicians sang in Russian, and each played an instrument—fiddle, accordion, and tambourine.

I was feeling alone and isolated, as if there was no one in the vast space. Maxim was standing under a tree, his expression oddly menacing in the beam of a red light cast on his face from a colored bulb. Then he wandered toward me and tried to strike up a conversation—how did I like Al Zahra, what was I majoring in? I answered him in monosyllables—I was majoring in literature and linguistics; I didn't like Al Zahra.

Then I noticed Tala signaling to me with one hand and pointing in the direction of the restrooms with the other. Relieved, I asked Maxim to excuse me and walked away.

"I'm so nervous," Tala said in the bathroom. "I've never lived apart from you."

"We will visit each other, go to our usual places . . ."

"Tala, hurry up, the car is waiting," Anton called. Tala kissed me on my cheek and left hurriedly to join him, and I followed.

Anton turned to me and said with a half-smile, "Sorry to pull the two of you apart." Up to that point, he had kept a distance from me. What was it about him that created such mistrust in me? Was it his charm that suddenly changed into a shifty manner, his eyes that became icy and expressionless at times?

Taking her hand, he led her outside. But just before she left my sight, I saw a dark glimmer of fear and mistrust on her face that added to my own similar feelings.

That night as I lay in bed, I imagined myself standing behind the door of the room where Tala and Anton would spend the night, and many nights to come. I could almost hear muffled sounds of clothes being taken off, of movements from them getting into bed, whispers. Would she tell him things she didn't like about me, or would she praise me? Would he tell her that he wished there was just one of us, urging her to disconnect herself from me in order to become a whole person? I imagined his hands caressing Tala's breasts and moving down to her navel and below.

I felt anxious about his discovering she wasn't a virgin, a trait so highly valued in brides. I found some solace in looking at the moon, so close to the tree before my window that it felt like I could touch it. Its face, though brightly lit, seemed to be hiding things I couldn't decipher.

I closed my eyes and drifted into a prolonged dream. In the dream, Tala was sitting at the edge of a well, looking down, her hair very long and falling forward. Leaves, flower petals, and butterflies fluttered in the air as if they had lost their way. The edge of the well was slippery, covered by algae. She could fall. I screamed, "Tala, Tala, watch out," but she just remained there, and in a moment, she fell into the well, and I could only hear the echoes of her falling. I woke with a feeling of foreboding.

In the morning at breakfast, Grandmother noticed me gazing at the empty chair next to me. "Don't be sad," she said. "Soon you'll be getting married too."

Tala was flying to Greece that day with Anton to spend a week there for their honeymoon.

Still, it seemed unnatural that she had left me and was sharing her life with this man who had unexpectedly entered our lives. I counted the days until her return.

As soon as she was back from her honeymoon, she wasn't restrained in complaining. She sounded pent up, saying, "On the trip when we should be totally immersed in each other, he got on the phone and talked to Maxim or other men in Russian, sometimes yelling at them. When I asked him what he was talking about, he said, 'A wife should stay away from her husband's affairs.' I told him it wasn't like that between Baba and Mum. He just shrugged and then said, 'Maybe they didn't tell you everything . . .'"

"Tala, I'm sorry."

Then I got to what was on my mind. "Does he know about . . ."

She knew what I was referring to. "I told him my hymen was broken when I fell down the stairway of our porch. I saw blood and Mum took me to a gynecologist . . ."

I said nothing but thought she was starting her marriage with a lie. As if reading my mind, she said, "Sometimes a lie is better than telling the truth."

After a pause, she went on, "Anton hasn't been entirely truthful with me either. For one thing, I think his work is illegal. I've gathered that from the way he whispers things to Maxim and others on the phone."

Then she tried to cheer us up. She said, "Oh, the hotel was amazing—stunning decor, the bluest pool, a view of the Mediterranean Sea from the room. And there was a valley of butterflies. If you whistle, they all fly out from their hiding places, and the sky becomes covered with their colorful wings."

After we hung up, I looked at the photograph of us on the mantel. I thought how broken our shared world had become now that she was married.

# Chapter 11

Tala dropped out of Al Zahra, and I stopped going too, knowing it would be even more unbearable there without her. We hadn't been interested in making friends with anyone, wanting to keep our exclusive world together. It wasn't easy to make friends anyway; there were no parties given at school, and none of the students wanted to socialize with each other after school. Most of them lived far away, some on the outskirts of Tehran, and had to go home as soon as possible before darkness would settle.

The degree from Al Zahra wasn't worth much anyway when it came to the job market. Priority was given to boys who graduated from boys' universities which offered technical courses. The University of Tehran opened up more job opportunities, but Tala and I didn't get in even though our father taught there. We had good grades throughout high school but didn't do well in the very technical *Konkoor* examination.

Instead, I enrolled in the Sepideh School of Languages to improve my Spanish and English. I went to two-hour classes four afternoons a week. I also found a part-time job working at a travel agency, speaking with customers who didn't know Farsi.

In the mornings, Grandmother went to the other side of the courtyard and collected eggs from the hens' shed and fried them for us. Sometimes she made pancakes, and we used the maple syrup she made from the sap of the large maple tree in the courtyard. When I had time, Grandmother showed me how to knit sweaters with yarn she bought from the bazaar. She made thread from caterpillar cocoons and showed me how to make silk handkerchiefs with it. She told me she learned those skills from her mother. She was happy growing up with a mother who doted on her. When the time came for her to marry, her mother was wise and careful in arranging a husband who was right for her.

"You don't need to love a man before marriage. That happens afterward," she said. "But we have to make sure he's from a good family and is honorable." After a pause, she added, "It is your turn now to marry. Suitors will come for you. We have to find out more about them than we did about Anton."

Her hair highlighted by henna, her voluptuous figure, and her lively way of speaking made her seem much younger than seventy years old. In spite of the age gap and different ways of thinking, I felt I could talk to her. Still, I was full of an aching loneliness, not having Tala there with us.

At dusk, she lit the two burgundy-colored glass shaded oil lamps she kept on the mantel in the living room, liking that better than the light from the ceiling bulbs. The lamps reminded her of her childhood days when they rarely had electricity.

I liked having Grandmother to myself, but still, I was lonely for Tala. I spent some time after school and work reading novels I got out of the library and writing ideas in a notebook that I wanted to one day make into short stories or a novel. Some of the novels I read were translations of foreign writers, opening windows into different worlds for me. I wanted to emulate styles of writing that were a mixture of reality and dreams, similar to *Blind Owl*, a surrealistic novel by an Iranian writer whose books were censored but possible to obtain from the black market. It was about a young man's despair after losing a mysterious lover. He drifts into frenzy and madness.

I was convinced that truth was a combination of reality and perception of that reality, that it could change like looking through a kaleidoscope. Tala's approach to painting was similar to mine to writing.

Once in a while, I looked at what I had jotted down, some long ago and some more recent.

*I am afraid of Tala abandoning me or dying as Mum and Baba did.*

*She is now lying in bed next to Anton. He is caressing her breasts. He asks her if she loves him. She doesn't answer and that prompts him to slap her. Or she answers in an ambiguous way . . . "I don't know what love is," and he accuses her of being cold like ice.*

She rarely visited me and Grandmother at the family house. When she visited, it was brief, just to fulfill an obligation. She didn't like being in the house—the place she had wanted to get away from by marrying Anton—I could tell she was afraid she would somehow be forced back there.

Grandmother excused her. She said to me, "She wants to get adjusted to her new life."

Tala and I saw each other about once a week at Sam's Café, which was usually filled with mostly students from the University of Tehran. We both liked its lively and less restrictive atmosphere. We usually went there when Anton went away to Natanz for his work, or occasionally to Russia for a brief time.

As was the case from the time we met him, Tala had a lot of ups and downs about him—he was too controlling, he wanted her to become different from me. He said it was freaky to have a lookalike. She had asked him why he chose her over me if he saw us as alike. He said there were subtle differences, and now he wanted the differences to be more pronounced. He became agitated, for reasons that didn't seem logical to her. She sighed and said nothing else. She seemed tired of either justifying or complaining about him.

As Grandmother predicted, suitors began to come for me. One was a seminary student in Qom whose family lived in our neighborhood. Of course, I wasn't going to marry a man devoting his life to religion and living in the oppressive, ultra-conservative city of Qom. The second suitor was twenty years older than me and owned a carpet shop in the bazaar. He had gold caps on his front teeth. I found nothing appealing about him.

"Do you love Tala more now because she's married?" I asked Grandmother one morning at breakfast, eating in the courtyard.

"You're equally precious to me." After a moment, she added, "She has a sly side to her."

Regretting criticizing Tala, she corrected her remark. "She's shy, doesn't express herself well."

Alas, I didn't get to have more such conversations with Grandmother.

One morning after breakfast, she began to throw up. After that, she wasn't the same. She had periods when she was incoherent. On the rare occasion when Tala came to visit her, she turned to her, then to me, and back to her again and said, "They lied to you, the egg never split."

After that, she was more fragile, and one morning she fainted and fell on the living room floor. I called emergency and an ambulance came. Two medics picked her up and put her in it. "We're taking her to Motavali Hospital," one of the men said.

"Can I go with you?"

"I'm sorry, but you have to go there on your own."

At the hospital, a nurse took me over to a doctor. He said Grandmother had pneumonia and she needed to stay in the hospital for a few days.

"Can I see her?"

"Unfortunately, not now. She's being carefully examined. Come tomorrow during visiting hours between ten in the morning and noon."

As soon as I was back in the house, I called Tala to tell her what happened. But Batul said Tala was away for a week. Anton took her with him to Natanz. She said she had no phone number for her. I asked her to tell Tala to call me as soon as she returned.

Smartphones had become available in Tehran, and Tala could certainly afford one. But she had told me Anton forbade her to have one, warning her that people could hack it and find out personal information. She added, "But the truth is, he doesn't want me to have a private phone separate from his."

In the morning when I arrived at the hospital, Grandmother was sleeping. I sat on a chair by her bed. Her soft, almost unwrinkled skin, her thick wavy hair, which maintained some of the dark strands among the gray, and her large amber eyes gave her the aura of a younger woman. Touches of her beauty—which, according to Baba, had given her the nickname *khoshgel*, meaning beautiful—were still there.

She opened her eyes and said, "Oh, Roya, you are here. Don't forget me. That way I'll be alive."

"I will never forget you. Neither will Tala."

"I'll be waiting for you . . . we'll see each other."

Did she believe that all of us were going to heaven and that she would be waiting there in paradise with its lush gardens, flowers, lakes, and birds, like in some of her embroideries? She must be thinking she wasn't leaving this world; she was only entering another one, a better one.

She turned her face to the side; her breathing became shallow, and she fell into silence. "Grandmother, Grandmother," I called, but she remained silent. I barely managed to ring the bell on the side of her bed. A nurse rushed in. Then she went and got a doctor.

The doctor took Grandmother's pulse and listened to her heart. "She's no longer with us," he said.

She looked utterly serene, though life had drained out of her.

"Can my uncle come and see her now?"

"How quickly can he get here?"

"Within two hours."

"You can call him."

I left to make a phone call to Uncle from the public phone in the reception area.

"Oh, my dear, dear mother," he lamented, beginning to cry. My tears silently mingled with his. After we calmed down somewhat, we tried to console each other. Finally, he said he would arrange everything.

He got off the phone to start the burial process.

He told me he would take her to Qazvin so she could be buried next to Baba's grave. Tala wasn't with us this time. She was still away with Anton.

After the burial, we ate out with some family members, then I stayed in a hotel room by myself. I felt pangs of loneliness without Tala to share our grief for Grandmother. Now with Mum, Baba, and Grandmother all dead, I felt even more need for Tala.

As soon as Tala returned and I told her about Grandmother's passing, she started to cry, and so did I. After a moment of crying, we each expressed how hard it was to have lost our parents and now Grandmother. Luckily, we still had Uncle Ahmad. I asked her to come to the house and take what had belonged to Grandmother. We discussed everything and we each took what we wanted.

Grandmother had very few valuables—two silk Isfahan rugs with paisley designs, a set of brass silverware with leaf designs, a silver tray and tea glass holders with intricate designs of birds and flowers, the burgundy lamps. The main valuable items were her jewelry, including a gold necklace with leaf designs, another necklace with floral designs and earrings matching it, and a set of thin bracelets. Tala said I could have all of them.

Grandmother had little money in the bank. When she moved in with us, she sold her house, not at a high price, since it needed repairs. She gave some of the money to destitute women in the neighborhood, and spent some of it on pilgrimages, visiting shrines in Karbala and Mecca. I had been using the money I inherited from Baba, but that was getting depleted. I had to get busy and rent out the house and move to a small apartment within my means.

Generously, Tala said I could have all the rent money, but she wanted me to keep the large room on the other side of the courtyard for storage. She wanted to put some of her paintings there and keep the door locked.

"Anton doesn't like to have my paintings in our house," she said. "He thinks paint poisons the air." She had more complaints, which she couldn't stop expressing even while we were engaged in the sad activities following Grandmother dying. "He spends one night a week at the Russian Club, usually with Maxim and some friends. I don't trust Maxim, I dislike him. Anton doesn't take me with him, saying sometimes men need to be together, away from their families. He's evasive about who the friends are or what they do. I still don't know exactly what he himself does. When I ask him, he says, 'Don't burden yourself with matters that shouldn't concern you.'" She went on and on. Even though he was secretive about his own connections and activities, he incessantly quizzed her about everyone, family, friends, acquaintances, teachers, neighbors. His questions were endless; he wanted to know all the details. She tried to see his good points. Of course, he was generous with her, lavishing her with presents, giving her money to spend on what she wanted. He was entertaining, telling her jokes and stories about growing up in Moscow, how he and his friends used to hang out in the evening in cafés and clubs or visit historical sites.

As she was leaving the house, she said, "I'm worried that he may be transferred to Russia to work in their office there. Roya, I don't want to go so far away from you."

"I hope that won't happen. I only have you now."

"I will try to resist going, but I know I don't have a choice."

I had no idea then that it would happen. But, of course, neither she nor I could have stopped that move.

# Chapter 12

Soon after Grandmother died, with Uncle's help, I rented out the house. I moved into a studio apartment in a two-story building. It was in an area near the language school where the population was more open-minded and didn't condemn a girl living alone.

I met Reza by luck when taking a different route to the language school.

On that day, the street I normally took to go to the school was being repaired, and I took a longer route. Halfway down Hospital Street, I came across the Baloochi Veterans Hospital. I was chilled at the sight of men on crutches, victims of the war with Iraq. One of them stood behind the wire fence, staring yearningly at passersby.

"Please help me," the man said.

I froze in my spot, wondering how I could possibly help him.

"What can I do for you?" a young man asked, stopping by the fence. He looked familiar—he was thin, of medium height, with a pile of curly dark brown hair and brown eyes.

"Can you mail this letter to my wife?" the veteran asked and waved an envelope he was holding.

"No problem. I'll mail it for you." the young man said, taking the envelope.

A tall, hefty orderly came over to the veteran and led him away from the fence.

"You're Reza Toorani!" I said, suddenly recognizing the man; he used to live in our neighborhood. Tala and I often passed him on the way to high school.

"Roya!" he said, recognizing me too.

A motor scooter zooming onto the sidewalk interrupted us.

"People are out of control," Reza exclaimed. "Of course, I don't blame them. Life isn't easy these days."

I nodded in agreement. "I haven't seen you in the neighborhood," I said.

"I was living with my uncle in Isfahan after I lost my father. My uncle could afford to send me to college there. I came back a year ago."

"You used to fly kites on your rooftop . . . I have to go to my class now. I am taking courses at Sepideh Language School, to improve my Spanish and English."

"I know where Sepideh is. The post office is on the way; I want to mail the letter. It's amazing we came across each other like this."

"Yes, I happened to be taking a different direction."

I was going to be late to my class, so I said, "Hope we'll see each other again."

"You've been in my thoughts all these years," he said. "And now I am seeing you face to face."

I said goodbye, and as I walked to Sepideh, Reza's words hummed in my ears. *You've been in my thoughts all these years.* When I used to see him with his kites of various shapes, going up and up and tangling high in the sky, I was riveted by him. Now, years later, running into him, the attraction rushed back. During the classes I was distracted, my mind focused on Reza, wishing I had been courageous and exchanged phone numbers with him. But he didn't suggest it either. He could have someone, maybe was married. I tried to push him away from my thoughts.

When I got to my apartment, I called Tala to tell her about the unexpected encounter.

"I remember him," she said. "We used to watch him fly kites."

She invited me to meet her on Thursday at 3:00 when Anton would be away overnight in Natanz. She suggested Arte Café. We had gone to it once before, mainly to see an exhibition in its basement.

The interior of the café was appealing; it was designed with old nostalgic artistic items and wooden furniture. It was frequented by intellectuals, artists, writers, journalists, university students.

In the café, Tala was already sitting at a table by a window overlooking a row of tall cypress trees. She was sketching on a pad, which she took with her wherever she went. Most of the tables were taken by young men and women. Some of them were wearing jeans with fake labels, Levi or Nike. Like the girls at Dizin Ski Resort, the girls observed the *hijab* in a loose way, letting most of their hair show. They were talking heatedly about America, how it had harmed Iran as well as benefited it by introducing fresh ideas. They were ignoring the notice posted close to the entrance door, saying: *Please don't talk politics.*

We ordered *café glace* and assorted pastries. As soon as the waiter brought them over, I was startled to see Reza sitting alone at a table in the back. He saw us too and came over. He sat at the table next to ours and I talked a little about the old days, while Tala started to sketch something in her pad. I hadn't seen Reza for years and now I was seeing him twice within a few days. Tala put down the pencil she was sketching with and walked away to the restroom.

"I could always tell you and your sister apart. She walked slightly behind you, kept her head down," Reza said.

Abruptly, he glanced at his watch and got up. "I have to go. Say goodbye to your sister for me." He looked deeply into my eyes, and I felt the tremor of attraction and sensed it in him too. But he didn't ask for a date.

When Tala came back, she turned the pad she had been sketching in to a page. "Look, I drew Reza."

In the drawing, an ugly man, nothing like Reza, was holding his head in his hands and staring into space. She had added a full beard, which he didn't have.

"This isn't very flattering. He's better-looking than this," I said.

"When we used to see him on our street, I sensed he liked you more," she said. "He looked only at you when we passed him."

"So? Anton chose you over me," I said.

"I wish he hadn't."

Then our conversation went in a different direction. "Anton wants me to get pregnant. I'm not ready for it. I've been trying not to, avoiding sex with him as much as possible. I hope you'll get married and then we can both become pregnant at the same time."

"What a great idea!" I said.

We talked for a while longer and finally, we got up, left the café, and went in different directions.

A few days later, I was coming out of the Sepideh Language School and gave a start seeing Reza standing under the sycamore tree across the street. He signaled to me and turned to the side alley. I joined him there and he asked, "Will you see a movie with me? They're showing *Children of Heaven* at Jomhouri Cinema. I've heard really good things about it. We could go to the noon show on Friday. It's empty at that hour. No one will see us."

"Yes," I said without hesitation.

We arranged that I would meet him a few moments before noon, and we would each buy a ticket and go inside separately and take seats in the back row.

I called Tala to tell her about Reza, him waiting for me by the language school, his invitation to see a movie with him. She said what she had before, "I hope you will get married to him so we can plan to have babies at the same time."

"You're jumping ahead. I will be going out with him for the first time."

"I'm sure this won't be the only time."

After we hung up, I kept thinking of Tala's idea of us getting pregnant at the same time. It seemed far-fetched to plan something like that. Anyway, I had no idea how far my relationship with Reza would go.

Hours went by very slowly till Friday. Before going to meet him, I stood in front of the bathroom mirror, studying myself. Did I look different enough from Tala that Reza liked me better than her? I could only see the barely noticeable coloring of our eyes and hair. It was probably something about my manner that drew him to me.

Knowing that he preferred me to Tala made me feel more equal to her since Anton had chosen her over me.

On Friday, as I approached the cinema on the Gholestani intersection, I saw Reza getting off his bicycle and then chaining it to a fence close to the wall, next to other bicycles. He was wearing a saffron-colored shirt and his hair was unruly from the bicycle ride. He had a light, happy aura about him that day.

Then he bought a ticket and went inside, and I did the same, as we had agreed to do. Movie posters hung on the lobby's walls. The air was filled with the scent of espresso coffee from the café on the second floor.

Inside of the theater, we joined each other in the back row, which was empty and dark. There were only a few young people sitting in different spots, some of them together, some alone. The movie had been banned in Iran. But after it won prizes at a film festival in Europe and got acclaim, it was allowed to be shown here.

The plot revolved around a little boy taking his sister's shoes to the shoemaker to be repaired, but he loses them on the way home. The siblings decide to keep the predicament a secret, knowing that their parents don't have enough money to spend on another pair of shoes, fearing they would be punished. They devise a scheme to share the brother's sneakers: the sister would wear them to school in the morning and hand them off to her brother at midday so he could attend afternoon classes. This uncomfortable arrangement leads to one misadventure after another, revealing difficult aspects of life in the poverty-stricken neighborhood.

In the darkness, Reza held my hand, and I felt my heartbeat accelerating. "You wouldn't know this, but when I was in high school, I used to detour going home so that I could see you coming out of your school. Sometimes I followed you, but kept enough of a distance," he whispered. "I didn't want to be like the *lati* boys."

After the movie was over, we took the metro to Tajrish. Walking on the crowded square with people going in and out of a bazaar, carrying bundles of food, and rushing to their destinations, we felt anonymous, more free to be together. After strolling for a while, we went to a kebab restaurant and sat in its garden. As we ate, Reza confided in me. His mother was diagnosed with depression and had to be on medication. His father had died a few years before in an accident when his car hit a post.

He was working as a journalist and taught part-time at a private boys' school. "When I was in college, I was arrested once," he said. "I was wearing a T-shirt with *Free Political Prisoners* printed on it. The *Basij*, noticing the words and assuming they were an attack on the government, arrested me and held me in their headquarters. Luckily, my uncle had some influence and bailed me out."

I told him about my closeness to my uncle as well, especially since losing both parents and then my grandmother. Tala and I were deeply connected to each other, but there were also times of friction and a desire to be separate, be distinguishable to others.

We got up after a while and took the metro back, getting out at the same stop since he lived close to where I did. Before parting, he gave me his apartment's address so I could meet him there. He asked me to go there separately so that the other tenants in the building wouldn't see us together.

His building was small, consisting of three floors. He lived on the third floor. He would leave the outside door open, and I could go up the steps to his apartment. I walked slowly to allow him to get there before me.

He opened the door for me and led me inside. I looked around as he went into the kitchen to get us something to drink. The living room was large with a high ceiling and a window overlooking a courtyard. The pale-yellow walls gave the impression of perpetual light. It was furnished with wooden items, some of them painted yellow or green. Several ornamental terra-cotta jars and bowls were arranged on a mantel. Potted plants—jade, ornamental palm, African violets—stood on the floor near the window. A case filled with books covered half of one wall. I looked at the books. They were mostly by ancient poets, philosophers, the kind of books Baba liked. He returned with two glasses of red wine and a bowl of pistachios. He said he got wine from an Armenian vendor. I told him my father used to get it that way too.

After having some wine and pistachios, we went into the kitchen and he began to make us supper, veal *goulash* and rice. He said he learned the recipe from a Hungarian friend in college. I offered to help with the preparation, but he said he wanted me to relax. I sat on a stool and watched him. He sliced the veal, cut up onions, put them all in a bowl, and shook paprika and salt on the mixture. He sprinkled olive oil in a frying pan, sautéed everything, then added water, covered the pan with a lid, and let the stew simmer. He cooked noodles, boiled them in a pot, and made a creamy sauce for them. He proceeded to make a salad and a vinegar and olive oil dressing.

I was impressed with his ability to cook, as most men stayed away from it. After we sat down at the table and ate and had more wine, talking rapidly at the same time, he took me to the hall, and we climbed the stairway to the roof. The sun was disappearing, leaving streaks of pink, red, and lavender across the sky. The kites danced upward, some tangling together, their bright colors blending into the dusk's light and then vanishing altogether as if they had melted. In the courtyard across the street, a young man was sitting on a rug spread under a tree, reading a book in the light of a lantern hanging from a branch.

"That man teaches in a high school, so does his wife. They have two children. I envy their harmonious life."

Back in his apartment, he put his arms around me and kissed me. His lips pressing against mine sent a wave of pleasure through me. "Stay with me tonight," he said after we pulled apart.

"I have all my stuff in my apartment." Eventually, I got up to leave. We made plans to meet on the following Friday to see another movie, which had a similar theme to the one we saw before.

After the movie, we went to his apartment, and this time we both let go of our inhibitions. We undressed and lay in bed, kissed, and went further. I didn't go all the way. He took some tissues from the side table and wiped us off. As we lay back, he asked me if I had ever had a relationship with another man. I told him about Henry and that we didn't go beyond kissing. He said he had a girlfriend in his first year of journalism school, but the relationship broke up when her parents found out she was seeing him. Soon she was married to a suitor they chose for her. Since then, he hadn't had any relationships with another girl. We kissed again and he whispered, "I can't wait anymore, let's get married. Soon—you agree?"

Resting my head on his chest, I whispered, "Yes, yes."

Later, in my apartment, I called Tala. "Reza proposed," I said.

"I'm so happy for you. I feel better that you have someone. And remember, we talked about getting pregnant at the same time."

I laughed. "It won't be easy to do that."

"We can try."

After we hung up, I felt sad for Tala, wondering if she had ever been in love with Anton the way I was with Reza.

# Chapter 13

Soon after Reza proposed, we began to prepare for a small, casual wedding. He introduced me to his four sisters and mother. His mother was living with his youngest sister, who hadn't married. They were very different from Reza. All his sisters, except for the youngest, married right after high school to men who were shopkeepers, similar to his father, who had been a blacksmith. Reza went beyond all his family members in education.

His mother, sisters, and their husbands adhered to the daily rituals of Islam, as Grandmother had. Reza was agnostic, more like Baba, Mum, Tala, and me. Still, he was close to his family, as I had been to my grandmother and was to my uncle, in spite of the differences between us.

We found an apartment, bigger than the ones we each were living in. I stopped going to the language school as the tuition kept going higher, and by then I was fluent in Spanish and English.

Tala offered me her wedding dress, but I thought it was too fancy, considering we were going to have a small reception in one of Reza's sisters' houses. Instead, I settled for one Uncle Ahmad's coworker's wife made for me, putting sequins from Uncle's own shop at its neckline.

We would have the wedding in Soheila's house so that we could have the guests sit in the courtyard. We went to the Grand Bazaar to look for wedding bands. Daylight came in through the small round skylights. Shoppers, porters, errand boys, brokers, and beggars roamed through the bazaar's lanes and went in and out of shops carrying jewelry, clothes, handbags, kitchen appliances, and produce. Donkeys heavily laden with merchandise made their way laboriously through the lanes. The air was filled with sounds of hammering of metal, the swish of shoemakers' tools, jingling of donkey bells. We found a ring with a woven design for me and a plain one for him.

The day before the wedding, we rented chairs and a large table and arranged them around the pool. We hung strings of colored bulbs on tree branches and added flowers to the beds and bought additional goldfish for the pool.

For the first part of the wedding, in the afternoon, we spread the *termeh* that Grandmother had used for Tala's wedding and arranged the symbolic objects on it, something Reza's family liked to do. The mullah who married Tala came to do the same for Reza and me. He asked Uncle and Hassan, Reza's sister Soheila's husband, if they approved of the wedding, and then asked Reza and me the usual questions.

After the mullah left, Reza's family members and friends, thirty of them altogether, came for the reception. Neither Anton nor Tala came, canceling just before the first part of the wedding. She called and said, "Anton says he has to work in Natanz for two weeks and he doesn't want to go without me this time. He said he absolutely had to leave today. It was an emergency situation. Not that I know what that would be. Forgive me . . ."

"But it's my wedding; you're my sister. Everyone expects you to be here."

"I'm sorry, but you know how Anton is."

Tala lowered her voice to a near whisper as she said, "Roya, this week, locked up with him in Natanz, I finally will try to get pregnant . . . you're getting married, and you can try too. We'll have babies close in age." Before I could respond, she had to get off the phone. I was stirred up by her request, and liked the idea—if we could control getting pregnant as we wished.

The guests were arriving, and my mind drifted to the party. The single men and women didn't mingle directly in respect for the more conservative guests, including Reza's mother and his sisters. But, as at Tala's wedding, the single men, Abbas and Hooshang, Reza's friends, eyed the single women—Afsaneh and another girl, Nooshin, friends from my language school. We had no musicians, in fear of the *Basij*. Hooshang began to play his violin very softly so that it would be hard to hear from the street. *You do not know who you are until you find the person you love*, he sang in a quiet tone.

The lights from the lanterns and the round, full moon were reflected on the pool, creating different shapes and images.

At the end of the evening, after all the guests left, Reza and I went to our apartment. We undressed and lay in bed, making love with abandon.

Reza, not afraid of me getting pregnant and in fact having expressed a desire to have children, didn't wear protection, and neither did I, thinking of what Tala suggested.

The following day we went to a little bucolic village that was less expensive than some other resorts. We stayed for three nights in a hotel perched on a hill covered by bright wildflowers. Our room overlooked a stream with crystal-clear water flowing in it. In the morning, roosters crowed, and the scent of bread baking filled the air. We ate breakfast on the veranda and had bread, jam, and *sarshir*, all made by the family who owned the hotel, and a platter of fruit from their garden.

After breakfast, we explored the village, walking through winding, shady garden lanes with a fragrant breeze blowing.

The air was clean and cool, a contrast to the polluted air in Tehran. Reza told me about an article he was going to write. I told him about a vignette I wrote based on the amazing coincidence that brought us together after years of not having seen each other.

"My grandmother used to call it fate. I think of it as coincidence," I said.

He looked at me in an utterly interested way that made me feel everything I said was important and said, "Yes, coincidence."

We came to a path along the river. We used the flow of the water as our guide. In a secluded area, protected by the high walls of a valley, we climbed down and swam naked in the river.

At night, we ate in one of the village restaurants where the food was prepared with local ingredients and served on plates made by the local artisans. After we left the restaurant, we strolled for a while on streets lit by lanterns hanging from tree branches and by the stars, which were very bright in the clear air.

When we returned to Tehran, we completed our honeymoon by celebrating at the Mar Mare restaurant in Shemiran. The owner had, at one time, introduced Iranian cuisine to Americans and other foreign tourists. It was inside of an eighteenth-century building overlooking a large courtyard filled with ancient trees and an abundance of flowers. The sitting area of the restaurant consisted of booths covered with green velvet cushions. The brick walls were decorated with Persian miniatures and framed calligraphic lines of poems by ancient poets, Saadi, Hafez, and Khayyam. Candles in brass holders were set on tables or hung on walls. The candlelight and the poems, mainly with themes celebrating love, which passed the censors because they were written centuries ago, created a romantic atmosphere.

Finally, in our apartment, we got undressed and went to bed. As we made love, I said to myself, maybe this is the night I will get pregnant, and so will Tala, in another city.

When Tala and Anton returned to Tehran, they invited me and Reza out to dinner at the Russian Club's restaurant, which was separated from the larger part by a colorful curtain. The atmosphere was lush, with a chandelier, vivid blue drops hanging from it, bright maroon chairs, and bouquets of flowers on each table. The people at the other tables seemed to be a mixture of Iranians and Russians. Anton ordered food that was enough for at least ten people—a variety of dumplings, beet soup, fish, and beef. He mainly engaged Reza in conversation, while Tala and I were quiet most of the time, listening to them talking and studying their reactions to what each said to the other. They talked about their work, Reza only mentioning his teaching and of course nothing about his newspaper. Anton only said he worked for the petrochemical company with branches in Tehran, Natanz, and Moscow.

Tala and I were on edge, eager for our husbands to get along. Both of them looked somewhat tense and defensive. As soon as we were finished with dessert—blini and porridge, along with fragrant tea—Anton asked for the check, paid, and we left. He drove us to our apartment. With him behind the wheel, Tala sitting next to him, and Reza and me in the back seat, we were all quiet.

In our apartment, Reza said, "I think Anton is involved in some illegal things. How do you think they manage to live like that?"

"You may be right."

I thought Reza's own involvement with the newspaper, writing under a pseudonym, was considered illegal by the government. But of course, it was of a different nature altogether, with humanitarian intention.

"You didn't tell Tala about my writing . . ."

"I did, but made her promise not to tell Anton."

"You shouldn't have told her."

"She confides in me about Anton. She doesn't trust that he's telling her everything about his work."

The subject was dropped. It was obvious Reza and Anton didn't have much in common.

The following afternoon, Tala called. "I'm sorry nothing developed between our husbands," she said. "They are so different."

I agreed with her, but before I could respond, she had to get off the phone as she heard Anton's car in the driveway. Reflecting on what we had said about how different Anton and Reza were, I realized they were similar in one essential way—they both were keeping a part of their work and activities hidden. Perhaps Reza's work was more honorable, but still, he had to hide and lie about so much that engaged him. It seemed Tala and I couldn't take steps too far from each other, as when we were children. Still, the other differences between our husbands pulled us apart in many ways.

We became close again when we both became pregnant within days of each other, miraculously, as she had wished and so had I.

# Chapter 14

My memories were interrupted by Reza calling me from the living room. I got out of bed to join him. He was making breakfast and listening to *Free Europe in Prague* on the shortwave radio he kept on the kitchen counter.

> *. . . A man who went to Rey Castle to search the rubble for any remnants of his family sobbed when he found his sister's gold necklace—her name was engraved on it . . . Red Crescent workers are searching for people's belongings.*

While I was in the hospital, Reza found out that people killed in the debris and not identified were buried in Paradise Zahra Cemetery in one huge grave with one stone and no names on it.

"I'm sure the numbers were larger than what was reported on the news. That's always the case. We're never told the truth when catastrophes happen," Reza said bitterly. After a pause, he added, "The doctor attending to you at the clinic I spoke to said you and Tala were lucky that you were enclosed in a part of the cavity that was larger, had more air coming in." He sighed. "Of course, lucky isn't the right word."

Reza's grief only intensified mine. "Can we go to the cemetery?" I asked.

"Are you up to it? You're still weak, need to rest."

"Yes, I'd like to go. We can spend a little time and come back." I was taking a strong painkiller that the doctor said was safe enough for a period of time, but I shouldn't take it unless I really needed it. I would take one before leaving for the cemetery.

"Let us go today after breakfast," Reza said. He served us eggs, *sangak* bread, and *sarshir*. He went to the patio and got mint leaves from the plant I had put there. He added them to the tea in the pot.

As we began to eat and drank our tea, we were silent, caught in our grief.

After breakfast, we got ready to go and took the metro to the cemetery's stop. The cemetery, at the southern edge of Tehran, spread for miles along a highway that led to a desert.

It was one of the hottest days in Tehran. Still, the streets were filled with people engaged in different activities. Men wearing black appeared on the wide avenue in front of the cemetery, mourning a popular mullah who had just died. They held a banner that said *You Instilled the Words of God in Us, May Your Soul Rest in Heaven*.

Close to the entrance gate, there was a cart displaying religious items—rosaries, clay *mohrs*, educational pamphlets. Other vendors sold flowers and fruit from their carts. Reza bought a bouquet of flowers, paying what was asked, not bothering to haggle as the other customers did.

Inside the cemetery, families were sitting in different spots, seemingly oblivious to acres and acres of graves. Since they couldn't bring the dead back to life, they seemed to be trying to soothe themselves by eating fragrant, tasty food and carrying on ordinary conversations. They must have already shed tears until their eyes ran dry.

*Aghounds* stood by the gravesides and read prayers for the dead from the Qur'an.

As we walked on, we came across a large area filled with graves of people who were executed when the shah was overthrown and a new regime took over. These gravestones had no names on them. A sign on a pole said *The Infidels*.

We passed *Golkhane-shahida* (flower garden of martyrs), the part of the cemetery devoted to the graves of some of the soldiers who fought in the war with Iraq. They were all automatically declared to be martyrs. On a banner between two trees was written *Victims of Saddam Hussein's brutality: 1980–1988*.

This section was well-kept with flowering bushes all around the graves and many signs saying things like *The martyrs are our saviors, The martyrs are children of God*. The stones had names of the dead and little histories. Some had their own shrines—sealed glass cases on stands, filled with photographs—a few showed the men were wearing helmets or bandannas and holding guns, and others seemed to be at their homes, stroking the family cat or a child. Some cases had war paraphernalia: helmets of fallen soldiers, dusty boots, blood-stained headbands, and worn, rusted diaries. Two gravestones, connected at the side, had the same last names and dates of birth and death, twin brothers who died at the same time fighting on the front. One of the photographs showed both of them in uniform. They were indistinguishable from each other. Would Tala and I die at the same time? I wondered, almost delirious at the tragic sights.

Seminary students in crisp brown frock coats and carefully clipped black beards sat cross-legged by the shrines, fingering rosaries and whispering prayers. Mourners passed platters of *Khoresh*, rice, fruit, nuts, and pastries to each other or to beggars who came over to them.

The vast number of graves only intensified my sorrow.

We reached the one-stone grave Reza had described. *May Their Souls Rest in Heaven* was engraved on it. Reza put the flower bouquet on the stone, next to others already there. I couldn't stop tears from pouring out of my eyes. He put his arm around me while crying himself.

More families started to come and collected around the grave, some of them crying, some addressing their loved ones buried there.

"My dear little girl, you could already read and write," a woman said, choking on her words.

A man was holding a photo of a boy. "My only son," he said, his voice quivering.

Oblivious to our suffering, sparrows chirped in tree branches, and sunlight shone on the large sycamore trees, making them glow with a vivid green color. The sky above was, for a change, free from smog and golden with a mirror-like gleam to it.

Finally, we wiped our tears off with a handkerchief I had in my handbag and left. Outside of the cemetery gate, I gave a start at the sight of Tala and another young woman, standing by the flower seller. There were some scars on one side of Tala's face. I still had a few too on my face and arms.

"Tala! What are you doing here? Why haven't you been calling me?" I asked breathlessly.

"Roya *joon*. I've been completely absorbed in caring for Tavoos. He was sleepless for a while, but he's getting better." She introduced her friend and said, "Simin's grandfather is buried in this cemetery. And I wanted to visit the grave of . . ." she stammered. "The one-stone . . ."

Tala had complained that she didn't have anything in common with Anton's friends' wives on the rare occasions they socialized with them. She seemed to have met Simin on her own, apart from Anton's circle. Reading my thoughts, she said, "Simin and her husband and son live a few blocks from me."

She greeted Reza and then embraced me. "I'm grieving for your baby. I should go now, but I'll call you, I promise." She said goodbye to me and Reza, and she and her friend went inside.

As we waited for the metro, I complained to Reza again about Tala having disconnected herself from me. He was silent, probably having nothing else to add to what he said once before, "She's the darker side of you."

"Maybe it's Anton's fault—making her separate herself from me. Can you try to have a talk with him?"

"What can I say to him, that he's a swine?"

We sank into silence. We got out on Mir Abad Square. He wanted to go to his newspaper's office. But our way was blocked by hundreds of young people, male and female, demonstrating. They held banners with statements, *Free Akbar Tavakoli, We Don't Allow You to Silence Us*. The very air around them reflected anger, suppressed yearnings, and an urgency to change things: arbitrariness, oppression, chaos, secrecy, and fear.

They began to chant praise for liberal leaders in Iran's recent history—Prime Minister Mossadegh and Barzagan. Some held posters with *Iran Freedom Movement* inscribed on them.

"I should join them," Reza said.

"Please, let's go home, I can't bear one more trauma," I said as I saw the *Basij* approaching the demonstration.

Reza might not have conceded had it not been for his awareness of my fragile state of mind, and his own too. In addition, Hossein had told the journalists working for him to stay away from joining demonstrations as they could be arrested and questioned, which could lead to the newspaper being exposed.

A little further down, we came across a group with another agenda. Their leader stood on a platform, holding a loudspeaker and saying, "Reform means an assault on our religion, means blasphemy. The playwright,

Farmaian, must die." The crowd standing around him cheered and then began to shout, "Death to the minister of culture . . ."

A few foreign journalists stood by, taking photographs and jotting down notes.

In Goo Alley, the mother of martyred Ghasam and the sister of martyred Ali were walking by. They disappeared into their houses, black flags hanging above their doorways to signify that someone inside was killed fighting in the war.

A little further, Saiid, "The Woman," came out of his house, cleared his throat, and walked past us. His nickname was "The Woman" because, according to the rumors, he had once been in jail, but had dressed as a cleaning lady and escaped. No one knew what his crime was. One theory was that when he still lived with his parents, he built a hidden pump that directed the *joob* water into his house's large reservoir, depriving others on his street of sufficient water. Some whispered that he was a homosexual based on the way he shunned eligible girls and their mothers, who tried to catch his interest.

So much in our society was shadowy and unpredictable that you never knew what was true or a lie, who you could trust, why a certain thing happened, or why someone did what he or she did. What was upsetting me now was how Tala had become shadowy; even her face was like a blank mirror. I couldn't read her feelings and emotions when I saw her by the cemetery. What is she hiding from me? Again, the question went around and around my mind.

Inside, Reza went to his desk to do some work and I went back to bed to rest.

# Chapter 15

My wounds from the accident had finally healed, and I decided to go to Tala's house, unannounced.

I waited until Reza left for work so that he wouldn't discourage me from going, then I took the bus and got off at the stop close to her house. I waited in the driveway, my heart beating hard as if I had run all the way there. Batul opened the door. "Oh, salaam, how are you? Tala *khanoom* went out with Simin. They took their babies to the park, but they must be on the way back already. She never stays out long. She's still in pain. Come in and wait." She spoke with a tremor in her voice and her head shook slightly too, making her seem much older than her age of forty-five. She worked for Anton before he married Tala. Perhaps he wanted someone weak, who would carry out his orders readily. But from a few interactions I had with her, I got a feeling that she was on Tala's side, not his, when it came to anything that needed meddling with.

In the living room, Batul asked, "Can I get you tea?"

"No, thanks, I just had some."

"I'm sorry about your baby . . . May God keep the devil away from us all." As Batul was leaving the room, she mumbled something that sounded like, "Anton, the devil."

My eyes went to the playpen in the corner. A mobile with wooden fish dangled from its side and a blue-colored ball with white stars lay on its mattress. I heard sounds of footsteps and then Tala walked in, holding Tavoos. The baby, wearing the navy-blue overalls that Tala and I selected together for him while we were still pregnant, was sleeping in her arms. At four months, his features were well-formed, and he had a pile of thick, curly brown hair.

Tala's face twitched a little as we stared at each other speechlessly. "I've been meaning to call you," she said finally.

She seemed remote, as if I weren't within inches of her. Then she wandered to the playpen and put the baby in it. She took off her *manteau* and sat next to me. "Since we brought Tavoos home, Anton hasn't left Tehran. I can barely breathe."

Now that she was not covered up by the *manteau*, I could see she had lost weight. She had also changed her hair color to blond. Noticing my assessment, she said, "Anton thinks I look stylish this way. He told me to join a gym. I met Simin there. Most of the others are spoiled, empty-headed girls, but Simin isn't like that. Do you want to hear something terrible?"

I stared at her, waiting.

"Anton said I should get plastic surgery so that you and I won't look so alike. It was his pressure that made me change my hair color."

"Remember when we were teenagers, sometimes you wanted to change your appearance so that we wouldn't be so identical," I said, trying to make my tone sound light, not sure if I could believe everything she did was because of Anton's pressure.

Tavoos began to cry, and Tala got up and went to get him. She returned, holding him, and sat next to me again.

"Dr. Moosavi told me Tavoos isn't recovered yet from the traumatic birth, but he'll be fine, a baby's brain is resilient. Here, hold him." She put the baby in my arms.

I put a finger in his hand, and he clamped his fingers around it. Then he smiled at me, a reflexive act, of course, but it felt like an acknowledgment. I kissed him on his cheek and rocked him a little in my arms. He looked at me intensely with alert eyes and he touched my hair gently. A surge of love for him rushed over me.

"He loves you," Tala said. "Anton would be so jealous. He notices things like that. He keeps saying to the baby, 'Don't you love your father?' Underneath his dogmatic, superior manner is a cavern of insecurity. He lifts up Tavoos in the air, hoping to get a reaction; Tavoos only cries then."

I cooed to Tavoos and he kept smiling. Then he laid his head on my shoulder.

"Do you know what Anton would have done to me if Tavoos was killed in the accident? He would somehow disable me and then divorce me," Tala said, and took Tavoos from me. "I should put him in his crib and let him sleep a little more." Holding him, she went to his room and returned shortly.

"Why have you been avoiding me?" I asked.

"Tala, I feel terrible. I was the one who talked you into going to Rey. And now you don't have your baby. I just can't bear the guilt."

While I was assessing what she said as being true or a lie, she went on to another complaint about Anton. "After all the rejections, one gallery in Shemiran accepted two of my landscape paintings. But then Anton forbade me to exhibit them. He's trying to stop me from painting. He says it's bad for the baby to be exposed to paint, even though I paint in the room all the way on the other side of the courtyard."

This was expected, Anton had only given her false promises about his admiring her being a painter.

"The other day I was passing the Burn and Trauma Clinic. For the first time, I understood why people try to commit suicide by setting themselves on fire."

"Tala, don't talk like that . . . Are you really that unhappy?"

"I am and I am not. Depends on the day. But the weight is heavier on the side of unhappy. At times I wish I could find my way out, ask for a divorce. But then I know the consequences . . . The court would give custody of Tavoos to him."

The sound of a car entering the driveway interrupted us.

"It must be Anton," Tala said. "He takes breaks from his work and comes home to see Tavoos."

We sank into silence as the door opened and Anton came in.

"Nice to see you," he said to me. He was trying to be friendly, but his expression was ambiguous. It was as if he had a *Do Not Disturb* sign on his face. He was wearing a suit and a tie, as usual. I had never seen him in casual clothes. That added to his aura of arrogance. He quickly went to Tavoos's room and came back with him in his arms. Only then did he look at me with a vague smile on his face, for a moment making him seem gentle, likable, which must have been what enticed Tala, in addition to his wealth.

I started to leave, and Tala followed me outside and kissed my cheek. "As soon as Anton goes to Natanz for a few days, I'll call you and we can get together."

Anton had parked his car, a silver Porsche, in the driveway rather than the garage. It seemed he would be going back to work soon. I wondered if I should walk around for a while and then go back inside. But I had second thoughts. Not only was I feeling tired, but I had also sensed Tala was nervous that I dropped in to see her. That could be why she poured out complaints about Anton and expressed suicidal impulses so that I would be understanding of her having withdrawn from me.

On the way home, I was feeling confused and, at the same time, concerned about Tala. She had sounded so intense. A bitter powerlessness exuded from her. Then I worried about Tavoos—how was all the unhappiness at his home going to affect the poor child? He had already been born traumatically. I fell into a daydream. Tala and Anton had left Tavoos all alone in the house and gone to Natanz together. It was dark, but I could see my way to Tavoos's crib. I picked him up and, holding him in my arms, ran all the way home.

I came back to reality as I reached the station near my apartment and got out. I felt a little calmer as I entered Goo Alley and heard the familiar hum of conversation from the teahouse.

Reza was home early. I told him about my concern for Tala, her expressing suicidal thoughts.

"That's upsetting. But what can we do for her? She's married; it is Anton's responsibility to attend to her problems."

"He's part of her problems." Again, I said, "Can you talk to Anton?"

"I have nothing to say to him. He isn't a child."

"If she leaves him, the baby will go to him by law."

"You're right. She's in a difficult situation." He came over to me, held me in his arms, and kissed me. "I know it's hard on you to find Tala in a bad situation. But it isn't in your power to help her with her marriage."

We talked for a while longer and, finding no solutions, went on to prepare dinner. We were both quiet while eating and withdrew to bed early.

## Chapter 16

Days went by and Tala didn't call to set an appointment. When I called her, she said she would call me soon, but then got off the phone in a rush.

Still, like a desperate child, one afternoon I went to her house, again unannounced, and rang the bell. No one answered. As I turned around to leave, my eyes caught a silhouette behind the curtain on the second floor. Was that Tala? Did she see me and tell Batul not to open the door? Heartbroken, I left.

I mistrusted her blaming Anton as the reason she was avoiding me. She could find time to meet me during the day when he was working. Dark, disturbing thoughts, some old, some new, filled my mind. It could be because she doesn't want me to spend time with Tavoos and is possessive of him. Or she is feeling such intense pity for me having lost my baby while she has hers that she can't bear spending time with me.

Hallucinatory images went before my eyes. I saw Tala and I covered by debris, our babies thrust out of our wombs, their umbilical cords broken. Then I had a vision of her pulling my baby to herself and pushing the baby next to her toward me.

Another image came to me. A rescue worker picked up a baby who was alive and crying. Tala, alert now, said, "Oh, that's my baby." In the confusion, the rescue worker took her word for it. The images were like a mirage, but still, they haunted me.

I have to try to go on with my life and wait for Tala to turn around and seek me out, I said to myself.

Hoping to get pregnant again, I set up an appointment with my obstetrician. It was required for women to have women obstetricians, but they were overbooked since the men obstetricians outnumbered them. I managed to get an appointment with Dr. Davoodi, who had attended to me during the pregnancy.

After I told her about the miscarriage, she squeezed me in for a quick visit.

Reza accompanied me to her office, and we sat on chairs in the waiting room. We were silent and sank into concern about what the doctor was going to tell me. Then it was my turn, and I was called by Dr. Davoodi's nurse to go into her office.

Dr. Davoodi was middle-aged and had a gentle manner. After offering condolences and asking me questions about the accident, she began to examine me. When I got off the table and dressed, she said, "Sit down, let us talk."

I sat on one chair and she on another. "I'm sorry . . . but your uterus was punctured and scars formed. The scar tissue has covered your abdomen and blocked your fallopian tubes."

"Can the scars be removed?"

"It is very risky, almost impossible," she said, and then she tried to comfort me. "You're young, have a life ahead of you. There are always new inventions in science that could possibly help you."

Still, I left the office filled with despair. In the reception room now, a few pregnant women were waiting their turn. Children hung around their mothers or stood by the fish tank in the corner.

"Are they alive?" a little boy asked Reza.

"Yes, they live in water," Reza said, his face lighting up at the child's curiosity. How sad that he might never be a father, I thought.

He got up and we left. Outside, I said to him, "My dear, I don't have good news."

"What is it?" he asked, looking a little shaken.

"Dr. Davoodi believes I can't get pregnant again unless there are new developments in science."

After a long pause between us, Reza said, "We should consult other doctors."

Then we went in different directions, he to his newspaper office and I toward the metro back to our apartment.

The next obstetrician we consulted, Dr. Mahnaz Hamadi, had a medical degree from England. She was highly recommended by one of Reza's colleagues.

Dr. Hamadi examined me carefully, but alas, she did not have better news. "I'm very sorry to say the damage to the womb is extensive, and the scars are large and deep."

Again, I had to give Reza the disappointing news.

The travel agency hadn't called me since I had taken three months maternity leave. I rang their phone number but there was no answer, and no new number was given. I decided to go there and hope someone would be in who I could talk to. The most direct way to get there was by bus. People had collected by the bus stop, shifting in their spots, mumbling complaints.

"Get in, miss," a taxi driver said to me, stopping at the curb. He already had four women in the taxi.

I shook my head. Taking a shared taxi was still more expensive than taking the bus.

"Sixteen hours a day driving this damn taxi. I only hope my son will have a better life than me," the driver said, and then put his foot on the accelerator and zoomed off.

There was no bus in sight, and I started walking. On Vali Asr Avenue, vendors had put stacks of dollars and other currency on low tables in front of them; they claimed to offer better rates in dollar to *tooman* than banks would. I passed an old-fashioned tailor shop with young girls working behind antiquated sewing machines. Large pairs of scissors hung on a wall behind them.

When I reached Homa Travel Agency, a sheet of paper was clumsily Scotch-taped to its door. On the paper was scribbled *Closed because of high rent*. Tourism had dropped because of various international conflicts with Iran and the rising prices of air travel.

Disappointed and wondering what other possibilities I could look into, I decided to go to a job agency. I had once passed one on this avenue, just a few blocks away. Perhaps it would have listings of travel agencies that were still open, or other jobs.

I walked in its direction and reached Negar Job Agency. By then, my scarf and *manteau* were covered by soot and dust; I felt a deep exhaustion that made me want to turn around, return home, and sleep. I willed myself to go inside and find out if anything was available. The women sitting in booths were wearing dark chadors, *hijab* being observed more strictly in offices. I went to one of the desks.

"Jobs are scarce," the young woman sitting there said. "Fill out a form and we'll let you know if something comes up." She handed me a form.

I sat on a chair next to a counter and filled it out and gave it back to her.

"A job might be available," she said. "Do you know how to knit?"

"Yes." I had learned it from Grandmother.

"Best Baby Clothes is looking for someone to knit children's clothing for them. It's only five blocks from here on the same side of the street. Speak to Mrs. Beyoglu, the owner. Tell her I sent you there."

I found it easily. On the wall next to the entrance door, someone had scribbled in English, *I love you, kiss me.* Inside of the store, the walls were covered by photographs of children at different stages of development—a baby holding onto a chair, children playing in an amusement park. An attractive woman, wearing a colorful scarf loosely, letting patches of her blond hair show, was helping customers. Two women who seemed to be mother and daughter bought several outfits, a few of them with Tweety Bird and Morris the Cat embroidered on them in English.

"Are you Mrs. Beyoglu?" I asked after the customers left.

She nodded. "May I help you?"

I told her my reason for being there and the job agency that referred me to her.

"I'd be interested in baby sweaters, outfits, hats. Here are some examples." She spread photographs of babies wearing different outfits and hats and sweaters that another freelance employee had knitted for her. Then she showed me patterns and yarns. "You can select any of these. I'd leave it to your judgment . . . If you agree with my terms, you can start as soon as you want."

She gave me the necessary papers, on one of which I had to agree to accept half of what each item sold for. The other form that she signed said she would be responsible for the expenses of yarn, pattern, and the commission to Negar Job Agency.

"I'm sorry that I can't pay more, the rent here is so high," she said.

"I understand," I said. In truth, one-half was more than I expected. I knew from people in the neighborhood that most other similar places paid only one-third.

I selected patterns and yarns to use and left.

On the way back home, Jordan Square was thronged with people gathering around the carts piled with merchandise—produce, plastic handbags and slippers, fake Levi's. People examined the items and haggled with the vendors. Lately, I bought from carts that charged less than shops as I hadn't worked for a few months and we were low on money. The income I had was from the rent I got from the family house, but some of that went to repairs and sometimes the house had no renters. Reza's salary from the high school and a very small sum from the newspaper didn't compensate for my lost income from the travel agency. I bought a handbag to put the knitting material in and headed home.

After a few blocks, I came across my friend Afsaneh, who I'd met at the language school.

"Afsaneh," I said.

"Oh, Roya, so nice to see you."

We filled each other in on what was happening in our lives. She was very sympathetic to me when I had the miscarriage, and had visited me often. But then we hadn't seen each other for over a year. She had gone to France to take courses in architecture to build upon what she learned at the architecture school in Tehran.

"I'm between jobs for two weeks," she said. "I'm just heading to see a play, *Shahr-e Qessa*, at the Jameh Theater; it got a good review in *Emrooz* magazine. I have an extra ticket. My friend canceled. Do you want to come with me?"

I had nothing planned for the afternoon and Reza was at work. I welcomed the distraction.

The theater was a modern round wooden structure with latticework decorating the top. There was a Picasso-like statue on the lawn in front. When we walked in, the auditorium was filled to its eighty-seat capacity, mainly with young people.

*Shahr-e Qessa* (*City of Tales*) was a drama, a parable about contemporary sociopolitical issues. In the interwoven stories, the corrupt, aggressive managers of various companies begin to take control of payment and benefits for employees, until finally the employees unite together and start fighting back. At the end, the employees win, a happy resolution to the sad story.

On the street after leaving the theater, Afsaneh and I agreed that the happy ending was a good idea after all the depressing scenes, though it wasn't necessarily realistic that employees would get their way.

We went to College Street and sat in a recently opened French café. The place was small and decorated tastefully, with a terracotta floor, rust-colored walls, beige chairs, and tables. We ordered cream puffs and café au lait served by a waitress who spoke with a French accent.

As we began to eat, I told Afsaneh how doctors had told me I couldn't get pregnant again.

"Oh, I'm so sorry. There's always hope for new treatments."

"That's what the doctors said." Then the hallucinatory images of Tala pulling my baby to herself when we had the accident, which haunted me in my dreams and daydreams, came before my eyes. "Afsaneh, I hope you don't think I am insane if I tell you . . ."

"What is it?" she said, focusing on me intently.

"I wonder if my sister stole my baby."

"What do you mean, stole?"

"When we fell under the debris in the collapsed building, she might have been more alert than me and could have taken my living baby."

"Oh, that'd be so terrible. Is she capable of that? You're so close."

"Her husband wanted a son, and demanded it as if she had some control over it. Maybe she was afraid of the consequences, of what he would do to her if her baby was dead."

"Oh, Roya . . . that would be an unspeakable betrayal . . ."

I felt tears collecting in my eyes. Maybe this was all due to my envy. We had tried to get pregnant close to each other and it had happened. We talked and talked about taking walks with our babies, visiting each other frequently. We shared ideas about what we heard was good or bad for babies. And now I didn't have a baby and maybe wouldn't get pregnant again. Tala had hers and she was leaving me out of her life as a mother.

"Maybe I'm just envious of her . . ." I said.

"DNA testing is available at the British Embassy, but they use it only to establish if a person committed a crime. It isn't allowed by the government to give it to anyone, on the basis that it would create shame and conflict."

"Of course, I could never bring myself to tell Tala of my suspicion and go for DNA testing, even if it was available. That would destroy my relationship with her permanently and infuriate her husband. It would have dire consequences for her."

We both sank into ourselves for a moment. Then she said, "There's something I've never told you. I don't want everyone to know about this, so please keep it between us."

"I promise I will."

"I'm not my parents' biological daughter. My father found me in an alley. I was on the sidewalk next to the wall, covered by a blanket. He took me home. They reported it to the police, and on their own put notices in *Daily Tehran* and other places, but no one came to claim me. So they adopted me. They were overjoyed to have me because my mother couldn't get pregnant."

I said nothing for a moment, startled by what she had revealed. Finally, I said, "You look so much like your mother, the same blue eyes."

"Yes, it's strange."

"So lucky that your father found you." I reached over and kissed her cheek.

"I never had a desire to find my birth parents." She paused, lowered her voice, and said in a near whisper, "Maybe my birth mother got pregnant out of wedlock. Maybe she was a prostitute . . . If my parents weren't so wonderful, I might have tried to find her."

A line of people wanting to get tables was forming in the restaurant. The waiter put the bill down on our table.

Afsaneh insisted on paying. I thanked her and we got up to leave. Outside, we promised to see each other again soon.

# Chapter 17

On the way home, an impulse came over me to turn around and go to Tala's house, hoping to find her and talk to her about that day of the horrific accident, one baby dead, one alive. Perhaps I would tell her honestly how confused I was, that I couldn't be sure it was my baby who died. But even thinking of doing that made me feel crazed. Then an idea formed in me; Reza and I could adopt a baby. Afsaneh had turned out so well, having been adopted by nice parents. I believed Reza would be a good, accepting father and I would be the same.

I changed my mind about going to see Tala and went in the direction of my apartment. On Khanat Abad Avenue, next to the old Karvansaray, a row of men in gray laborer's clothes were sitting and leaning against the wall, eating sandwiches and drinking imitation colas, either taking breaks from their jobs or waiting for someone to come by and offer them jobs. I was startled as I recognized one of them, with an angular face and a full beard, to be Jalal Mohammadi, a journalist who was imprisoned for a year and let go after he signed a statement that he would never write anything "inflammatory," which meant criticism of the way certain things were handled by the government. His photographs were in newspapers for days.

When I got home, Reza was in, sitting at his desk. He got up, held me in his arms, and kissed me.

I pulled away, and almost breathless, I managed to tell him I had seen Jalal Mohammadi sitting against a wall along with a few laborers. I added, "Reza, do you want to end up like him? You should quit before it's too late."

Clearly, he wasn't in the mood to pursue the subject. He said, "I'm in the middle of writing something." Then he sat down again at his desk.

He was totally committed to his work. I thought of how he and his colleagues took turns distributing copies of the newspapers to newsstand owners who were willing to take the risk. They also put them in lobbies of universities when no one was looking. In the office, they stuffed the newspapers in large burlap sacks, the kind used in old-fashioned shops for storage, and drove them to places in a car that the publisher left at their disposal. When it was Reza's turn, he would wake even earlier than usual, have a quick breakfast, and dash out. I was always full of trepidation. Sooner or later, the newspaper office would be discovered and he and the others working there would be arrested.

I left, went to the small patio extending from the living room, sat on the chair among potted plants I had put there, and started to knit a baby sweater. The patio overlooked a usually empty alley with a dead end on one side and its other side blocked by an abandoned building project. The scent of the mint plant I had grown in one of the pots mingling with the scents from the flowers in another pot filled the air. So often I envisioned bringing the baby to the patio for fresh air.

As it began to grow dark, I went inside to get dinner ready.

Reza and I prepared dinner together and sat at the dining table. As we started eating, I thought about my talk with Afsaneh. "Why don't we adopt a baby? I met Afsaneh today. She told me she was adopted. She has turned out to be a wonderful, accomplished girl."

"I wish we could," he said promptly. Obviously, he had thought about it and dismissed the idea. "They'd do a background check and might find out about the newspaper, the pseudonym I use."

His words felt like blows. "Our life is hell . . ." I couldn't stop myself from saying.

We sank into silence for a moment. Then he startled me, saying, "I forgot to tell you, Tala called me this morning in my office."

"She called you, why is she calling you . . ." I asked, astounded. "How did she get your phone number?"

"I'm not sure. You must have given it to her."

"What did you talk about?" I asked, recalling giving her the number during our pregnancies in case something important came up and Reza wasn't home to answer the phone.

"She said she wanted to tell me; it was harder for her to tell you."

"What was it?" I asked, confusion swirling through me.

"She changed her mind. She couldn't bring herself to say it."

"Are you telling me everything?" I barely managed to ask through my constricted throat.

"Of course I am."

After we finished eating, as usual, he went to his desk to work.

I recalled a conversation I had with Tala when we were sitting together in a café.

"Are you still happy with Reza?" she asked.

"You know my life with him is difficult," I said, repeating what I had already told her. "I'm always on edge that he's going to be arrested."

"But you love him," she said wistfully, as if envious that she had fallen out of love with Anton, if she had ever loved him.

"Yes," I said.

Did she have a pang of jealousy of me that she couldn't bear? Had she at moments wanted to make love to Reza, to experience what I did, as she claimed was her reason for having sex with Henry? I tried to push away images of her and Reza meeting in a secluded place and making love and promising each other they would never tell me about it. But then why had Reza told me she called him?

Feeling stirred up and confused, I dialed Tala's number. Batul answered and said Tala was resting, a typical response.

I felt utterly empty—in twenty-four years of my life I had lost my mother, father, grandmother, and baby, and now Tala had become inaccessible to me.

I lay on the sofa and closed my eyes . . .

*Tala was wearing a dress in a saffron color, with rectangular designs of blue scattered on it and a belt tied in the back at her waist.*

*"You are wearing my dress," I said.*

*"I wanted to try it on, but I don't like it, it's poorly sewn," she said, taking it off. "Look at the crooked collar, mismatched sleeves."*

I woke with a start, and when I managed to fall back to sleep, I had another, more disturbing dream.

*Tala and I were in an unfamiliar room, leaning against cushions. I realized with a start that we weren't the only ones in the room. Reza was there too. Tala reached over and held one of Reza's hands. Then the two of them lay down and she spread a sheet she picked up from the floor over both of them. I could tell they were undressing from the way it showed through the sheet.*

*"What are you doing, he's my husband," I said to her, and to him, "She's my sister."*

*Reza was silent.*

*Tala said, "He's in love with me, you understand, don't you? We can share him. I wish Anton would die."*

I woke to the sounds of an argument between two men in the alley. That was just a dream, I realized, but felt no relief.

Ever since Reza told me that Tala called him in his office, everything around me seemed to have a secret meaning—the phone ringing once and then stopping, him leaving the apartment earlier than usual. I questioned him again and again about that phone call, and each time he answered calmly, "All I know is what I already told you. She said she wanted to tell me something that was harder for her to tell you." Only once he burst out, "Will you stop questioning me? You have to ask her what her motive was."

My suspicion faded gradually every time I heard Reza's sincere tone and saw how much his usual involvement with his work consumed him. He didn't seem capable of such a betrayal. He had always questioned Tala's character, said she was the dark side of me. The person I needed to confront was Tala.

Finally, I decided to once again just drop in on her.

Batul opened the door and said Tala was out with Simin and had taken Tavoos with her. "Come in and wait for her."

I had just sat down on the sofa in the living room when sounds of footsteps reached me and Tala walked in, holding Tavoos. Tala's face twitched a little as we stared at each other speechlessly.

She put Tavoos in the crib, came back, and sat next to me. "I've been meaning to call you," she said finally.

"You called Reza." The words flew out of me with intensity.

"I'm sorry . . ." She looked utterly lonely, as if she was talking to herself, as if I weren't within inches of her. "I wanted to tell him how bad I felt for him and you . . . about the loss. That it was my fault we went to the castle."

"But you could have given that message to him through me."

"It was an impulse—I know it was out of line for me to call him . . . But I had no intentions beyond just offering an apology. I promise I will never call him again."

There was no point in pursuing the subject, so I went on to another one that was on my mind. "Tala, I have a big problem. I can't get pregnant again. I have thick scar tissue in my womb. I consulted two doctors."

"Oh, I'm so sorry. But what doctors are telling you now may not be the case all the time. There are new developments . . . At least you're lucky that Reza isn't like Anton. Anton would certainly divorce me. Not only the nature of his job, but his background is also kept from me. Only once after I kept questioning him, he told me his father was in jail for years and died there."

"Really? On what charge?"

"A very strange reason. After the shah was overthrown, the airplanes he'd purchased from America became useless. So Anton's father, who was a pilot, stole some of the useful parts of the old abandoned planes and sold them back to American companies, keeping the money."

We stopped talking as we heard a car entering the driveway and Anton came in.

I said hello to Anton, and he nodded at me. I said goodbye and left. All the way home I thought about what Tala had said, in a sincere tone, was her reason for calling Reza. I would try to accept it, I decided, unless Reza's way of acting or treating me changed, pointing to guilt.

Days went by, and since Reza hadn't changed in his work habits or his treatment of me, I began to believe Tala's reason for calling him was what they had both told me.

# Chapter 18

I worked hard knitting baby clothes, even though anything connected to babies pained me. I realized that along with the pain were some moments of pleasure in the idea that a mother would like my work and buy it. When I had a little time, I wrote in my notebook, stories which were based on real events or made up. Often, they went in the direction of how accidents or coincidences could irrevocably change the course of one's life, how illusion and reality were often interwoven, indistinguishable.

Reza, involved with his teaching and writing articles, was always overworked, making it easy to avoid discussions that would lead to disagreements or accusations and doubts—such as Tala's phone call to him.

One evening he came home, looking uplifted. He said, "Hossein gave us a bonus today. He's happy that the threats have stopped. Let us eat out tonight. We haven't done that for a long time."

We both changed our clothes and left for the restaurant.

On the way to Beheshti restaurant, after we got out of the metro station, we passed Revolutionary Square, crowded with people roaming around, cars racing, and drivers shouting at each other. Billboards showing Sony, Coca-Cola, David Beckham, and portraits of Khomeini were visible beyond the minarets of Friday Mosque.

In the restaurant, we were seated at a table overlooking the Church of the Holy Cross, still preserved after the Revolution that led to the destruction of many buildings and monuments. In its little garden stood a statue of the Madonna, holding a baby in her arms, her face serene. I felt a pang of loss and turned away from looking at it.

We ordered lamb kebabs, Shirazi salad, lima bean and dill rice, and nonalcoholic beer. The waiter brought everything and arranged it on the table.

I noticed two bearded men sitting at a table on the other side of the room with briefcases by their sides, their eyes focused on Reza.

Reza noticed them too. He whispered, "Those men are making me nervous. Let's leave."

He paid and we left. Outside, the silhouette of the mountains surrounding the city dissolved and a blade-shaped moon appeared in the sky.

The men followed us as we walked to the metro station. But then they turned around and went in a different direction.

"I guess it wasn't me they were looking for," Reza said and sighed with relief.

But when we went to bed, we had a hard time sleeping. The sight of those men lingered with us, taking over our other concerns. Reza tried to calm us down. He said, "We're overreacting. They realized their mistake."

We finally fell asleep.

The following day, dusk was approaching as I walked home after doing some shopping—buying a new scarf and tights from a cart that would be less expensive than a shop.

On Jamaly Avenue, a dark cloud of diesel fumes, coming out of old exhausts, hovered in the air, mixing with scents of chive, basil, and parsley from the produce stores. Pedestrians were wandering in and out of shops. On the sidewalk, a man was boiling sugar in a massive pot set over an open fire to crystallize it. A little further, peddlers were hawking a variety of merchandise. "Two *toomans* for a kilo of freshest mulberries," "Roasted corn . . . ," "Flowers that soothe your dear ones' souls."

I stopped by the cart that carried vegetables and fruit and bought some. As I was paying, Gholam, the toothless old man, who was there daily with his cart, said, "Reza *Agha* was just here. A car stopped by him. Two men got out and forced him inside." Then, staring into my eyes, he said, "*Khanoom*, it was a black Mercedes . . ."

His remark shook me. The *Basij* drove Mercedes provided for them by the government. Could they have been those men who were watching us in the restaurant? Just a few weeks ago, a teenage boy living with his family in one of the alleys near us was arrested on some obscure charge. I saw him being handcuffed by two *basiji* and taken away. His old mother followed them, using a cane. "Please, he's my only son, my sweet innocent boy."

What were those men going to do to Reza, where were they taking him? I thanked Gholam and walked home rapidly. In the apartment, I dialed Reza's office number in case the men had let him go and he was there now. It rang and rang but he didn't answer. He had told me firmly I should never go to the office to look for him. He took me there only once, after dark one evening. It looked like any modern office, with new equipment and fluorescent lights. The press was in the basement, but the clanking of machines reached the office.

"Can't people passing on the street hear this?" I had asked.

"The basement has thick stone walls. The sound comes through the ceiling," Reza said.

Now, as I waited anxiously for his return, I went to his desk to look at notes he had taken for future articles. I found a pile of sheets, compositions written by students in the high school he was teaching at. I figured out what the assignment was: "Write a story about what your dreams are for the future; aim high." The school was filled with children of liberal, educated parents and Reza wouldn't get into trouble for trying to lead them to aim for higher education, to think critically, and try to solve problems.

Next to them, I found notes he had taken for articles to write.

*Is the architect hired to restore old buildings competent?*

*Does a country need to "acculturate" and "guide" her people?*

*Why do two women count as one man?*

*If Coca-Cola is bad, why is it being bottled in the holy city of Mashad?*

*Why do mullahs hide satellite dishes at their home but forbid them to others?*

Then I reread one of the cuttings of his articles in *Ayande*, the newspaper he wrote for, always under a pseudonym.

*March 5, 2020*

*Ayande, PROTEST, by Jahangir Le Blanc*

*On the soccer field, a pop band took the stage. One of the singers announced, "I'm dedicating this song to all the journalists who have been arrested and put in prison and kept under terrible conditions." The singer had an Iranian flag around his shoulders. The streets near the stadium were packed with police. Members of the Revolutionary Guard Corps, wearing fatigues and holding rifles, rushed into the stadium as the audience began to chant. Many people among the audience were beaten and arrested.*

It wasn't that I didn't agree with most of Reza's ideas, but I wasn't willing to take risks like he was. I took the notes, the cuttings, and some banned books from the shelf on the wall behind the desk and put them all in two shopping bags. My hand was shaking as I carried the bags to the cubicle in the basement, one allowed to each tenant for storage. Luckily, I didn't encounter anyone.

I had dark images of Reza being taken to Evin, the notorious jail for political "criminals" that stood on a winding road off the expressway. It had iron walls, low architecture, rows of narrow, dank cells inside, and interrogation chambers. When pregnant, Tala and I had gone to Luna Park, one of the parks we were checking out to potentially bring our children to. When we got there, we found out that Luna Park, a little less than a mile from Evin, was the base for shuttle buses taking visitors to the prison. When a prisoner was about to be released, the family had to wait in the park. The sight of the anxious families and all the police around prompted us to leave immediately.

Reza's sisters had moved to an apartment complex in a newly developing neighborhood where phone lines were not installed yet. Soheila's husband had a phone in his shop, but that would be closed at this hour. I didn't have Reza's friends' phone numbers. Waiting for him to return home and not being able to reach anyone to ask if they knew the cause of his delay was unbearable.

A knock on the door startled me. I was afraid to open it. Could it be the *Basij*, coming to search our apartment as I feared? More, louder knocks followed.

"Open up, it's me." It was Reza's voice.

I ran to get the door, feeling a surge of relief.

"The men who were watching us at the restaurant were waiting for me on Jamaly Avenue. I don't know why they left me alone then, but today as I was coming home, they forced me into their car. They took me to their headquarters, questioned me, and slapped me. Then another guard came in, said something to them, and suddenly they let me go."

"Have they found out about the newspaper?" I asked, my heart beating violently.

"No, they thought I was connected with a team organizing Tehran University students to demonstrate again," he said.

"Reza, are you keeping something from me?"

"No, I had nothing to do with any of that."

"Sooner or later, they'll find out about the newspaper."

"Why should I be one of those passive half-dead people?"

"Remember, we picked names meaning 'happy' and 'safe' for our children. We put happiness and safety above everything for them."

"Mindlessness, passivity, isn't happiness."

"I want a half-normal life."

"A half-normal life here is being half-dead," he said, flushing.

"Can't you at least get work in a reformist newspaper?"

"Those papers are like clubs now. They give work to people they know. You can't just go through the front door; you have to find a back window to go in from."

"I don't want to wait for everyone else in the world to be happy first . . . Reza, do you still love me?"

"What kind of question is that? You know I love you," he said.

When we finally went to bed my sleep was dreamless, blank, and dark. I woke from the sound of the pool faucet being turned on for tenants to do ablution. I felt the throbbing I used to have in my forehead during the pregnancy. Any day he could be arrested, and we would be torn apart.

Reza wasn't in bed. I heard him humming a song to himself in the shower. *Don't give up your dreams . . .*

He stopped singing and soon he came into the dining room wrapped in his bathrobe.

I served us tea, bread, jam, and cheese, and as we started to eat, he asked, "What happened to my notes and other stuff?"

"I put them in storage. I was afraid they'd come and search."

"Good. But where are the students' papers?"

"They are in the drawer."

He got up. "I have to go to work. My teaching is for the whole week."

"Are you well enough to work?"

"I think so."

After he left, conflicting thoughts took over me. Was something wrong with me to criticize Reza for striving to make a change? He and others like him were flickering candles in a dark landscape. But how do you balance self-preservation with self-sacrifice? Where do you draw the line between idealism and strayed, useless expression of anger? Reza was soft-spoken, gentle, and had a sense of humor, but anger churned in the deep well of his existence. When he started a new article, he stayed at his desk all night. He skipped breakfast so that he could work on it. He rushed out of the apartment unshaven, wearing mismatched clothes, in a hurry to share what he wrote with his coworkers. Did he ever truly love me, or were ideals his true love? Even his desire for children was tinged with his ideals. "I want to raise them in the right way." He tried to influence his sisters' children, and read books to them that he hoped would make them aware of right and wrong in our society. He had said so many times, "Journalism is my life."

I was influenced by Baba's belief in putting the protection of loved ones over chasing after change through protests and activities that endangered them.

One of the few times I actively participated in a political protest was in my last year of high school. On March 8 of that year, Tala and I joined the large number of women demonstrating at Jaleh Square. Some of the women were wearing armbands saying *We want freedom of speech* or *We want equality with men*. Tala and I joined a group shouting, *Our people didn't pay for the Revolution with their blood to create a new prison*. The *Basij* appeared and first went to the ones with armbands, beat some of them with sticks, and pushed them toward their cars. Guards began to spray water on us and make more arrests. Tala and I managed to get away.

When we returned home and heatedly told Baba about our participation in the demonstration, he told us, "I'm not a man of action. Even my objection against the shah's brutal regime was no more than verbal protest and adding my name to petitions. I didn't take the risk that masses of people who swarmed the streets, protesting loudly, did; some of them were arrested and some executed. That was so that I could be here for my family. I put the protection of my loved ones over idealism. I don't know if that's right or not but that's my preference. My dear Roya and Tala, I loved you and your mother more than my ideals. I wanted to take care of you."

Did Reza put his idealism above anything else, even my safety? Did he love me the way Baba did, or were his emotions when it came to his love for me faint compared to his ideals? I had no answer to these troubling questions.

# Chapter 19

Soon after Reza left the apartment, I went to Best Baby Clothes to drop off the sweaters I had knitted. Mrs. Beyoglu's face brightened up as she said, "Your twin sister was here yesterday and bought a few outfits for her baby."

I was startled. "How do you know she was my sister?"

"She looks exactly like you. Only the color of her hair seems to have been lightened. I asked her if she knew you were working for me and showed her two of the outfits you made. She looked at them carefully but selected other items and left the shop quickly."

Feeling pain, as if Mrs. Beyoglu had thrown icicles at me, I said nothing. After she examined what I made for her and she paid me, I selected more yarns and left. Tala had been shopping for her baby, but did not want what I had made, though they most likely would have fit Tavoos. Besides, she could have asked me to make whatever she liked for Tavoos instead of going to the shop.

When I reached home, in the courtyard, the young muscular swarthy Afghan man, Emir, who came in once a week to take care of maintenance chores, was pruning the trees and bushes. Mina, the landlord's fifteen-year-old daughter, was hanging clothes on a rope tied between two quince trees to dry in sunlight. She kept taking glances at Emir, a man her father would never let her to marry, considering him below her level.

I went up to our apartment and found Reza was already there, sitting at his desk.

"Tala was shopping at Best Baby Clothes," I said.

"So? Nothing wrong with that."

"She could have asked me to make clothes for her baby."

"She probably thought you wouldn't accept payment from her."

"At least she could have selected the ones I gave to the store. They would fit Tavoos."

"Stop obsessing about Tala. She has her own life now, separate from yours."

I walked away since the discussion wasn't getting anywhere.

Over the next few days, I made two sweaters, one in blue and one in white and maroon, about the size that would fit Tavoos. I packed them in a box I bought from the stationery store near me, went to the post office, and mailed it to Tala. I waited anxiously for her to call.

She called five days later. "Oh, it's so nice of you, my dear Roya, to make these. They fit Tavoos perfectly," she said in a sincere tone.

"I didn't have the chance to give you a present for him sooner," I said.

"Of course, it's understandable. You were traumatized, as I was. Anyway, don't worry about it."

Before I could say anything else, she said she had to get off the phone because she heard Tavoos crying. She was always the one who got off the phone.

Nowruz holidays were approaching, and for the following days, I was busy preparing for them.

Nowruz started on March 21, celebrating the beginning of spring and the renewal of nature, with a set of beliefs handed down from Zoroastrianism. The government hadn't been able to suppress the holiday, though it was secular—it was so deeply embedded in the culture.

Trees were full of new leaves and blossoms. Tulips and daffodils filled the flowerbeds. Birds sang cheerfully in tree branches or flew upward to the sky. The snow that made walking difficult in our narrow street had all melted and sunlight shone on the remaining puddles. Florists displayed flowers in wooden boxes for customers to buy. Mostafa, the landlord, and his wife, Golnar, planted new flowers in the courtyard. He put the goldfish, kept in an indoor tank over the winter, back in the pool.

In preparation for the holiday, Reza and I cleaned, shook rugs to remove dust, and put the wheat plants we had grown from seeds on oval platters on the windowsill.

We had to finally face giving up the baby's belongings. Even after I miscarried and was told by doctors that I wouldn't be able to get pregnant, we kept the baby's room intact—the crib, the little unisex outfits on one shelf, and toys on another shelf.

Since another obstetrician I visited told me there was no hope for me to get pregnant, I asked Geraleh, a pregnant woman living in the alley, to come and take away everything that we put in the room for the baby.

Geraleh already had five children; she and her husband made a bare living from his fabric store. I had seen her coming out of the Center for Needy Women with bags filled with food—bread, eggs, milk, cheese.

She came to our apartment with her two teenage brothers. "You're such kind people, God will reward you in ways us mortals may not be able to understand or predict," she said.

Gradually, her brothers took everything out of the room—the crib, the receiving blanket, the small bureau filled with baby outfits, bibs, bonnets, and socks—to take to her apartment.

After they all left, I helped Reza move his desk, chair, and bookcase from the corner of the L-shaped living room to what was meant to be the baby's room. We moved the dining table and chairs to the space where his desk had been.

Reza, sad and on the verge of tears, left the house. I took refuge in looking at different objects that had histories for me, the ones I chose from Mum's and Grandmother's belongings—silk Isfahan rugs with paisley designs, brass silverware with leaf designs, blue ceramic plates, the two lamps with burgundy shades. Would Tala and I be who we were now if Mum hadn't died when we were so young? Maybe she would have prevented the mistrust between us. I recalled again what she asked me and Tala. "Will you promise to always be best friends?" She looked at me and then at Tala and said, "Yes, stay close."

Then, inevitably, my mind went to Tala being a mother to Tavoos, she with her unstable nature. What kind of influence she would have on him?

Reza returned home late. "I went to see Abbas. He needs help. He's been smoking opium."

"Oh, that's upsetting."

"I gave him a lecture about it, I don't know if it did any good."

We ate a quick dinner without saying much else and withdrew to bed, engaged in our own thoughts.

On Nowruz day, he put on his navy-blue woolen sweater and I put
on the blue silk scarf we had given each other as presents, and we left
for Reza's sister Soheila's apartment, where she and her family moved
after selling their house. We carried a variety of presents for his family
members. On the street, voices of children talking and laughing and
the sound of music reached us from inside of houses.

Someone was singing in the adjacent alley, *In the spring, the heart is
restless, my beloved, come and warm up my cold heart.*

*Eid Mubarak* was written on the walls or doors of stores that were
closed for the holidays. Bright pink and yellow blossoms were visible
on trees.

On Hassan Martyr Alley, a couple with ten children, starting from
age two, rushed out of their house, filling the narrow alley. Two of the
little girls, who were below the age of nine and didn't have to cover up,
were dressed in shiny patent leather shoes, with ribbons in their hair
and the belts of their full-skirted dresses tied in the back, just like Tala
and I did at that age.

On Jamaly Avenue, we waited for a long time for a bus and finally
decided to take a taxi, a luxury we rarely allowed ourselves, as no buses
were in sight and the metro was closed for the day.

As the taxi moved easily through the streets, I could tell Reza was
tense about visiting his family. Ever since the miscarriage and my in-
ability to get pregnant, there was a covert criticism of me among his
sisters. It was as if they were silently saying, "You were foolish to take
that chance going to Rey," reflecting what I knew Reza still felt to some
extent.

When we arrived, his sisters, his mother, cousins, aunts, uncles, and
their numerous children were already in the apartment. They all got
up and we kissed and said *Eid Mubarak.* The apartment was sparsely
furnished, in keeping with the Muslim tradition, which Reza's family
observed and Reza had rebelled against, with only rugs on the floors,
one table to hold the food, and no chairs. On the walls were posters of
mosques and framed calligraphic *surahs* from the Qur'an.

Soheila had set an elaborate *Haft Seen* on a table, following a tradition
that included putting at least seven items, their names starting with the
letter S in Farsi, on a table, each symbolic of something. My eyes went

from one item to another. *Sabzi*, wheat or lentil seeds grown in a tray prior to Nowruz, represented rebirth. *Senjed*, the dried fruit of the lotus tree, represented love. *Samanu*, a sweet pudding made from wheat germ, symbolized affluence. *Seer*, garlic, represented remedy. *Seeb*, apple, was symbolic of beauty and health. *Serkeh*, vinegar, represented patience. *Sekkeh*, coins, forecast prosperity and wealth.

She had added extra symbolic items as if to make sure to provide maximum protection for the coming year: painted eggs, representing fertility; goldfish, representing life; rose water, having magical cleansing powers; candles, representing enlightenment and happiness; a mirror, to bless reflections of what was in the space outside of it.

I thought of the Nowruz when Tala and I were eight years old, and she was sick in bed. I had picked up the mirror from the *Haft Seen* table, which Mum set, even though she was raised in a different culture. I found no reflection of myself in the mirror. Grandmother, who was present, said, "My dear, it's because Tala is sick, and her face is covered by a sheet."

I had no trouble now seeing image in a mirror and so Tala must be well, I thought, following Grandmother's logic. I brushed away the absurd thoughts and got up to help Reza's sisters spread a long rectangular cloth on the carpet and arrange plates, silverware, and glasses on it. Then his youngest sister, Niloufar, and I went into the kitchen to help.

We brought out a variety of rice, *koreshes*, thick homemade yogurt, chopped salad, and much more, and arranged them on the cloth. Then all of us, including the children and husbands, sat around the cloth, cross-legged, and began to eat.

Soheila suddenly said, "Any news for us?" She was looking at my belly to see if there was any sign of pregnancy.

I shook my head.

Niloufar, kind by nature, said to me, "Don't worry," and patted me on the back.

We exchanged some presents, and when it was time for Soheila to put the children in bed, Reza and I got up to leave. Outside, he said, "I'm sorry Soheila is inconsiderate."

I just shrugged. We walked for a while until a taxi stopped and we got in.

In Goo Alley, the Ramadan Teahouse was teeming with men. A few men staggered out as if they were drunk or had taken opium.

When we arrived in our building, I found a package in front of our apartment. I was happy to see Tala's return address on it.

I took it inside and opened it. I found a rose-colored vase. I took it out of the box and put it on the table underneath the window. Sunlight shining on it brought out the glittering rose color.

The phone rang and I picked it up. It was Tala. "I'm sorry, Roya, I just haven't been myself. We'll see a lot of each other again when I feel better." She gave excuses every time I wanted to see her. She had a headache. She was fatigued. She was depressed. At times, she didn't even try to give excuses.

"Did you get a package?"

"Yes, I just opened it. It's beautiful."

I had also bought a present for her that I hoped to give her in person.

"I have something for you too," I said.

"What?"

"An art book, modern European and American painters. I'll give it to you when I see you."

"I don't know when that's going to be." Then, in disjointed sentences, she said, "Anton told me we're going to Moscow for a while for his work." Her voice sounded different, as if someone else were speaking. "There are things I haven't told you."

"Tell me now."

"I will one day."

"Can I see you before you leave?" I asked.

"There's no time. We're leaving tonight, flying."

"You could have told me sooner . . ." I said.

"I didn't know until yesterday that we were going away." Then she said goodbye hurriedly and got off the phone.

As I walked away from the phone, my elbow hit the vase. It fell on the floor and shattered into pieces, making me feel brokenhearted.

It felt like it reflected what had shattered between Tala and me.

Reza, who had already gone to his desk to do some work, came to my help to put the pieces in a garbage bag.

"Anton is taking Tala to Russia; his work is taking him there."

"A period of separation between you and Tala is healthy. You know how upset she makes you."

I nodded in agreement, though I wasn't sure how I would bear the vast distance between us. In spite of our conflicted relationship, at least I could see her once in a while. Now she would be out of my reach.

# Chapter 20

After the holidays, I went to Best Baby Clothes and gave what I had knitted to Mrs. Beyoglu, got my check and, as usual, picked up new yarns and patterns. I didn't linger to talk since customers were coming in.

The shop was close to Tala's house; impulsively, I started walking toward it, hoping to find Batul at home. She may have a phone number for Tala's home in Russia.

I knocked on the door and Batul opened it. "Oh, my dear Roya, how are you?"

"Not too bad. I'm happy to see you. I want to ask you something. Do you by chance have a phone number or address for Tala and Anton? She left hurriedly . . ."

"No, nothing. I'm staying on here to watch the house. Tala *joon* wasn't happy about the move."

"I thought so." I thanked her, said goodbye, and left. On the way back to my apartment, I was surprised by a realization that I was actually happy that Tala was now far away from me and Reza. I had tried to push away my anger and suspicions about Tala's phone call to Reza, and most of the time I managed not to think about it. But now it came to me again. Was that the only time they had a private conversation? In this state of mind, I wondered if Reza was Tavoos's father—he resembles Reza more than he does Anton. But since Reza told me about the phone call, he had been so involved in his work, so sincere and considerate toward me—it was out of character that he would betray me.

The days following Tala's departure were filled with small and large incidents and traumas, and they took my mind off her.

One day on the way back from grocery shopping, I noticed the stationery store on Jamaly Avenue had on display in its window a variety of Valentine cards and chocolates wrapped in silver paper with red hearts on them. A vague imitation of the West's Valentine's Day was about to take place for the young who wanted to be in step with the "freedom-loving" world. Boys and girls who knew each other from their neighborhoods secretly exchanged gifts, even though most likely they didn't dare to be intimately involved.

Florists had set up their carts on the sidewalk with bouquets, gift-wrapped for the occasion. I felt the urge to buy a bouquet for Reza. Now, with Tala having become inaccessible and still feeling the vacuum of having lost my baby, Reza had an even larger space than ever in my heart.

In our apartment, I took the wrapping paper off the bouquet of mixed flowers and a card slipped out of it. On it a message was written crudely by hand, *Love, Sex, Forget Plato, go with Bacchus, Be Meat. If you want to meet me, give your number to the vendor.* An idle boy must have slipped the card inside the wrapping paper when no one was looking. I tore the card into pieces and threw it, along with the flowers and the paper it was wrapped in, into the garbage can. It was as if the words had contaminated the very idea of the celebration.

Reza came in soon after I was home, and I was about to tell him what I found inside of the bouquet, but he looked upset and distracted.

"What's wrong?" I asked.

"The newspaper is getting more threats—unsigned letters, anonymous phone calls..."

"Oh, it's time to quit the paper, Reza. You can't go on like this."

He just shrugged, noncommittal.

After a tense dinner together we went to bed, tossing and turning until we managed to take refuge in sleep.

That wasn't the worst of it. The following day when I came back from buying fish, Reza was standing by the outside door. "Oh, here you are," he said and went inside. I followed him to our apartment. As I was unpacking the fish, he said, "Roya, I have to go into hiding. The *Basij* had gone to the newspaper office, confiscated everything, and arrested Hossein. They are keeping him under observation in his own house he shares with his brother. They didn't imprison him because he has connections with some *basiji*. Luckily, I was out in the library, and so were two of the other journalists. One who was still at the office escaped before the *Basij* noticed him and came to tell us what happened."

"How are we going to hide?" I asked, hearing the thumping of my heartbeat.

"Hossein is planning to move the office to an old farmhouse near Abyaneh where no one would be aware of or keep track of the newspaper," he said. "He's looking for places for us, me and three other journalists, to live in. I don't know for how long we will have to be in hiding."

"What are we going to do with the apartment? Pay rent on it and rent something else?"

"Our lease on the apartment expires this month. Hossein is taking care of our rent in Abyaneh."

Since we had rented the apartment furnished, we only had our personal belongings to take, he added.

He seemed to have thought about the move and come up with a plan. "The other three journalists aren't married and will share a house. There's a high school in Kashan, an hour away. I'm sure I can do part-time teaching there too, and maybe you will find a consignment store nearby."

This was the beginning of hurried and furtive days of getting our affairs together. That night, after a quick dinner, we withdrew to bed, both restless and having a hard time going to sleep. We kept talking about what steps to take. Reza would inform the landlord that we wouldn't continue with the lease as Reza's job was taking him to another city. We would pack our belongings and take the train to Kashan and from there find a way to go to Abyaneh.

We finally stopped talking and managed to get some sleep.

We continued with the details of the move in the next few days.

He would say goodbye to his best friend, Abbas, whom he trusted and would confide in about the move. He wouldn't tell his sisters the reason for the move, nor would he tell them where we would be relocating. I wanted to spend a little time with Afsaneh before we left, but when I called her home number, her mother said Afsaneh was away on a tour in Istanbul.

I went to see Uncle Ahmad, the only person other than Tala who knew what Reza did. I gave him the address of the house we would be living in, which Reza had already gotten from Hossein, and asked him to collect the rent from the family house and send it to me there as soon as I opened a bank account. I thanked him for all the help he had always given me, and we parted with tears in our eyes. Even if Tala was in Tehran, Reza would forbid me to tell her why and where we were going. He was afraid Tala would break down and tell Anton everything.

The day before leaving, I stored some items we might want in the future in the storage room in the family house where Tala had put her paintings.

That afternoon, Abbas came to our apartment. He and Reza talked about what they always did, reform. "They want blind obedience and submission," Abbas said, his voice full of passion even though they had already expressed that many times. "What are our lives worth if we have to hide our ideas?" He was thin, with chiseled features and long dark hair, an attractive man, except when his face tensed up with bitterness.

They lamented the state of affairs in the country as if by mere repetition some solution would eventually pop up. Like Reza, Abbas was usually not the kind of man who in the evenings would go to a teahouse and smoke a water pipe, the tobacco sometimes laced with opium. He made little money from his gift shop and never married, saying he couldn't afford it.

Finally, they embraced. As they pulled apart, Abbas said, "Don't let go of your ideals."

"Of course I won't."

Then Abbas said goodbye to both of us and left.

When it was time for Reza and me to leave, as we were about to walk out the outside door for the last time, Golnar, our landlord's wife, held a Qur'an first over my head and then over Reza's to bless our journey. She recited lines she knew by heart from the Qur'an.

> *May the blessing of Allah be your companion all through the journey. Allah will bless you beyond your expectation, and guide your way in life. May Allah send along with you angels that never miss their focus; may they be the ones to hold your hands while you arrive at your destination.*

Reza and I, not adhering to religion, still felt comfort in her words and her kind gesture.

Riding in a taxi to the train station, I had a feeling that the weakened rubber band that held Tala and me together was in danger of snapping now, with her in Russia and me going to a remote town. We would be look-alikes in different parts of the world.

## Chapter 21

To save money, we took the five-hour bus ride to Isfahan rather than the one-hour plane ride. In Isfahan, we transferred to another bus going to Kashan. In Kashan, we had no choice but to take a half-hour taxi ride to the house in Abyaneh.

Abyaneh, a 2,500-year-old market town, surrounded by mountains, a river running through it, and the air reddish from the clay that houses and buildings were made of, was like a different world, with an instant calming effect on Reza and me. It felt like we were safe now, away from our usual concerns and tensions.

The roofs of some houses seemed to serve as courtyards for other houses higher up on the slope. Sumac bushes, bright cacti, sunflowers, and asters were in bloom, visible on the rooftops and the tree beds on the streets. On one roof stood a row of quince trees with pink flowers and yellow fruits. Women going by on the streets, most of them old, were wearing colorful dresses with full or pleated skirts and shawls with floral designs embroidered at their edges wrapped around their heads and shoulders. Men, most of them old too, wore grayish suits and felt hats.

The taxi stopped by a three-level structure consisting of three houses, one on top of the other, the way all the houses we had passed were set up. Reza and I got out, each holding our suitcases. Zobeideh *khanoom*, who was expecting us, was sitting on a chair behind a desk in a small room near the entrance door of the house, level with the sidewalk. She lived in that house and rented the upper two, Hossein had told Reza. She was middle-aged and was dressed similarly to the women we passed by on the way. We introduced ourselves and she said, "Welcome," with a local accent. "I will take you to your house."

She led us up a set of stairs to the middle house, the size of a small apartment, above the first floor.

"You can find everything on the main street. Let me know if you have any questions or need anything," she said and left.

The interior of the house was cheerful with green and white walls and framed nature photographs and paintings hanging on them. A hand-woven bedspread and a carpet on the floor added to the color. It consisted of a large room with an L-shaped alcove and a kitchenette. The bed, in the L, had a metal bedstead, and a wooden chest stood next to it. A small sofa and two comfortable chairs were set against the wall in the main part of the room and a wooden dining table and two chairs behind it stood in the middle. The high ceiling and a large window with a view of the mountains made the place seem spacious.

A bowl filled with fruit stood on the dining table as a gesture of hospitality. The kitchenette was equipped with a refrigerator, an oil-burning stove, a kettle, dishes, and silverware. She had put bottles of *doogh* inside the refrigerator for us. We had already eaten during the long hours of the travel and skipped supper. We had some fruit and glasses of *doogh* and went to bed early.

But we kept ourselves up by talking about the suddenness of the move to a place we had never been to and where we had no friends or relatives. He would meet the other journalists from his newspaper daily, but I had no one. We were in hiding and were not sure for how long.

In the morning, we started our routine. For just the beginning of fall, it was already cold out, and we put on our heavy sweaters. First, we went out to shop. We were immediately struck by how ancient ideas and customs dominated the village. The houses we passed each had a pair of doors, like the one we were now living in, with distinctive knockers. Later we found out from Zobeideh that men and women who lived in Abyaneh all their lives and obeyed the tradition used different knockers, with each making a different sound in order to signal to the house owner which gender should be answering this visit. Most of the houses had balconies with colorful flowers painted on them. We kept stopping and looking at the verses from the Qur'an and poems carved on some of the doors. We recognized two poems, both on one door, by the revered ancient poet Ferdowsi.

> *Listen: this story's one you ought to know,*
> *You'll reap the consequence of what you sow.*
> *This fleeting world is not the world where we*
> *Are destined to abide eternally*

*We keep seeking, suffering, and treasuring,*
*We fill our hearts full of desire*
*Finally, we inherit just soil.*

It was amazing that the population of this town was so interested in poetry. Not only did they carve it on their doors, sometimes they recited it as they were walking.

There were few cars on the streets. People were shopping at a general store and at an open market that carried fruit and vegetables, probably local, a variety of fish, and *barbari* bread. Everyone spoke in the local dialect, and we missed a lot of the exchanges between them. We bought bread, fruit, vegetables, and fish to take back with us.

On the way, we took a different street, which was emptier. We passed the remnant of a Fire Temple left from Zoroastrian times when they built fires and worshipped around their flames, and then a large mosque with turquoise minarets.

Back in our house, as soon as we unpacked the food, we had breakfast and then took out everything from our suitcases and put it in the large closet that was practically hidden behind the kitchen.

Then Reza left to go to the old farmhouse, at the outskirts of the town, where they would produce the newspaper. Reza would take the long walk to it.

After Reza left, I went out to try to find a consignment shop. I walked down several narrow alleys and then I entered a side street, parallel to the wider main street. A few stores stood on one side—a general store carrying groceries, a hardware store, a butcher shop, and a laundromat. I went inside the laundromat to find out if I could bring clothes to be washed. A man with a Turkish accent said he had recently opened the place but didn't have enough customers. He said the small population of the town did their own laundry by hand, and he was going to close soon. So I would need to wash our clothes and hang them on a line on the roof, the part that wasn't covered by the house above it, and let them dry in sunlight as the others did.

A little further, I came across a children's store, *Daste Baaf* (hand-made), written on its canopy. I went inside and the young woman sitting behind the counter received me with a friendly smile and asked me what I needed. I gave her only my first name and she also introduced herself as Mehri. I told her why I had come to the store, and she was receptive. She said she could use some sweaters for children and adults. "Babies are scarce here. My main buyers are tourists. They like to take sweaters back as souvenirs. Are you living in Abyaneh?"

"My husband and I are here . . ." I hadn't prepared what to say. After a pause, I said, "We needed to get away for a while from our hectic life in Tehran. Just being in a quiet, beautiful place is healing."

"I live in Kashan. Not married. My fiancé was killed in a demonstration; I can't bring myself to warm up to another man."

"I'm so sorry."

"He'll always be with me."

She gave me a few patterns and I chose some yarns. She offered me one-half of what would be sold as Mrs. Beyoglu had, but I didn't need to fill out a form. I said goodbye and left, glad to have found some work. If I didn't have to hide the real reason we came to Abyaneh, I could have possibly become friends with her, I thought, feeling a pang of loneliness.

On the way back, taking a different route, I passed the Friday Mosque made of wood and brick. Its octagonal columns were topped with capitals engraved with different motifs. Some of the columns seemed damaged either by an earthquake or fire. It took my mind to that day that Tala and I visited Rey Castle when it began to collapse and trapped us in a cavity. But as I walked on, the intertwined alleys rich with blossoming trees and flowers and the murmur of the water in the river had a soothing effect.

Back in our house, I went to the roof and started to knit a sweater, in a rush to get it done, to bring in a little income. All the houses across the street were quiet, with no signs of activity. Though I liked the atmosphere of the town, still the silence, the solitude, only added to my feelings of loneliness. This period will be temporary, I said to myself. It can't last forever. Reza and his coworkers would have to move again, in fear of being discovered.

# Chapter 22

Days, months, went by, and Reza and I kept the same routine. He spent four days a week at the farmhouse and three days a week teaching. I never met his colleagues. All three were single and living together in a house close to the office.

On the days Reza went to Kashan, he took a pile of newspapers with him to put in lobbies of different institutes, as he did when we were in Tehran. His coworkers did their share of distributing the newspapers in Kashan or Isfahan. None of them put them anywhere in Abyaneh for fear of being caught.

I did the household tasks, cooking, knitting sweaters, and other items. I did my knitting mostly in a shady corner of the roof. As I sat on a chair I put there, I looked at the slow activities on the streets. Sometimes I saw other women on their roofs washing clothes, as I had started doing. I could hear bells from the city hall and, at different intervals, the voice of the muezzin from the mosque's minaret, calling people to prayers, *Allah o Akbar, come and pray, come and pray, God is great*. Parrots, sparrows, and mourning doves among trees that lined the street below added their songs.

At my breaks from knitting and other tasks, I continued writing vignettes in the thick notebook I had kept for a long time, now mostly about what I observed on my walks. The whole town was like a museum. Every time I noticed something new, I thought about how Tala would use that for her paintings. Then I imagined her in Moscow, visiting galleries and museums with displays of great art. What else is she doing there? Maybe she and Tavoos, out of necessity, take courses in Russian, go to parks together, and speak in Russian with other mothers and children and when home with Anton. In her Tehran house, Batul did all the cooking. Does Tala have a maid now who cooks for her, maybe Russian cuisine? She had once taken me to a Russian restaurant in Tehran where she and Anton ate often. She ordered for us what she believed was the best on the menu—beef stroganoff, borscht, sweet and sour cabbage. Now, in Moscow, her life must be full of new discoveries and stimulations.

She was keeping herself apart from me. Why, why, I asked myself again. I thought of her betraying me with Henry, but then bursting out and confessing to what she had held back. Will she one day do the same, burst out and tell me what she is hiding from me? Again, the list of possibilities I had thought of paraded before me. She feels intense pity for me. She doesn't want to share Tavoos with me. She and Reza have done something behind my back, though that idea was pale by now. How long is it going to take before she feels compelled to tell me why she is avoiding me? She could find out from Uncle Ahmad where I am now, get my address and phone number from him.

I imagined what Tavoos could understand and do at his age, now close to four. He would ask questions. Why is the sky blue? Why do birds fly? He is able to name familiar colors. He can remember part of the stories Tala or Anton read to him and put together puzzles. Does he have a recollection of me from the brief interactions we had?

Abyaneh was the opposite of Moscow. The population was small, and most people living there were old, their children, when grown, having left for bigger cities to go to school or for job opportunities.

Although the population of the town was small, people weren't like a happy family, nor did they seem interested in letting someone into their lives. Each family kept to itself; I could tell from the fact that I rarely saw anyone entering another person's house. When I came across someone I had passed by before on the street, there was no flicker of recognition or acknowledgment on his or her face. Even the woman on the first floor of our house, who attended to us when we arrived, said very little and showed no curiosity about Reza and me, perhaps honoring our privacy. She didn't volunteer information about herself either. All we knew was that she had a husband her own age, about fifty, I guessed, who took her place in the evenings until midnight, then he closed the doors. Privacy was what Reza and I were seeking too, so we accepted the distance everyone kept. After the brief conversation I had with Mehri at the shop, we rarely exchanged anything personal. I just handed her what I made, she paid me, I chose more yarns and patterns, and left.

I was often struck by stabs of loneliness that transferred themselves to a yearning for Tala in conflicting ways. I wanted to confront her and make her confide in me the way she used to. Was she thinking of me, missing me? I kept going up and down about whether I envied her for living in a major city, full of cultural activities, having enough money to buy whatever she wished, and having a lovely son to take care of, or the opposite, as she was far away in a city with no friends, married to a man she vacillated between tolerating and hating. What was she doing at that moment? Was she strolling the city, holding Tavoos's hand?

If and when I was with Tala again, would we ever be close like we used to? I could take this to be like the periods when she withdrew from me and then sought me out again. I thought of that beautiful glass bowl she sent to me as a Nowruz present. My elbow hit it. It fell on the floor and shattered into pieces. I wondered again if that was a symbol of our relationship being shattered. Could it ever really mend?

Fall ended and a cold winter arrived. Heavy snow began falling. With my rooftop covered by snow, I did everything inside of the house. Looking out of the window in this season, the streets were practically empty, with no visitors or tourists present. The drama was from the sounds winter birds made, the thrashing of tree branches, mournful mewing of stray cats. The men or women who used to display their own hand-made merchandise—kilims, pottery, shawls—spread on cloths in front of their houses were now absent from the streets. My mind went to Tala and me collecting snow that had fallen in our house's courtyard, making it into balls and throwing them against the wall, each time followed by our laughter as if we had accomplished something important. I couldn't stop myself from complaining to Reza about my loneliness, the limitation of our lives. Once, I burst out with what I had already said a few times, but now with even more urgency, "You just have to quit the newspaper. We have to live a real life."

"I'm so sorry. I know this is hard on you. It's hard on me too. But if I quit now, Hossein will be upset and angry. He would be capable of giving my name to the *Basij*. I will be arrested wherever we go."

Then spring came, followed by summer. Finally, it was fall, a year since we came to Abyaneh. But still, I had no connection with Tala. Once, I looked at myself in the mirror hanging on the wall and was shocked that no reflection of me appeared. I remembered again that when we were children, Tala became sick and stayed in bed all day. I had looked at myself in the mirror on the living room wall but found a blank image. I said to Grandmother, "I can't see myself in the mirror."

"It's because you're separated from Tala; she's sick and covered up," she said. "When she gets well and is out of bed, you'll see yourself again."

It had sounded logical then. But could I believe it now, that Tala was sick and that was why my face was blank? I realized I was still influenced by those words and began to be concerned for Tala.

My reconnection with Tala happened in an unexpected, traumatic way. It was almost a year after we came to Abyaneh and I was still feeling like a tourist. I carried on with my routine—doing the household chores, knitting, and taking walks. When the sun was about to set, I would start to return to the house.

On one evening, Reza was late, so I made a *kuku*, rice, and salad, ate some of it, and saved the rest for him.

I went to bed, tired from having taken a longer walk than usual. The sky outside of the window above the mountains was bright with numerous stars and a full moon. I never pulled down the shades so that I would be able to see all the dramatic changes in the sky. I had just drifted to sleep when the phone rang. Anxiety swept over me, wondering if something happened to Reza. I picked up the phone quickly, but the voice saying "Roya" was Uncle Ahmad's.

Before I could greet him and ask him questions, he said quickly, "I hate being the bearer of bad news. Tala . . ." His voice was tinged with sadness.

I waited, my heart beating hard.

He went on in a somber tone, "Tala is at Azadi Hospital in Tehran. Anton is dead. They returned from Russia a few days ago. The accident happened when he was driving Tala and Tavoos somewhere. After the accident, Maxim took Tavoos and went away with him."

It was hard to absorb and believe all that. I mumbled, "Is this real . . ."

"The *Basij* found my number in Tala's address book in her purse."

In a state of shock, I fell into silence.

"Can you come to Tehran and see her? She begged me to call you."

"I can't believe it . . . I will try to come."

The connection became weak, and we could hardly hear each other. He said he would call in the morning. After I put down the receiver, still incredulous, I wondered if this was a ploy by Tala to try to get me to go to Tehran, but no, it couldn't be that. Uncle wouldn't make up something so horrendous.

I was filled with questions. I knew from Tala that the nature of Anton's work was shady. Was he driving recklessly, pursued by government agents?

My thoughts were interrupted by Reza turning the key in the door and coming in. I rushed over to him. "Reza, I have terrible news," I said as he was taking his jacket off.

He turned to me sharply and said, "What? Tell me."

"Tala . . ." Slowly, with a shaky voice, I told him what Uncle Ahmad told me.

"That's terrible news . . ." Then he asked what had gone through my mind. "Are you sure this isn't a ploy?"

I said to him what I had to myself. "Uncle would never participate in a lie like that."

"I wouldn't stop you from going to see her," he said.

As I warmed up the food I had saved and sat with him to eat, we talked more about what had happened, Tala being in a sanatorium, Anton dead, Maxim taking Tavoos away.

"I need to go there soon," I said.

"Yes, you have to."

Finally, we went to bed, and after tossing and turning, we fell asleep. I was awoken by a disturbing dream . . .

*I was in an ink-black room and trying desperately to escape through a door, turning the handle. The handle came off and fell on the floor with a loud thud. I knocked and screamed,* Open, open . . . *A tree branch was banging against the window, moving back and forth like an erratic heartbeat.*

I woke with my heart beating hard. A rooster's crowing and the voice of the muezzin from the minaret sounded in the air. Men and women would get up and do ablution and pray. Were the people in this town at peace with their lives, or did they have wishes they asked God to fulfill as they prayed? I hadn't felt peace and tranquility as far back as I could recall. Being tied to Tala, I had to bear her pain as well as my own, the anguish her betrayals created in me, then the periods of her withdrawals. But the news Uncle gave me about the accident wiped out my negative feelings toward her as if by a magic wand.

# Chapter 23

At breakfast, Reza and I talked and talked again about the accident and my plan to go to Tehran to see Tala. After he left for his office, I called Uncle Ahmad. The connection wasn't good, but I managed to tell him of my plan—I would come to Tehran in two days, needing that time to wrap up what I had to do here. I would stay for two weeks. Uncle said he would prepare my childhood room for me in the family house since the tenants left a month ago and he hadn't yet found reliable people to rent to. He offered to meet me by the bus. But I knew the bus could be hours late. I asked him to leave the key above the entrance door of the house and if the phone was working, I would call him as soon as I got settled in. He said he hadn't disconnected the phone.

I began to get ready for the trip—I quickly finished what I was in the middle of knitting and gave it to Mehri, bought a ticket for the bus, and packed my personal necessities. Reza accompanied me to the bus in a taxi. As I looked out of the window, dandelions were floating in the air. A shepherd was walking his goats and sheep on the mountain road. At the bus station, I said goodbye to Reza, feeling nervous, and I could tell he was feeling the same way.

The bus was half empty and I had two seats to myself. The scenery outside, sometimes arid and sometimes lush with wildflowers by the roads and fruit visible on trees, was similar to the early fall day when Reza and I came to Abyaneh. But knowing that Tala was hospitalized and Tavoos taken away by the villain Maxim gave everything a dark tinge.

I remembered when Tala and I were children how lights and shadows created continuous changes in the meaning and character of every object for us. Even sounds—a cat mewing, a bird singing—became different as the light changed. Everything looked like mere reflections on water, ever-changing.

Grandmother told Tala and me that we should never let our images blend into each other in their reflections in water—it would lead to one of us diminishing. For a fleeting moment, I thought I must have caused Tala's demise. One day, in Abyaneh, exhausted from walking, I sat on a rock next to a river and looked at the flowing water. A leaf spiraled down from a tree and fell into the water, creating ripples. I saw Tala's reflection mingling with mine, what Grandmother said we should never let happen.

I was so absorbed in my thoughts that I was startled by the driver's voice announcing, "Tehran station. Collect all your belongings before getting off the bus." I picked up the duffel bag I had packed and got off.

Outside the station, I took another bus to the family house.

The drowsiness of siesta time was over, and shops and offices were opening up and vendors were setting up their carts.

On the narrow Aria Alley, where the family house was located, children were engaged in different activities—throwing balls against the walls, playing hopscotch, and jumping rope. A few boys were flying kites on a rooftop. I remembered how I used to watch Reza do that.

Years ago, a couple with ten children lived in the house next to ours. Grandma had said of the mother, "It's a marvel, pregnant every year." The woman, I remembered, was thin and short but her breasts were large, you could see through her *manteau*. Grandmother said to Tala and me, "Her breasts are full of milk. One day you'll have children too and you'll have milk in your breasts." Tala never breastfed Tavoos. She told me she didn't have enough milk, and most mothers fed their babies with bottles these days anyway.

The dove-gray wooden door of our house and its round knocker were intact, despite all the renters. I picked up the key that Uncle had left for me on the top of the doorway and opened the door.

Entering the house, my heart was heavy. I was returning to death and tragedy: Mum, Baba, Grandmother, all dead. And Tala, whose existence was entwined with mine, was severely injured now and was in the sanatorium.

I looked for the phone to call Uncle. I found it in the living room on the table next to the sofa. He picked up quickly and we talked for a few moments and arranged to meet at the entrance of the Azadi General Hospital at ten in the morning, the beginning of the two-hour visiting period.

I walked from room to room. They were all small and stood in a row like square boxes, as they were when we lived there. The features I liked had remained—friezes along the edges of the ceilings, fruit designs on the fireplace mantel, stained-glass windows above the French doors opening to the porch. After Mum died, Grandmother moved to the end room that was used for guests. Baba's study stood at the other end and, next to it, his and Mum's bedroom. Tala's room was next to theirs, mine next to Grandmother's. The bookcase in Baba's study was no longer there. Once, it was filled with books in English, Spanish, and Farsi. Other items of furniture were replaced as they gradually got worn out or were damaged by renters.

From the large French doors, I looked at the courtyard, with a round pool at its center, four flower beds around it, and a row of trees against the wall. The shed where we kept chickens was still there in a corner. In the fall and spring and summer too, when the weather was cool and the air was fragrant with the scent of flowers, we sat in the courtyard on a carpet we spread under the trees to eat. A lantern was hung on one of the trees and was turned on as it began to grow dark.

Rooms that belonged to Tala and me were now painted white. Until we were six years old, we slept in one of those rooms, first in cribs and then in beds next to each other. Before we had language, Mum would hear us jabber to each other, communicating in that way, incomprehensible to everyone else but us.

A row of photographs stood on a dresser. Uncle must have put them there for me to see before he rented the house again. One was of Tala and me when we were about ten or eleven, standing in the courtyard with our arms around each other. Another one was of Baba and Mum when they were young. Mum's hair was a light shade of blond, her eyes dark blue. Her skirt came to just above her knees. Baba was wearing a T-shirt and khaki pants and was smiling. He had the same mild, unassertive aura about him as he did later in life. Next to that was one of our grandmother and our grandfather. They were standing next to their sons, Baba and Ahmad. Grandfather was wearing a blue suit and a black bow tie. He had Baba's laid-back smile and the hefty, laconic posture of Uncle Ahmad. Grandmother was wearing a black skirt and a white shirt with black and blue stripes. It fascinated me to look at Grandmother in that photo which, somehow, I had never seen before. She was dressed stylishly, and her hair was parted on the left, some strands curved to the side of her face.

Grandmother, looking so different in that photo from the way she did later, made me wonder if she changed in her beliefs as she grew older.

Next to that photograph was one of our grandparents on Mum's side, also at a young age. Sophia was petite like Mum but with darker coloring. William was tall, with blue eyes and blond hair. On a family visit to Olivera when Tala and I were six years old, there was an air of quiet and sadness about their household. Both of her parents were ill at that time. Mum hired someone to take care of them.

Vague, blurry images of the visit came before my eyes. Tala and I spent most of the day in one room, where we also slept. Grandmother Sophia, though ill, had made sure to get us a present: a large dollhouse with many rooms and a variety of furniture and miniature dolls, which we moved from room to room. Mum didn't want to leave her parents at home and go out during this critical period and we never saw the camping grounds, the swimming pools, bars, and sports fields that she had told us about.

On the mantel stood another photograph of Tala and me that he must have put there too. Our hair was long and parted on the left side and held back with barrettes. We both were wearing blue velvet dresses with belts tied in the back and Day-Glo-colored shoes.

It was hard for me to know which was Tala and which was me.

Looking at the photograph, I was saddened again by how broken our language, our shared world, became as we grew older. I asked myself, why did I leave Reza even for two weeks to be with Tala, considering our conflicted relationship for the last few years? Was it merely to comfort her with my sisterly presence, or to try finally to have a conversation that was long overdue about the unsettled questions floating through my existence like dark threads? Would she be lucid enough before I had to leave Tehran for us to have a real heart-to-heart conversation? Would she want that? Is that why she begged Uncle to talk me into coming here?

I went back to the living room and tried to reach Reza. He didn't pick up his phone and I left a brief message, telling him that I arrived safely. His cell phone was provided and paid for by Hossein and was meant for communication between them; Reza rarely used it for any other purpose. I rang our house's phone, but he didn't pick up. He probably was staying in the office longer than usual now that I was not there for us to share dinner, talk about our days.

Uncle had put fruit, cheese, bread, and other items in the refrigerator. But, having no appetite and feeling worn out, I took a shower in the turquoise-tiled bathroom and went to bed, covering myself with the quilt that Grandmother made years ago with pieces of fabric in colorful floral designs. Uncle must have kept it and put it out for me to use while staying there. The crickets and night birds were carrying on like a chorus. From the window, I could see the sky had turned black and stars were scattered across it like shiny pieces of glass.

My mind drifted to when Tala and I were children and Mum sang a lullaby to us in Farsi, her Argentine accent still apparent.

> *Go to sleep now, close your eyes, and dream this night*
> *The moon and stars watch over you*
> *Close your eyes and peaceful dreams are soon to come*
> *Stars bathe you in soft white light*
> *Moonbeams whisper goodnight*
> *The moon is on the rise. The sleepy sun has closed her eyes*
> *Sail away on waves of the sea and oceans*
> *Realize all your dreams.*

Now, years later, I was soothed by the recollection of that lullaby and Mum's voice and soon drifted to sleep.

## Chapter 24

I woke at dawn to the cacophony of sounds from the alleys. I left the bed and looked out of the window. Lights of a minaret on an adjacent street were still lit, shining brightly in the pale dawn air. Illuminated signs on Jamaly Avenue advertising a bank, a TV store, and a teahouse blinked in blue and violet. On a building hung the Iranian national flag, green, white, and blue with an emblem—Allah's letters shaped into a red tulip, representing young people who died for the country during the eight-year war with Iraq and the Islamic Revolution that overthrew the shah.

Down below, a few little girls walked in tandem, with two adults at the beginning and end of the line. When I turned around, my eyes found the carpet spread on the floor next to the bed. A quotation from Ferdowsi was woven on its margin in ornamental script: *The world is a scale where people are weighed.*

How would Tala and I be judged if we stood on a scale weighing our worth?

My thoughts were interrupted by the phone ringing. It must be Reza, I thought. But it was Uncle. He welcomed me, and then after a pause and in a hesitant voice, he said Tala had been transferred to the psychiatric unit.

"Why is that?" I asked, shaken up.

"We'll talk when I see you. She isn't in the most restrictive section for severe cases. They will let you visit her in her room." He explained that they allowed only one hour for visiting in the morning or afternoon, not both. The visiting hours in the morning were ten to noon, he added, so I should get there at eleven and meet him outside after that. He had visited Tala the day before, but today he was tied up with his work and couldn't get there until after the visiting hours. He lived in Darband now, an hour away from Tehran. He had moved there because expenses were lower and also because there was more demand for sequins from people living there.

He said I could take flowers to Tala, but no food, and that the number one metro would take me to the hospital. I should allow half an hour to get there. He would meet me at eleven by the door of the hospital.

After we hung up, I was so devastated by Tala being taken to a sanatorium that I had no appetite. I skipped breakfast except for a cup of black tea, dressed, and left.

On the way to the metro station, a pale sunlight was glistening on drops of water on tree leaves. It must have rained while I was sleeping. Broken-down pieces of tree branches and withered leaves covered the ground.

The metro came promptly, and I got in. I found a seat between two women. Some passengers were talking and laughing, but my mind traveled to the traumas that Tala endured at different stages of our growing up. I had pushed aside some of the harsh incidents from long ago and buried them under newer happenings. Now, confronted with the fact that Tala was admitted to the psychiatric unit, some harsh details moved forward. My mind paused on the cool spring day when we were eight years old and Mum took us out for a short walk. As we were passing Bank Melli, a group of demonstrators poured into the avenue from a side street and shouted, *we aren't getting what we were promised, we are cheated of our rights*, which were frequent complaints. The *Basij* appeared on the scene and soon the air was filled with smoke from the gas grenades they tossed at the demonstrators. A gunshot shattered the bank's front window and pieces of glass fell down like hailstones. Embers from burnt trash floated in the air. Panic-stricken passersby screamed and ran in different directions.

Mum, holding our hands, tried to get us out of the area as quickly as possible. Tala started crying and when we turned to look at her, blood was streaming down her forehead.

"Help, help," Mum screamed, rushing to the curb of the street and raising her hand for a taxi. Vehicles raced along the avenue, enveloped in smoke. Finally, one stopped, and we got in. Mum told the driver to take us to the nearest hospital.

At the hospital, Mum asked me to stay in the waiting area and, holding Tala in her arms, she followed a nurse inside. In the waiting room, women, men, and children fidgeted in their seats; some cried. Finally, Mum and Tala came out. The doctor had removed a piece of glass from Tala's forehead, put a Band-Aid on the wound, and prescribed a painkiller. He recommended that she rest in bed after taking the medication.

When we got home, I was forbidden to go near Tala. Though by then we each had our own room, we usually slept in the same one, climbing together in one of the beds. But now that wouldn't be possible. I stood outside her room's door, hoping for signals from her. But there were no sounds from inside.

Soon after the accident, Tala began to act strangely. Once, she believed she was a boy and told Mum and Baba that she wanted them to buy her boys' clothes and change her name to Teymour. She eventually snapped out of that phase, only to replace it with other disturbing behavior regarding her body and self-image. "I'm so ugly," she'd say. "I hate myself."

Mum took her to another doctor, an American-educated psychiatrist. Dr. Motavelli confirmed what the previous doctor said, that trauma was the cause of her strange behavior. He didn't recommend medication. He believed drugs at our age could often make things worse. He advised that all family members act calm and try to redirect Tala with remarks like, "Are you sure that's really true?" or, "You must be tired, you're imagining things."

Grandmother used her own methods of healing her. She prepared homegrown tinctures, put them in cherry juice, and gave them to Tala to drink. Since that didn't help, Grandmother thought a *jinn* had gotten into Tala. She gave her cold showers to force the *jinn* away.

I tried my best to influence Tala, to make her return to her usual self, but with no results.

Mum took her to Dr. Motavelli again. "Separate the sisters from each other for a week or two," he advised. "Tala may be trying to get more attention, competing with her twin."

After consulting with Baba, Mum sent me to live for a week with Grandmother, who had her own house then, to see if Tala would improve. Grandmother's house was modestly furnished—no chairs or tables, only rugs on the floors, cushions against the walls to lean against—in keeping with the Muslim belief in living simply. But there was a lot of color in the rugs, kilims, and cushions, mostly in different shades of green, which in Islam is associated with paradise.

Being separated from me, Tala recovered from the strangest of her behaviors, and I went back home. Then some new ones took their place. She went from being neat to being unkempt. She no longer organized everything on the shelves or in the bureau in her room. She just dumped them all on the floor.

From bits and pieces of our parents' conversation, though they spoke in quiet tones, I was able to patch together what the doctor said on subsequent visits. Dr. Motavelli had asked Mum if Tala was sexually abused at any time. "I was so embarrassed," Mum said.

Yes, almost, I thought. Not long before the accident, Tala and I had gone to the bazaar close to the house. We liked the drama there—vendors opening burlap bags full of merchandise brought over on donkeys, the colorful displays of produce, a blacksmith polishing a pot with a little fire aimed at it, a man dipping yarn in pots containing different color dyes.

On the way back, we reached a wooden fence blocking the way. On it was painted in red: *Dangers for girls. Don't enter. You'll fall into a trap you won't be able to get out of.*

We turned around to go home from a different direction. It was already getting late, and we walked rapidly. You rarely saw girls or children out on the streets when it was dark. Only occasionally a teenage girl, unable to hold back desire, refusing to be a prisoner of rules, would slip out and meet secretly with a boy. Or you might see a prostitute furtively peeking out of the half-open door of a shabby house.

As we entered a narrow street, an odd-looking man dressed in rags jumped out of a doorway. He grabbed each of our arms, forcefully pulled us inside the hallway, and shut the door. We kept screaming as he pulled down his pants, exposing his large, hardened penis, and whispered, "Touch it, touch it." Someone knocked on the door and the man suddenly stopped. I quickly went to the door and opened it. Whoever had knocked was not there. Holding Tala's hand, we ran all the way home. We never told anyone about what happened; we had snuck out of the house without asking permission. Tala seemed more disturbed than me by what happened. She brought it up to me, asking, "Why did he do that, was it our fault?"

And hadn't Anton been abusing her, keeping her almost a prisoner? When we met him the first time in Dizin, had he, just by looking at Tala—her shy manner, avoiding eye contact with him—assessed that she would be easy prey to his demands, which quickly slid into abuse? I tried to push the thoughts aside—what difference did it make now? He was dead. I was jolted out of my thoughts when the train came to a stop at the station close to the psychiatric unit.

# Chapter 25

The unit Tala was in was on a narrow street, in a three-story building with a brick facade. A cart with bouquets of flowers on it stood in the middle of the street. I bought a bouquet of mixed flowers to take to Tala. Next to the psychiatric center was a blood bank and across the street from it was a small two-story building with a sign that simply said *Residential*.

On the wall next to the entrance door was a plaque with "Azadi Psychiatric Center" written on it. Even though Tala had had periods of instability and strange behavior, the words "psychiatric center" and the fact that she was locked up inside still shook me up.

Finally, I gathered my strength and went up the two steps in front of the door and rang the bell. The door opened and I entered the reception area. A woman was sitting behind a desk. "May I help you?" she asked.

"Yes, I'm here to see my sister, Tala Arjomandi-Alexandrov."

She looked in a notebook that had the list of patients and she asked me for identification. I showed her my birth certificate and then she gave me a visitor badge that I pasted onto my blouse. She said I had to wear it while in the unit. She asked me to give her my purse to hold until I was leaving, but I could take the bouquet of flowers to Tala's room.

"Go up the steps to the second floor. She is in room twenty-two."

I went up the steps and entered a long hallway. It was pristine, with spotless peach-colored walls. The floors were covered by pale green tiles. The medicinal smell in the air sent a wave of nausea through me.

I passed a sink with a mirror above it that seemed to be for ablution before prayers. The mirror was covered by reddish spots; my face stared back at me looking distorted, disfigured, the way I used to see it as a child when I was apart from Tala for even a short period of time.

Since Uncle called me about the accident I had counted the minutes until I could be with Tala. Now, standing in front of the door to her room, I had an urge to bolt, fearful of the condition I was going to find her in. Finally, I knocked softly and walked inside.

Tala was lying in bed sleeping. Her hair was lank, her skin sallow. She was wearing a drab gown that was given to patients. A pad and crayons stood on a side table. A nurse must have brought it at Tala's request, or Uncle had done so. I put the flowers on the table too and sat on the blue leather chair close to her bed, hoping she would wake by herself. The walls were pale blue, the same color as the gauzy curtains on the locked window, overlooking a courtyard. I noticed an unframed photograph of Tavoos on the table, half hidden behind the bouquet of flowers. He resembled Tala, and me, of course. And he still had the pile of curly dark brown hair like Reza's. I felt the troubling, painful pang of the thought that Tala had taken my baby when we were in the cavity. Could it really be true? How can I be angry at her now, while she is injured, suffering at all levels, body and mind? In a white shirt and blue pants, a thoughtful expression on his face, Tavoos looked older than his age of four years. I wished I could hold him in my arms, rock him, look into his gentle eyes, and see a smile slowly appearing on his face.

A bathroom with a toilet and sink extended from the room. A poster of deer roaming in a field hung on one wall. But, in spite of the pleasant decor of the room, being in close proximity to Tala in this condition made me feel a physical pain, adding to my distraught mental state. My eyes went to a pair of crutches against the wall. Memories blocked the sight. *Tala and I ran in a jade-green field, yellow daisies scattered in it, and in the middle of them a cherry tree redolent with fruit. We reach up and pick a few cherries. Dandelions float in the air. "Come back, Tala, Roya," Mum calls to us. We hold each other's hands and run back, our long hair swinging over our shoulders. On another day, we walk on stones with pink and dark blue veins at the bottom of a wide stream. A little farther away, dragonflies dart back and forth above the stream, and one alights on a stone. Hours later, we lie under a mosquito net on the rooftop of our house. Numerous stars twinkle and the round moon sails by. Fireflies glitter on the tops of tall tree branches . . .*

Clearly, after all the time of separation and the conflicts between us, she was still a part of me. We had good times and bad times. We were inseparable, but then were pulled apart.

"Tala," I whispered, deciding to wake her, knowing I didn't have much time to be with her on visits.

Slowly, she opened her eyes, and a flicker of a smile appeared on her face. "Roya," she said. "You're here." Her voice sounded different, tinged with pain.

I leaned over and kissed her cheeks one after another.

I tried to keep my voice upbeat to hide the terrible feeling I had just looking at her anguished face. "Tala *joon*, I came as soon as it was possible."

"I was hoping you'd come."

"Of course I'd come. I missed you so much."

"I missed you too. Do you believe me?"

"Yes," I said.

She sank into silence.

I pointed to the photograph of Tavoos and said, "He's adorable."

She nodded. Then she said, "Living with Anton in Moscow was hellish. He kept trying to keep me down and said I had a low IQ because I was a twin. What triggered his insults and anger was partly my fault. I couldn't hide that I no longer loved him, maybe never did."

I wondered, as Tala finally admitted she was not in love with Anton, whether he would admit the same thing if he were pressed. Maybe for him too this was a marriage of convenience. It was better for him to be married, a family man, as far as his job was concerned and among his colleagues. To them, that meant stability, trustworthiness. In retrospect, it was odd that only after meeting her once he came over and told Baba he was smitten by Tala. Again, it went through my mind that he saw Tala as the weaker of the two of us, easier to manipulate and mold.

"My loneliness in Moscow made me more needful of him, and that always led to fights. Roya, I told him the truth. . ."

A nurse came into the room and said in a firm voice, "Your visiting time is over."

I got up and told Tala I would visit her the following morning. I kissed her on her cheek and left. What did she mean when she said she told Anton the truth? Did she tell him about Henry, that she had given her virginity to him?

In the corridor, I looked at my face in the mirror above the sink for the use of patients who prayed and needed to perform ablution. My image reflected back in a blurry way. I thought of another one of my grandmother's beliefs, which she expressed in a variety of ways. "You are created alike so that when one is in need, the other can come to her to help." I was here to help Tala, and I had to be strong, not let myself diminish.

I decided to walk home. At that moment, the sky was gray, but bands of light were scattered on the horizon and the mountains were visible. The gay voices of children playing ball or jumping rope in the back alley poured in. Again, I was thrown back into the rushing, undulating river of memories. I saw myself and Tala in the alley branching out of our street, jumping rope together or playing with marbles our grandmother brought us from Karbala, the holy city she visited, or the stones we collected from the *joob*. After a while, we would leave and sit at the edge of the round pool, dangling our feet in the water. Butterflies, their wings saturated in bright colors, sipped the nectar from flowers, and sparrows chirped in tree branches. Sometimes, we collected jasmine flowers growing on bushes in a corner of the courtyard and with strings made fragrant necklaces and hung them around our necks. We made crowns with gold-colored paper, strung flowers around them, and put them on our heads. Then we looked in the mirror, startled each time by the identical faces looking back at us.

I came across a row of art galleries on Vali Asr Avenue. What if I brought a small painting by Tala as a sample of her work to find out if any of them would be interested in exhibiting her art? Now that my resentment of her had mostly abated, I thought I would do something that would please her.

When I reached the house, I went to the storage room, where Tala had put some of her paintings. I remembered Anton didn't want them in their house, telling her, "It's bad for Tavoos. They poison the air."

I looked through the ones stacked against the wall of the largest room. Two of them were of women with empty eyes, represented by dark holes; the figures were surrounded by overlays of minuscule circular and rectangular mirrors, glittering white like moonbeams. One was titled *Drowning*—it depicted two young girls sitting under a wild sumac tree by a stream. The girls looked identical but bore no resemblance to Tala and me. One of them was leaning over the water, her long hair flowing down; she seemed to be contemplating drowning herself.

A little further, I found her older paintings, ones I had already seen. One was oil-based, with birds, angels, and mythical animals hovering above a romantic scene, with men and women in embraces and one of the men giving a goblet of wine to a woman as they stood under a willow tree. A small painting depicted waves splashing against black rocks, creating a pool of foam in which red and yellow fish floated. It was both turbulent and beautiful. I selected that one because it was small enough to carry. I left and walked back to Vali Asr Avenue.

I stopped by galleries and looked at their window displays. They were mainly showing photographs of religious or historic subjects. Then I came upon the Mirmiran Hall of Paintings, which had opened recently. There was nothing displayed in the window. I went inside and was immediately filled with joy at the sight of many other young people there, roaming in the long narrow space of the gallery.

The paintings displayed were by five painters, two of them women. They each had their own unique approach. One was filled with colored clouds. Another was of a bucolic landscape but with broken-down huts in the foreground, showing the harshness along with beauty. Another was of a group of flat-faced cows with dots of red blood on their skin. I went to the back of the gallery, where a young woman was sitting behind a desk.

"May I help you?" she asked.

"I have a painting by my sister I'd like to show you."

"Unfortunately, we're not accepting anything new. You could come back in a few months and talk to the owner."

I tried other galleries, and they all rejected the painting for one reason or another.

A café that Tala and I used to go to was just a block away. I went in and found our table. I remembered the spot because it was the only one with a view of a back garden. As the waiter put my order of a lamb kebab sandwich and a glass of *doogh* on the table, a peasant woman entered the restaurant, holding a basket with varicolored glass bracelets in it. I bought one and put it on my wrist. It was deep green, red, and blue, reminding me of a prism Mum had given to us. I used to hold it against sunlight and watch the colors change.

During one lunch with Tala here, we made fun of our husbands and their quirks. Now her husband was dead and she was locked up in a sanatorium, and my feelings for her fluctuated like the colors refracted by the prism. Again, one of my grandmother's remarks rushed back to me. "There's a reason for everything in creation. You and Tala can look at your reflections on each other's faces and correct what you don't like or learn something about yourself." This was a variation of what she told me at that time when Tala was sick: "If you keep yourself well, she'll recover soon." We were sitting on a carpet in the courtyard, having tea. She turned to the goldfish floating in the pool, bright red in the sunny part, faded in the shade. "They're all the same color, but how different from each other they look when one is in shade and the other in sunlight," she said.

I asked myself, Am I now in sunlight or am I in the shade?

Finally, I paid and left. I walked back, going through Haftom Square, which was lined by dozens of women's clothing stores and food stands. Laborers—Iranian, Afghani, Pakistani—sat against a wall, waiting for someone to offer them work. High school boys were out, kicking car tires and enjoying the sound of alarms going off. A song came on from a car radio, engaging me with its words and melody that reflected my own state of mind.

A male singer sang:

> *When I open my eyes, you are not here*
> *the distance is daunting*
> *I wait under the street lamp*
> *in the orange-pink glow, I see you coming . . .*

Now, thinking back, I wished I had made an effort to stop Tala from marrying Anton, a man that seemed untrustworthy.

## Chapter 26

When I visited Tala in the morning, her first words after greeting me were, "Anton didn't treat Tavoos in the way I approved of. He pressured him to perform everything to perfection, scolded him, and kept saying, 'You can do better.' Now he's with Maxim, his evil cousin."

"I'm sure Uncle will do his best to get him back. He promised he'd do that. He has always been so kind, helpful."

"Yes. We are lucky to have him. He wanted to bring me some clothes so I wouldn't have to wear this drab robe. I told him not to. I'm hoping to be out of here soon."

I noticed she wasn't wearing her diamond-encrusted wedding ring. Was it off because of the hospital's rules?

I asked her that.

"No, I took it off and threw it out of the window before Anton put his foot on the accelerator."

She threw away the ring that she valued so much and had shown off to me. Was it her way of ridding herself of the side of her which blinded her to Anton's faults when she accepted to marry him? Who found that ring and was wearing it now? Or did it fall into a *joob*, travel by the flow of the water, and finally sink into a hole?

Of course, her marriage was doomed from the beginning.

"Roya, I told him the truth . . . Remember Henry?"

"Of course I remember."

I wanted to ask why she told him after all these years. She answered before I brought out the words.

"I wanted to hurt him," she said. "That threw him into a rage. He put his foot on the accelerator. He wanted to kill me, but he killed himself." Her face reflected the terror of the accident.

I had created a horrific picture of the accident ever since Uncle told me about it. The car swerving out of control on the busy Gholabadi Avenue and hitting a lamppost. Anton's head crushing against the steering

150

wheel, blood pouring out. Tala and Tavoos screaming, fear and help-lessness and pain enveloping them. Tavoos crying, "Mother, it hurts, it hurts." Tala losing consciousness and waking up in the hospital and ask-ing for Tavoos, being told he was taken away by Maxim. No one knew where they were; it amounted to kidnapping.

I came out of my thoughts through Tala's voice, speaking in monosyl-lables, telling me more about the accident, using words, then only half words that I patched together into something coherent. Tavoos was in the back seat and, as a result, was the least injured. It was amazing that she herself, sitting in front, wasn't killed. As soon as the car began to swerve out of control, she managed not to let terror paralyze her and turned her attention to Tavoos, managing to reach out to him to hold him tightly . . .

I conjured up the rest from the pieces that Uncle told me. The *Basij* and then an ambulance appearing on the site, medics taking the bodies out of the wrecked car and rushing them to the nearest hospital. From there, Anton was taken to a morgue. Then Maxim went to the hospital and, as Anton's closest relative, was allowed to take Tavoos with him. Tavoos only had slight injuries.

"We were going to stay on in Tehran, for Anton to go back to work in his office here."

Her mind went to something else. "Roya, I look at you and feel myself recovering. Don't cry for me, or else I will be crying. There are so many things I want to tell you; they weigh me down . . . but I can't put them into words . . . I feel so weak."

Hearing her words, "Don't cry for me . . ." I felt a pang of pain, think-ing how different she was from me now. She had lost weight, her hair was not properly cared for, and with the injuries on her face, the re-semblance between us had diminished. What will become of me now? Will I too soon be crushed by something I was not aware of? I tried to push aside the thoughts. As much as I had suffered from loneliness, losing my baby, and Tala's withdrawal, I was able to keep my physical appearance intact.

I held her hand in mine to stop her involuntary trembling. When I let go, the shaking stopped; I felt a rush of relief that I had that effect on her, that we were still connected at a deep level. But how sad that it took a terrible trauma to break the barrier that stood between us.

We were interrupted by a nurse coming to the door and telling me it was time to leave.

"I'll be back tomorrow," I said to Tala. She nodded and turned away to the window.

In the corridor, the same nurse said, "When she's better, you can visit in the morning and afternoon as well. But for now, her doctor believes visits only make her more agitated."

I asked her if I could talk to Tala's doctor. I wanted to discuss her condition, the medications she was on. She said I would need to make an appointment. She could make it for me for tomorrow. He was booked up for the rest of today. I followed her to the nurses' station, and she made the appointment for ten in the morning.

Then she walked away, looking forlorn, her steps wobbling. How could the sadness, regret, and anger hovering in the air, the strange sounds, moans, coughing, and pleading, not penetrate and become part of the caretakers' state of mind?

As I continued walking along the corridor, I came across a patient sitting on the floor, whimpering, "This is a cardboard box . . . I'm going to smash it and enter the real world."

A nurse rushed to her and, taking her hand, lifted her up and led her to a room. The woman moved along without resistance, as if she had been hoping for this attention.

Another patient came over to me and said, "It's nice out, not so much smog. Can you give this to my son?" She handed me a folded sheet of paper. I walked out with it, holding it in bright sunlight, hoping to see something written on it that I had missed. But there was nothing—it was blank.

Uncle was supposed to meet me across the street from the sanatorium in half an hour—he wasn't able to come earlier. I walked a few blocks with the sheet of paper before I could bring myself to discard it in a garbage can.

I was enveloped in a haze of anxiety for Tala, but the atmosphere of the street, a contrast to the melancholy and wrenching sadness inside the sanatorium, lifted my mood somewhat. The weather was mild, making it easy to walk, and many people were out—couples walking together, mothers pushing their babies in strollers. I went to the park a block away and sat on a bench, feeling weak from my anxiety for Tala. From my spot, I could see a row of buildings, looking like cubes or rectangular boxes, all alike, almost indistinguishable.

The tree branches were covered by birds jumping around and chirping. A woman sitting on another bench near me was throwing seeds on the ground for them. Sparrows collected around the seeds and pecked frantically. A cat had curled up under a tree and was sleeping peacefully in spite of the cacophony of sounds the birds made.

It was time to go to the sanatorium's entrance and meet Uncle. Around me, usual sounds continued—bicycle bells, cats mewing, a child's voice calling her mother. But what was normal had become jarring. I came out of that state, seeing Uncle waiting for me.

His shoulders stooped as if he were not strong enough to bear the weight of Tala's sad condition. An expression of melancholy was embedded on his face. We embraced, kissed, and expressed how much we had missed each other since I left Tehran.

Then we walked to a restaurant nearby. Ali Bagi *chelo kebabi* restaurant was crowded with families. The children's voices and laughter, the pink glow from the rose-colored lamps hanging on the walls, and the maroon curtains on the windows gave the room a warm atmosphere. The authentic food—*kooshteh koobeh,* almond pudding, and yellow translucent honey-filled pastries—were colorful and fragrant. But Uncle was weary, in the grip of the same concerns and sorrow as I was.

He had been supervising Tala's affairs since the accident, in spite of all his own burdens, having moved to a small village because he couldn't afford to live in Tehran anymore. He had been sorting out Tala's finances, arranging her admission to the sanatorium, and trying as best he could to track down Maxim.

As we ate, he told me about his efforts to find Maxim and Tavoos and his concerns for Tala. Of course, Tala had reason to be deeply depressed, he said—the accident; Anton dead, traumatic even though they were alienated; her son taken by Maxim, a man she mistrusted— and so did he from the little he knew about him. The law was in his favor, him being the closest male to the child's father and Tala having psychological problems severe enough to be admitted to a sanatorium. His efforts to track down Maxim and Tavoos with the help of Family Affairs, the police, and Tala's lawyer hadn't led to anything yet, but he would continue trying.

A question was pressing on my mind. "Where was Maxim when the accident happened? And how did he get hold of Tavoos?" I asked.

Uncle explained that Maxim had arrived at the general hospital where Tala was taken, along with Tavoos and his dead father. He got permission to take Tavoos home—the child had only very minor injuries, just some scratches. He sighed and added, "Tala's lawyer, Parvaneh Jahanbani, has settled many cases in favor of women. She's going to work on this case."

"Uncle, I wish I could be of more help to Tala. But I will be leaving soon. I have left Reza to himself."

"Yes, you have a responsibility to yourself and your husband. You're lucky you married a nice man."

"I don't know what I can accomplish for Tala while I am here."

"Just your presence, the fact that you cared enough to come to see her, makes a difference to her. Batul is in her village now, visiting her family, but is planning to come back and live with Tala once she's released from the sanatorium. She is eager to."

"I'm really happy about that," I said.

"And I'll continue to supervise everything closely. We have to hope for the best."

"Should we consult with more doctors?"

"Azadi has the most qualified doctors in Iran. They all have degrees from the best medical schools. We just have to have faith that our dear Tala will come out of this state." As if willing himself to be optimistic, he added, "She will, for Tavoos's sake."

He told me what I didn't know from Tala—that she had been planning to take Tavoos and escape from Anton. She was setting aside money from what Anton gave her for expenses and she already had the large sum of *mehrieh* that was in the marriage agreement. She was keeping the money in a bank near him in Arak. He used some of it for her hospitalization but there was still a good sum left.

"I knew she didn't like Anton's association with Maxim," Uncle went on. "She said the two of them were involved in some illegal work, but she didn't know what. If Maxim gets caught, he could be put in jail."

I felt a heart-throbbing pain again, thinking of Tavoos being raised by Maxim.

Uncle and I agreed that Tala wouldn't be allowed to get custody unless she was discharged from the sanatorium with a letter stating that she is well enough to take care of her child.

We skipped dessert since he had to drive back to his shop and home in Arak. Anyway, in the grip of sorrow, neither of us had much appetite— we left half of the food we ordered. The waiter brought over the check. Uncle paid and we left.

# Chapter 27

Outside the restaurant, I asked Uncle, "Is there any way we could go into Tala's house and check it out—Maxim could have gone there and taken some things."

"We aren't allowed to go there until her lawyer gets things resolved for her." After a pause, he said, "Let me drive you to the house."

"I'll walk around for a while before going to the house."

As we were parting, he said he wouldn't be able to come to Tehran to visit Tala for a few days. His assistant at his sequin shop had to go away for a week and he himself needed to be present.

After saying goodbye, I spent some time walking on the wide Soltani Avenue, bustling with people going in and out of shops, cafés, and galleries, and my mood lifted a little. When dusk was approaching, I took the metro back.

In the house, I left a message again on our landline phone asking Reza to call me back. He worked even later hours now that I was not with him. I waited anxiously for his call; my concern for the threat he was under intermingled with my concern for Tala, if and when she was going to recover. To my surprise, Reza called back within minutes. He said, "I left work early tonight. I went to the office at 5:00 in the morning."

I filled him in on my visit to Tala, her condition, my conversation with Uncle. He listened and then said, "I'm sorry I'm not with you."

We had to get off the phone quickly as he was expecting to hear from Hossein, who called every day to find out what he and the others had accomplished for the newspaper.

I skipped dinner and got ready for bed. I tried to brush away the range of emotions I was feeling toward Tala now, mingled with the ones in the past—pity, sympathy, mistrust, and love.

From the window next to the bed, I could see the glow of real life at a distance—the sign above a store saying *Tehran Cola*, the gleam of an ad for TVs. But when I fell asleep, nightmares plagued me. Rows and rows of pills were lined up on the top of a rafter. I was desperate to take them and put an end to the ache I felt all over my body, but they kept receding. A hand pushed my face, and I woke with a jolt, shaking.

Outside of the window, a full moon, surrounded by blinking stars, stared down as if watching over the activities on the earth.

I closed my eyes, and this time, I fell into a dreamless sleep.

In the morning, I left for my appointment with Tala's doctor. I would visit her after that.

At the sanatorium, again I went through the routine of showing my birth certificate to the receptionist, a different woman from the one who was there the day before. She gave me a badge, which I pasted to my blouse, and I gave her my purse. Then I asked her where the doctors' offices were. She pointed to the corridor on the other side of the reception room.

I walked over and came across the nurses' station. A nurse was standing there, and she led me to Dr. Saggami's office.

I knocked on the door. The doctor opened it for me. I introduced myself and he said, "Sit down," and pointed to a chair. Then he sat behind his desk.

A bunch of pink carnations in a vase on his desk and a large print of a landscape of a pasture with cows grazing on it on the wall gave the room a serene atmosphere.

He was tall, slim, and wore thick glasses. His full beard had strands of gray, as did his hair.

"I'm glad you're here. We need to talk," he said.

"Yes." He gave the impression of self-confidence and kindness at the same time. I immediately felt I could trust him about what he would tell me about Tala.

"It isn't an easy situation for you, I'm sure, to find your sister in the shape she is in." He spoke with precision, and yet his manner was patient and calm, bringing down my level of anxiety. "It's for her own protection we are keeping her here." He looked downward, avoiding my eyes, and said in a hesitant tone, "She was suicidal."

"Suicidal . . ." A sense of dread took over me and I sank into silence.

"For a person in clinical depression, all colors fade to gray; morning light becomes indistinguishable from the darkness of night. A wish to die takes over, not just for your own sake but for others too. You believe the world is better off without you."

I listened, thinking again of that period when Tala acted so unstable, full of ups and downs, and our parents separated us for a week.

"In the hospital, before she was brought to this unit, she collected her medications and swallowed them. They had to pump her stomach. As careful as nurses are, patients still cheat. Their urgency enables them."

I felt tears welling in my eyes from the impact of his words. I managed to ask, "How long does she need to be here?" In spite of all the ups and downs Tala had as far back as I remembered, I didn't expect her to sink so low, into this desolate condition. This was at a higher magnitude than anything she went through before.

"We may keep her here for another week or so. Then she needs to be under close supervision at home."

"Can I ask what medications she is on?"

"It is a long list. We observe the results and change them according to her needs. The main ones are Prozac and Celexa. I know how close you and your sister are. She told me she was regretful that you had periods of separation, guilty that it was mostly her fault."

I said nothing, in the grip of sadness mingled with helplessness.

"She's very upset about her son being in the hands of someone she doesn't trust."

"Yes, for good reasons."

He took out something from a folder and slid it toward me. "She drew this a few days ago. It's disturbing, but still good that she let her feelings come out this way."

It was a black-and-white pen drawing of a large cavity with two naked girls, their bodies elongated and floating in liquid, their hair like clouds around their rigid, eyeless faces. In a far corner there were two minuscule babies, naked too, with their eyes closed, and in the opposite corner was a shadowy figure of a man, holding a knife in his hand, his eyes red, his hair disheveled. The drawing added to my anxiety for Tala.

"Your uncle filled me in about your sister's marriage, your family life."

"Who's her therapist, I'd like to speak . . . ?"

"I am. We don't have therapists; we only have psychiatrists. That way we can prescribe the right medication, judging by our observations during sessions with patients." He went on, "Yesterday, when I visited her in her room, she expressed excessive guilt over the accident, for having started a fight with her husband. Her son has lost his father and she blames herself for it."

There was a knock on the door. A gray-haired man was behind the door and the doctor told him to come in. I got up to leave.

In the corridor, I passed a young girl clinging to an older woman's arm and crying and begging, "Mother, take me home, take me home." A nurse came over to them and managed to separate the girl from her mother and led her up the stairway to the second floor. The mother walked away to the exit door silently, her shoulders stooped, her eyes kept downward.

It was almost visiting time, and I went to Tala's room. She was sleeping and I waited for her to wake up.

"I'm cold," Tala said, opening her eyes.

The room wasn't cold, and she was covered by a blanket. "Do you want me to get another blanket for you?" I asked.

"No, don't leave the room."

"I can ring . . ." I said and rang for the nurse to come.

A nurse came in promptly. "I'm so cold," Tala repeated.

"I'll bring you an extra blanket," the nurse said. Looking at me, she went on in a low tone, "Last night a woman tried to commit herself to this hospital, faking being suicidal. Just having food and a warm bed is a luxury for some people."

"She can take my place," Tala said.

The nurse left and Tala began to list her daily activities: she woke in the morning, groggy from the sedatives they fed her the night before. They gave her more pills. She had breakfast in bed, then there was the shower and a series of tests. She ate her lunch in bed too, not wanting to join the patients eating in the day room.

"There's too much pain clogging the air in that room," she explained. But last night, a group of musicians was brought in to play in the day room and she went there to listen. The musicians were young women, students of music at universities. Some of the patients jumped up and danced. One of them took off her clothes and danced naked until a woman orderly came in and forced her to put her clothes back on. Every day after lunch, a nurse took her to the courtyard in the back of the building for an hour and then brought her back inside.

As I was encouraged by her articulate description of her activities, she said, "Oh, I'm hoping to leave this place soon." But her next words contradicted that. "I want to die." She stopped talking and closed her eyes.

She fell asleep again and was oblivious to my presence.

The sound of the door opening and a nurse walking in woke Tala, and she opened her eyes. The nurse, a different one from the one I had met, was holding a tray with two paper cups, a few pills in each, and a glass of water on it. She was tall and exuded efficiency. "I'm sorry to interrupt but it has been a very busy day and we were understaffed." She turned to Tala. "I have to give you your pills now."

They were purple and pink. How pretty they looked, and how frightening at the same time.

"I don't want them," Tala said. "They make me feel strange."

"Honey, it's for your own good," the nurse said. Then, as if to make the pills appealing, she added, "They're imported from America."

Finally, Tala put the pills, one after another, in her mouth and took a few sips of water.

"You didn't swallow them. Here is more water . . . go ahead . . . That's a good girl."

Tala swallowed the pills. She was like a child. What if she stayed in this state permanently, I wondered with dread.

"Can I take her out to dinner later today?" I asked the nurse.

"I'm so sorry, but we don't have permission for that yet." Turning to Tala, she said, "Dear, your sister will take you out when doctors approve."

Tala looked at me and said randomly, "They did a CT scan yesterday and x-rayed my head from every angle again."

"Try to get well quickly so that you and your sister can go out to dinner," the nurse said to her.

After the nurse left, a faint smile came over Tala's face. "If I get my sweet son back, I won't be cold. Will you help me?"

"I'll do what I can . . . Uncle is doing everything now."

"I'm sorry, Roya *joon*, that I wasn't more help to you after you lost . . . your . . ." She sank into silence.

Through the half-open door, I saw a patient wandering into the corridor, then beginning to circle around in an out-of-control way. She screamed, "Open the door, or I'll kick it open." A nurse went over to her and led her away. Then she came to Tala's room and said to me, "I'm sorry, but this is the end of your visiting hour. Tala has an appointment with Dr. Saggami. I have to take her there."

I got up, kissed Tala's cheek, and left.

As I walked along the corridor, it was as if my brain couldn't tune out what didn't matter; everything was equally vivid, equally important. I saw patients playing cards at a table in the day room. A young woman wearing a red bathrobe instead of the sanatorium's uniform said to no one in particular, "We can wear red here." I noticed a few of the other patients were wearing their own clothes too.

The TV hanging on the wall was showing a nature program; images of a lush green area around the Caspian Sea flickered on the screen, with deer and sheep grazing on vast pastures. The bucolic scene didn't seem interesting to the sad women locked up here. Odd, I thought, that the name of the hospital was Azadi, freedom.

A little further down the corridor, a young girl with disheveled dark hair was leaning against the wall. She asked me, "Can you give me a cigarette?"

"I'm sorry, I don't have any cigarettes," I said. As I walked on, I heard her shout, "Coward."

Coward. The word hummed in my ears, penetrating my thoughts. Was I a coward? Couldn't I just take Tala out of the sanatorium? But, of course, it wasn't safe and probably wasn't up to me to make that decision. Still, my state of mind was dark from the helplessness I was feeling.

As I was about to climb the steps down to the lobby, I heard the sound of music from the day room.

*I don't want your love, I don't want your love to break me down . . .*

The record seemed to be scratched. The same line repeated over and over again. *I don't want your love to break me down.*

## Chapter 28

In the house as I lay in bed, in the light of the side lamp I picked up the novel, *The Blind Owl*, again, never tiring of reading it. Each time I discovered new meaning in the sentences and the plot.

Finally, I put the book aside and tried to sleep.

I woke at dawn; the room was filled with a pale light. I got out of the bed and looked out. The sky was streaked with orange, giving dew drops on bushes an orange glow.

As soon as I had breakfast, I rang our home number in Abyaneh and was able to reach Reza. We talked for a while about Tala's condition, the uncertainty of her coming out of the state she was in, and the possibility of Maxim being able to keep Tavoos. He had no more answers to what we could do to help, but just hearing his sympathetic tone soothed me somewhat.

After I put down the receiver, Uncle called and said he would be able to meet me at 11:00 at the sanatorium for us to visit Tala together.

Uncle and I sat on chairs by Tala's bed, and he went over issues that most concerned her—he would continue trying to track down Maxim and Tavoos. He promised her that we would take her out of the sanatorium as soon as it was approved by the doctors attending to her. "Don't worry, my dear, we all want you to be well and out of here as soon as possible," he added in his usual kindly tone.

Then he got up to leave. "I'm sorry I can't be with you a little longer," he said. "My worker is still absent, and I have to be at my shop full-time until he comes back." He kissed Tala's cheeks, and mine too, and left.

Tala was quiet during his visit, hardly saying anything in response.

After he left, she came out of herself and said, "Roya *joon*. Will you go to the petrochemical company, you know, where Anton worked and Maxim was working part-time? Maybe they'll tell you something about Maxim's whereabouts that they haven't told Uncle. I hope they'd trust a twin sister."

"I can do that," I said, wanting to be useful in any way I could. It was the end of the time I was allowed to be with her. I kissed her cheeks, said goodbye, and left.

I took the metro to the petrochemical building. It was a new skyscraper, with an atrium filled with trees, parrots, and other birds flying among the branches and a fountain at its center. Two narrow pools flanked the stairway leading to the main entrance. An artificial tree with silver leaves stood in the middle of the larger pool.

Inside, I went over a young, pretty woman, covered in *hijab*, sitting behind an ornate wooden desk.

I introduced myself and asked if I could have Maxim Alexandrov's contact information. "He is my twin sister's husband's cousin. Her husband was killed in a car accident and my sister was injured and is hospitalized. She needs to speak to Maxim."

"I am so sorry about such huge tragedies," she said in a gentle voice, "but we aren't allowed to give contact information to anyone."

She must have noticed the sadness spreading on my face. She said in a whisper, "We believe Maxim Alexandrov is hiding in Natanz or Russia."

Although she didn't reveal anything that would help, I still felt better to have come there and done something.

Tala's house wasn't far from the company, and I decided to go and look at it; a thought suddenly came to me that Maxim could be hiding there with Tavoos. Then, quickly, I realized the thought was absurd since he would easily be caught there. Still, I felt an urgency to go to the house, hoping Batul would still be there and I could ask her some questions.

As I stood in front of the house, I was shocked to see no flowers in the pots that stood next to the doorway, the lion heads chipped. No sound came from the inside, but I still rang the bell a few times. There was no answer. It seemed Batul hadn't moved back in yet or she would have attended to the flowers.

As I started to walk back, I saw Simin opening the door to her house, just five blocks away. I was struck by an old jealousy of Simin—that Tala almost substituted her for me after I lost my baby, the two of them taking their children to Mellat Park.

I crossed to the other side of the street and joined her.

"I'm Roya," I said.

She stared at me and then said, "Oh, Roya. Come in. I'd love to talk to you."

I followed her into the hallway and then to the living room. I sat on the sofa, and she went to the kitchen to get us tea. The clanking of dishes filled the air. She returned, holding a tray with tea glasses and sugar cubes, and put it on the coffee table.

She sat next to me on the sofa and said, "What a tragedy . . ."

"Yes, very upsetting. Have you seen her since the accident?"

"At the sanatorium. I saw her once, but then I had to go to Rasht. I just returned yesterday." An expression of sadness spread over her face. "I hope they can find Maxim . . . Of course, it's devastating to Tala that he has Tavoos with him."

"Yes, she's very upset about it. Our uncle is trying his best to find out where they are."

We took sips of tea and continued talking.

"My husband periodically goes to Natanz for his work. I urged him to ask around about Maxim's whereabouts. But so far, nothing."

She brushed aside her long brown hair from her forehead, a gesture similar to Tala's, and then said, "Tala was very upset about you losing your baby; she said it was like she had lost her own. Once, she said she wished she could give Tavoos to you and your husband. She thought you'd be better parents."

My heart gave a squeeze at Simin's remark. An image of Tavoos, when I was visiting Tala and held him in my arms, came to me—him smiling at me, the feeling of his skin as I kissed his cheek. I had so yearned for that baby, would have run away with him if I could. The thought came back: could Tavoos be mine?

"Simin, I know this may sound absurd, but how did rescue workers know which baby was mine and which Tala's?"

Simin wasn't surprised or taken aback by my question. She said, "Tala had the same doubts." After a pause, she went on, "She was tormented that there was no proof one way or the other, that she hadn't given you the chance to protest."

"You know how afraid she was of Anton, of what he would have done to her if he found out she lost their baby," I said.

Simin nodded in agreement.

"I found out about the car accident in the middle of the night. Our uncle called me. It was a hard blow."

"It was such a shock to see the report in *Etellaat*. It's lucky she and Tavoos didn't get killed. My boy misses Tavoos." She walked over to the mantel and came back with a framed photograph and handed it to me. It was of Tavoos and another little boy; they had their arms around each other as they stood by a lake with ducks on it. Tavoos looked serious, while the other boy was smiling.

"That's my son, Mohsen. I took the photo in Mellat Park. I would love to talk to you more, but I have to leave now to pick up Mohsen from a friend's house."

"Do you want to go with me tomorrow to visit Tala?" I asked.

"I exchange with other mothers taking care of each other's children. My turn is tomorrow. Then we're going away for a week or two for my husband's mother's ninetieth birthday. They live in Babolsar. Maybe we can go together when I return."

"I'm not sure if I will still be here. My husband and I moved away. I came to Tehran for two weeks to be with Tala."

"Oh, so we can't go together." She accompanied me to the door. "I'm happy we talked. Kiss Tala for me. Assure her I'll be there as soon as I can."

"I will tell her." I said goodbye and started going to the metro.

# Chapter 29

I opened my eyes to the pale rays of dawn. Rain began to fall heavily, splattering the windows with flat silver drops. Tragic images of Tala, a composite of my visits to her at the sanatorium, passed before my eyes. Tala with crutches beside her, the tremor in her hands, the expression on her face becoming sorrowful when mentioning Tavoos, Tavoos being taken away by a man she didn't trust. She was now someone different from the sister I had resented so much after my miscarriage. I wondered how I could return to Abyaneh while Tala was in the condition she was in. But if I stayed longer, I would be neglecting Reza. We were able to speak on the phone only three times, as his cell phone and our home phone didn't always work, the town being surrounded by tall mountains and not having a good enough signal. I couldn't find an easy solution other than discussing it with Reza, assessing his feelings.

I decided to walk to the sanatorium instead of taking the metro, hoping to burn the agitated energy inside me. A cool breeze was blowing, creating music as it passed through trees lining the streets, mingling with the gentle murmur of water flowing over colorful pebbles at the bottom of the *joobs.*

When I arrived in Tala's room, she was sleeping, oblivious to my presence. Thinking of her attempting suicide took my mind to the seminary student's words at Grandmother's funeral.

*What is it to die? It's to say goodbye to everyone and everything you know on this earth—family, friends, houses, clothes, jewelry. You leave with just a shroud to protect you . . . But may heaven be your living place.*

Tala, do you really want to die not believing in heaven? Was your suicide attempt just a plea for attention? Weren't you afraid of dying after the shard of glass hit your head? Weren't we warned all our lives against dangers surrounding a person? Don't stand at the edge of the roof, you'll fall and die. Don't go too close to the pool, you will fall in and drown. Don't go out alone, you can be murdered by that odd man who carries a cloth-covered pail in his hand; he cuts up the person he kills and puts them in that pail. Don't play with matches, they can create fire and burn you. Be wary of *jinns*; they steal children or get inside them, killing them . . . These were words uttered in urgent tones by Grandmother, by other women in the family and neighborhood, and even at times by Baba and Mum.

When Mum got sick, we said to each other, "No, she won't die, she'll get well."

During her sickness, while Baba was with her, we stood behind the half-open door and could see him getting up periodically and going to the window, looking out as if he couldn't bear the pain permeating the room. Once, he was holding a cut-glass tumbler filled with wine. Wine was forbidden by the government, but he could get it from an Armenian vendor. He held it to Mum's lips and said, "Our wise poets called wine an elixir. I love you so much; you must get well, for me, for our daughters and my mother, for everyone who loves you."

I thought again of Mum telling us, "Stay close." How can we stay close if you die?

I remembered a vacation to Shiraz Mum and Baba took us on before she became sick. Baba, interested in poetry, chose Shiraz, where the revered ancient poets Hafiz and Saadi were from and had their tombs.

As Baba drove on winding roads, the rice fields, the patches of colorful wildflowers we passed were enchanting. We stayed two nights in a hotel in the center of the ancient city, Tala and I sharing one room and Mum and Baba sharing another next to ours. During the days, we visited its famous sites—Hafiz's tomb, an elegant structure, a vast garden, a large ornate twisting bazaar, silent and peaceful alleys with old brick houses and buildings. Trees with clusters of grapes from which wine was made and imported to countries where alcohol wasn't forbidden.

The first night in the hotel, the howling of foxes, screaming like women in labor, frightened Tala.

"Nothing to be afraid of; we're together," I said.

Alas, I couldn't say that to her now and hope for good results.

The voice of a woman in the hallway shouting, "It's my turn!" flowed into the room, waking Tala and interrupting my memories.

"Tala, I went to the petrochemical company, but they wouldn't give me the contact information for Maxim."

"I thought they probably wouldn't. But I still hoped."

I filled her in on my visit to Simin.

She blushed, perhaps remembering how she had left me out of their friendship.

She jumped to another subject. "If something happens to me, will you try to find Tavoos and care for him like a son of your own?"

"Don't worry, nothing is going to happen to you; you'll get well," I said, trying to sound cheerful.

A nurse came in and said to me, "Visiting hours are over," which happened almost every time I came to see Tala. I wanted to stay longer and see as much of her as possible.

I kissed Tala on her cheek and left. I went to the nurses' station and the nurse sitting there said, "Dr. Saggami is in his office. You don't need an appointment. He's free now."

In his office, as soon as I sat down, he gave me some hope, telling me I could be sure my sister was in good hands. "She's better on some days and then she lapses, you must have noticed. We've started to gradually lower the dosage of all her medications."

"When can she go home?"

"It's still hard to set a definite date."

He didn't seem to be able or willing to offer any more opinions. His phone rang and as he picked it up, I waved at him and left. Walking down the hallway on my way out, a patient, her face smeared with food and her gait unstable, said to me, "Give me your wallet."

A few feet later, another patient said flatly, "His penis was too big." Then she screamed, "Didn't I tell you not to ever come here again?"

An orderly rushed out and forced the woman inside a room. I continued down the hall.

I took the long way home. It was one of those rare days when the Alborz Mountains were visible through the haze.

A row of shops carried massive straw bales of colorful spices. In one of the shops, men sat cross-legged on a carpet, leaning against spice bales and drinking tea. Life around me was familiar, was as usual, but it had a new glare of melancholy, reflecting my own state of mind.

Back in the house, I decided to go to the storage room and look for what else Tala might have put there in addition to her paintings. Maybe I would come across some things that were valuable to her or could cheer her up and take them to the sanatorium.

Next to the main room where she had put her paintings was a smaller one. As I entered it, I noticed a suitcase that had to belong to Tala since it was made in Russia. I opened it; it was filled with Tavoos's outgrown baby clothes and toys that, for some reason, Tala had kept.

A large envelope lay at the bottom of the suitcase. I took it out and sat with it against the wall. It contained sheets of paper with notes on them. On one sheet, Tala had scribbled a chilling sentence:

*I've been half-dead for a long time.*

I turned the sheet over and found a list with no date on it:

> *GOOD THINGS ABOUT MY LIFE:*
> *Beautiful son*
> *Money*
> *BAD THINGS ABOUT MY LIFE:*
> *I live with lies*
> *I hate myself*

The words cut through me. I took a few deep breaths to calm myself.

I searched for what lay at the bottom of the box. I was startled to see an envelope addressed to my apartment in Tehran, one that obviously was never sent. The envelope was unsealed, and I quickly took out the letter. The stationery was blue; at the top left was a picture of a wrecked rowboat half hidden in the mud. It seemed Tala designed the paper herself.

> *My twin Roya joonam,*
>    *I wish we could look at each other as I tell you my deepest feelings, bottled inside me . . . Remember we used to talk in code so that no one could enter our world? I yearn to be back to that time again, in that cocoon with you. I'm getting ready to tell Anton the truth. Why? Because that will certainly prompt him to divorce me if he doesn't kill me instead. He looks at me suspiciously*

*sometimes, making me feel that inadvertently I've let something about Henry trickle out. He asks me questions and I remain silent and then his patience ebbs quickly and he begins to scream, "Have you lost your voice? Are you deaf and dumb . . ." Then, repentant, he holds me in his arms and says, "I love you; you know that, don't you?" I melt a little, starved for his love but repelled by it too. Repelled because it's tinged with the underlying violence in him . . . I have forgotten how to smile. If I die, you must stay alive and carry on for me . . .*

The sadness of the letter, of her notes, was making me faint. I wanted to talk to Dr. Saggami again and tell him about the disturbing notes. Then I decided against it. They were private to Tala and the doctor already was aware of her suicide attempt.

I put everything back and searched in the boxes set against a wall. One of the boxes was filled with different items—two broken dolls from our childhood mixed with some toys that seemed to belong to Tavoos. The dolls were identical and were the kind that opened and closed their eyes when we moved them. At one time, during the period when Tala had her ups and downs about wanting to be like me or be different than me, we tried to make the dolls that Mum gave to us look different from each other by cutting one doll's hair very short and taking off one of her legs. But then what we did upset me, and I threw the dolls into the large garbage pail in the hall. Tala must have found them and hid them somewhere, so thoroughly that I never saw them until now.

I recalled what she once said years ago, *sometimes it's necessary to keep things secret.*

Seeds of secretiveness were sown in both of us since childhood. People lied to cover up the truth and expected others to be doing the same. Fear of disapproval by neighborhood people, or of something that could be interpreted as anti-government, led to warnings: "Don't tell anyone," "It has to be kept a secret," and "It's our secret."

Again, the question came to me—what would be the consequence if Tala told Anton that her baby died when the castle collapsed? He would pick up a heavy object and fling it at her head, killing her. He would divorce her. He would get another wife. I was struck by other, more painful thoughts. What if Tala had hated me and that was why she took my baby away? What if those attempts she made to separate herself from me after we fell into the cavity and she had Tavoos and I didn't have a baby were only a glimmer of deeper, more powerful emotions? From a recess of my memory, a conversation I had with her came to the forefront.

"Do you ever wish me dead?" she asked me one day as we walked back from high school.

Her question shocked me. "How can you ask such a question?"

"If you killed me, you'd have your own identity. You wouldn't be a copy of me or I of you."

"You're the one who always tries to distance yourself from me." Then I asked, "Do you wish I were dead?"

"No," she gasped. "I'd kill myself first."

I was feeling ravaged but forced myself to continue looking at what was there. One sheet of paper had a poem on it; it was by Forugh Farrokhzad, a feminist poet who was both praised and condemned by society. She died in a car accident, leading to questions about the cause of it. A fanatic, disapproving of her spreading what was called immoral ideas through her poems, could have run into her car, intending to kill her, since the details of the way the accident weren't revealed. One of the English teachers at Al Zahra, who was more liberal and was an admirer of Farrokhzad, believed family laws were unfairly on the side of men. Her expressing her views must have gotten her into trouble because at the end of that semester, she quit or was fired, and we never saw her again. Now reading Tala's notes made me wonder if Forugh had tried to kill herself by bringing on the accident and succeeded. She might have forced the car to hit the pole. Perhaps Tala had come to the same conclusion and was trying to emulate Forugh.

On another sheet, she had written down Forugh's famous poem, a farewell to her son when she was leaving her husband, who would by law get custody of the child, as would be the case if Tala left Anton.

> *I am composing this poem for you*
> *on a parched summer dusk . . .*
> *This is my final lullaby*
> *at the foot of the cradle where you sleep . . .*
> *My forehead tight with pain*

> *I have rested against a dark door . . .*
> *When your innocent eyes glance*
> *at this confused beginningless book*
> *you will see a deep-rooted lasting rebellion*
> *blooming in the heart of every song . . .*
> *A day will come when you will search for me in my words*
> *and tell yourself: my mother, that's who she was.*

Why did Tala copy the poem in her notebook? Was it because she hoped I would find it one day and, when Tavoos was older, I would give it to him? Was it meant to be a message to me? Did she copy that when she had suicidal thoughts and intentions?

Another poem by Forugh followed.

> *No one is thinking about the flowers,*
> *no one is thinking about the fish,*
> *no one wants to believe that the garden is dying,*
> *that the garden's heart has swollen under the sun,*
> *that the garden's mind*
> *is slowly being drained of green memories.*
> *And the garden's senses seem an abstract thing*
> *rotting in solitude in a corner or the garden.*

I had given Tala a collection of Forugh's poetry because we thought of ourselves as feminists, though the restrictions imposed on us didn't always allow us the freedom to be who we wanted to be or choose the best paths for ourselves. Now, reading the poems we both admired made me feel my heartbeats were coordinating with hers, though we were far-flung now in the paths we found ourselves on.

As I crossed the courtyard, beneath my feet, the dry yellow maple leaves had turned the ground to gold. A red ball lay abandoned under a bed of maple leaves. It must have belonged to Tavoos and fell out of his hand when Tala came to the storage room with him to store some things. I picked it up to take it inside the house.

As I walked, a flock of sparrows crossed the sky. Some of them descended on the maple tree and began to chirp. I watched them for a while.

Then my eyes caught an owl sitting on the parapet. It stared at me with somber eyes. Grandmother had said sparrows brought good news and owls were bearers of bad news. Now both were present. I wished she were here to predict what good news and bad news awaited me and Tala.

# Chapter 30

I had slept late and missed the morning visiting hours. I would have to wait until the afternoon. When I got to her room, to my disappointment, it was empty. I went to the nurse's station and found the nurse Parvin there. She told me that Tala had a visitor and she allowed them to get a pass to go out. "Who was the visitor?"

"Simin Baluchian. She said she was an old friend."

Strange that I felt a pang of jealousy as I did when I saw her with Simin in Behesht Zahra cemetery. Then that feeling gave place to relief that she had Simin as an attentive friend, that she was well enough to leave the sanatorium for a period of time.

"How long is she going to be out?"

"We gave them two hours."

"Can I take her out tomorrow?"

"We allow one outing a week. This is new—she wasn't allowed to be taken out before."

"Is it because she has recovered enough to go out?"

"Dr. Saggami thought it may speed her recovery to be out of here, even for a short time, and see the outside world again."

"I'll wait for her in case they return sooner."

She didn't object. I sat in Tala's room, which seemed even more desolate without her presence. But she and Simin didn't come back before it was time for me to leave.

After I left, I walked for a long time, stopped at some galleries, and ate in a café, but none of that calmed me. At night when I went to sleep, I had many nightmares; I woke from each shivering, though I was covered by a blanket.

I only remembered one dream. Two fetuses were tangled together. One was trying to separate itself from the other, but the first one held on, not letting go. I woke, my heart beating violently.

Is Tala going to get well and be able to be with Tavoos? In the midst of jumbled emotions, I found myself thinking, we'll share him. He will belong to both of us. We will love him together.

In the morning, I tried to reach Uncle, but no one picked up at his shop or house.

Alas, when I went to the sanatorium to see Tala, her health had declined even more steeply. The nurse told me I shouldn't stay with her for more than half an hour.

I went in and sat on the chair by her bed. "Tala," I called.

She opened her eyes and said, "Oh, you are here. Roya, I have no illusion that I will be living much longer."

"Things can turn around for you," I said, trying to be hopeful and give her hope.

"Tala, promise me to take care of Tavoos. I'm going to die, I know."

"Of course, I promise." I finally came out with what I thought must be burdening Tala, as it was burdening me still. "Tala, remember after we miscarried, we rarely saw each other? I had a feeling you were avoiding me."

"I felt terrible that your baby died. It was hard for me to face you."

"I had nightmares that you took my baby."

To my surprise, Tala didn't seem upset or angry. Instead, she said in a calm voice, "Roya *joon*, I had the same type of nightmares, that I had stolen your baby. It weighed on my heart so much that finally, before we left for Russia, I went to Dr. Semnani at the hospital they took us to after we miscarried. I wanted to ask if such a thing was possible given the state I was in. She said it wasn't. That after the miscarriage and being covered by debris, there was no way I would have the strength and ability to do that. Also, I was unconscious when they found me."

I said nothing, trying to absorb all that. After a moment, I said, "I wonder how one baby survived."

"I asked the same question. She said Tavoos must have just rolled out of a gap in the debris."

I was silent for a moment. Of course, this is what Reza believed too and had confirmed by talking with the nurse and the doctor at the maternity hospital.

"But I tormented myself that maybe they were all wrong," Tala went on. "Finally, I've stopped feeling that way."

"Oh, Tala, I know I was wrong to think that. I am so sorry . . ."

Then, on her own, she answered some questions I had meant to ask. "Roya, the accident was horrifying. Anton is dead because of me. I was the cause. But what if Tavoos becomes Maxim's victim . . . Even Anton wasn't a good father. He adored Tavoos but he was too controlling, and Tavoos would turn away from him. Roya, do you promise to treat Tavoos as your own child?"

"Of course I will. I'm sure your lawyer will be able to help with the family affairs so I can take care of him until you are well and out of here."

She went back and forth, trying to bring her thoughts and feelings into the open. She said again, "Roya, I love you. I'm so happy we're talking . . . Will you forgive me for abandoning you?" In the expression on her face, I could see shame, guilt, and love intermingling.

I couldn't possibly confront her now for causing me so much pain.

"Tala. I missed you . . ."

"I missed you too during those months, more than you can imagine."

Again, she closed her eyes and drifted away from me. Layers of memories were tearing apart and clearing the way again back to our childhood, so connected, inseparable, feeling and seeing what the other did. Back to when we would climb together into one of our beds and talk and talk, in our own language, using words we had invented so that no one else would hear or understand us. Not that we were doing anything we could be punished for. It was more so that we had our own world to ourselves.

She suddenly seemed exhausted and closed her eyes.

I got up and left, feeling somewhat calmer to have told her I would take care of Tavoos.

I took a different street back. I came to Azadi Tower. It struck me for the first time how many monuments and institutions had the name Freedom, which was so far from the way I and many other people felt, most strongly Reza, who spent his efforts trying to gain freedom.

Tala had wanted to visit the Azadi Tower that day, but we ended up going to Rey Castle because its museum was closed for repair. How different me and Tala's situation would be if we had been able to go to Azadi Tower instead.

The tower's structure, made of white marble, gleamed in the sunlight, inviting. I went inside. The museum was still closed, but I climbed the stairway to the rooftop, which was open to visitors. At the top, some tourists were taking photographs of the vast view of the city visible from that spot. I stood there for a long time, looking at the view— mountains surrounding the city, cars racing by on the streets. When I climbed down, I paused on a step and watched the light show of the colorful fountain in the center of the first floor.

Finally, when I left it was already siesta time; shops were closing and people were going inside. But the café I had been coming to since I came to Tehran was open. I sat under the shade of a large maple tree on a platform over the wide *joob* running along the sidewalk. In the serene, quiet atmosphere, my mood was uplifted. I thought Tala would get well and we would be best friends again, united by our mutual love for Tavoos. I had Olivier salad, spinach, yogurt, and lemonade. Then I had ice cream with pieces of hardened vanilla in it.

Two young girls came to the platform and sat, leaning against cushions and whispering about politics, but their voices were loud enough for me to hear some words—how people were arrested for the slightest criticism of the government. It made me think of Reza, at that moment writing articles that would sooner or later get him into trouble.

After I finished eating and paid, I walked to the house on Vali Asr Avenue. I passed Mellat Park, recalling again how Tala and I had talked about bringing our babies there in strollers.

That visit to the sanatorium was the last time I saw Tala and heard her voice.

# Chapter 31

Uncle's phone call to tell me Tala died came late at night, the same as when he called me in Abyaneh to let me know she was hospitalized. What he said sounded like a hallucination. But there was no denying it as he filled me in more—the hospital informed him that she was dead and had been taken to the morgue, where she would be kept overnight. The cause of death was not established. Dr. Saggami told him that though the wounds from the accident were healed on the surface, the internal bleeding might have continued. The thought that my future was going to be without Tala was shocking and disorienting, as if I were taking a walk in a jungle and had lost my way.

After a pause, he said he had known Tala wouldn't be living much longer and he had arranged a grave in Paradise Zahra Cemetery, which was open twenty-four hours a day, and he had started the burial process, hiring grave diggers. A stone was also ready to be placed once she was put into the earth and covered by it. As he rapidly told me all that, I was silent, enveloped in grief and feeling a little betrayed that Uncle had been certain Tala was going to die and he hadn't expressed it to me. "I wish you had told me," I said, as politely as I could manage.

"I'm sorry that I didn't prepare you. At least our dear Tala is no longer in pain. May her soul rest in heaven." He talked the way Grandmother did, and though I didn't have their belief in heaven and hell, his soothing tone calmed me somewhat.

"Will you come to the cemetery at 4:00 tomorrow afternoon?"

"Yes," I said, then I heard a man's voice asking Uncle something. Uncle said to me, "I will pick you up at 3:00," and we said goodbye. I knew little of Uncle's personal life. But he was always there for Tala and me; he treated us as if we were his own daughters.

I rang Reza's cell phone, but the mailbox was full, taking no messages. I called him at our home number, but he didn't pick up. We didn't have an answering machine on it for me to leave a message.

I lay back in bed, enveloped in a hazy state of mind, not quite knowing if I were asleep or awake. Every word Uncle told me kept fluctuating, leading to different questions. Was Tala really dead? Will I die soon? Or am I going to stay strong to do what Tala no longer can, try my best to get custody of Tavoos, look after him?

Finally, I drifted into sleep and woke up with a jolt from a nightmare that seemed so real that it felt like it was happening.

*I pick up a clay pot and throw it at Tala's head from the window and scream, "Tavoos is my baby." Tala screams back, "You are killing me so that you can have Tavoos to yourself."*

I sat up and took a few deep breaths. In the dark state of mind I was in, I questioned myself. Did I wish that Tala would die so that I could have Tavoos? The disturbing thoughts were finally pushed away by my keen awareness of how deeply I missed Tala, in spite of all the resentments and conflicts of recent years.

I managed to fall back to sleep.

In the morning, I called Reza again at our home phone number. As soon as he picked up, I started crying.

"What happened? Tell me, talk to me."

I told him that Tala had died.

"Oh, Roya, I know how hard that is on you. Come home as soon as you can."

I thought of his saying, "Tala is the dark side of you." Did he feel there was some benefit to me from Tala's death?

"I have to wait to see what I can do for Tavoos."

"I hope it won't be long."

"I'll be there as soon as I can. You know I miss you."

Finally, we said goodbye. I couldn't ask him to come to Tehran. Since Hossein had been under house arrest, the *Basij* were looking for the rest of the journalists connected to the newspaper. A few years ago, a photograph of them as a group was printed in a local newspaper, which was no longer in print, but the photograph could still be available.

At 3:00, Uncle picked me up, and we went to the cemetery together. We were both quiet for a while. Then he broke the silence, telling me what seemed to be occupying his mind. "We have to do our best to get Tavoos back from the scoundrel."

I nodded in agreement.

At the cemetery entrance, Uncle bought a bouquet of mixed flowers from the vendor who displayed them on a cart.

Inside, again some women were sitting together on a cloth they had spread under the shade of the large willow tree. They were sipping *sharbat* from glasses and taking pieces of *sohan* and eating them. Why is it so common to see this gathering of women in the cemetery, eating, talking, and drinking *sharbat*? Maybe they wanted to be near the graves of people they had been close to, hoping they would get a signal from them, that their soul or a part of it would appear in the sky or the top of the trees.

Uncle led me to where Tala's grave was. We waited for a short time before the workers, two tall, muscular men, brought over the coffin from the morgue, adjacent to the cemetery. They lifted the coffin and put it inside the grave with her head toward Mecca. I had to control an impulse to jump into the grave, be with Tala, the way as children we sometimes moved into each other's beds and how we shared Mum's womb. I came out of that state by the touch of Uncle's hand on my arm and his voice saying, "Watch out."

The men began to fill the hole with dirt. Adept at quick burials, and with Uncle having started the process even before Tala died, the grave provider affiliated with the cemetery had already put Tala's name and date of birth on the stone. Only the date of her death would need to be added. Two doves facing each other were carved above her name. Now, a mason Uncle had asked to be there began adding the date of her death. I put the flowers on the stone and then fell into that state where I had a hard time separating myself from my identical twin: was it me or she who was being buried?—the kind of confusion that had been with me since our childhood.

It was a lonely burial, with no friends or family members other than Uncle.

Uncle had already paid all the workers, and they left. Wiping our faces, wet from tears, with handkerchiefs, we left the cemetery. He took me to a restaurant nearby.

After we ordered and tried to force ourselves to eat, he said, "Tala named Tavoos and you as the beneficiaries of the money, including the *mehrieh* she saved in the bank near me. Most of it is in Tavoos's name, but what is left to you is a good sum too. Originally, she hadn't named anyone to inherit the money. She changed it recently, soon after the accident, while in the general hospital. Her lawyer has to go over the details with you."

I was surprised that Tala included me in the inheritance along with Tavoos. Even if there were legal obstacles for me to get the money, it was her intention that counted. Then I thought, she must have known she might die soon, and she hoped I would get custody of Tavoos.

Uncle filled me in more on the process of getting custody—he believed it wouldn't take long now that Tala was no longer alive.

After he paid, as he always did, we left, and he drove me to the house.

Inside, I called Reza. As usual, I had a hard time reaching him. Both his cell and the landline seemed to be out of order, which happened often in Abyaneh.

A little later, as the sun was about to set, I tried our home phone number. This time he picked it up. I filled him in on what Uncle told me, Tala leaving money for me in her will.

"She always tried to . . ." he started and stopped himself from saying, "to buy you."

"She was hoping I would get custody of Tavoos, so she left me money to be able to manage," I said.

He said nothing.

"Would you be happy if I got custody of Tavoos?" I asked.

"Of course. We will treat him as our own child."

I thought, he may be our own child, but I stopped myself. No time now for such speculation or discussions.

# Chapter 32

In the morning, I had just finished breakfast when Uncle came to the house, unannounced. He told me breathlessly that Maxim was found by the *Basij* in Natanz. He was being held in a cell until his guilt was proven. Tavoos was brought to Tehran and was in Mercy Home, a place for homeless children.

"Oh, Uncle, that's such good news about Maxim," I said, while feeling pain at the idea of Tavoos being in such a place. What was it like in Mercy Home, what were the other children like? The questions went through my mind rapidly. I asked Uncle the questions. He said, "It's supposed to be a good place, well-funded by philanthropists. Can you go to Parvaneh Jahanbani's office this morning? I checked with her receptionist. She's willing to see you at 11:00. She's making time for you in her busy schedule."

I said, "Yes, of course," and he gave me her address. After we got off the phone, I was filled with an urgency to meet Tala's lawyer. In fear of getting there late, I gave myself a lot of time and was half an hour early.

I told the receptionist, a young woman wearing a scarf and a *manteau*, I had an appointment. She looked my name up and said, "Please sit and wait for your turn."

There were several offices in a row with their doors shut. A few women were sitting on chairs and a couch, shifting in their seats, looking anxious. Finally, a young woman came over to me to tell me that it was my turn, and she guided me to Parvaneh Jahanbani's office.

Parvaneh was sitting behind a Formica-topped desk cluttered with documents. Her hair was covered by a scarf, and she had on a *manteau* in conservative colors. She seemed to be about forty and had a grave expression on her face. She greeted me and asked me to sit down, pointing to a chair across from her desk.

As soon as I sat down, she said, "I'm happy to meet you. We have a lot to discuss. Most of my clients' cases have to do with family disputes over custody."

She glanced at some papers on her desk. Then she looked up at me and said, "Once, I visited Tala at the sanatorium. Even in her condition, she resembled you strongly. It would be so good for Tavoos if you could get custody of him."

"I am eager to have Tavoos with me."

"Do you live in Tehran?"

I shook my head. The need for secrecy took over me. "I live in Kashan with my husband," I said. "I can take Tavoos there with me."

"I don't think they'd agree for the child to be taken away from Tehran yet. They would want to supervise how he's being taken care of."

"I'll stay in Tehran if I need to," I said.

"Unfortunately, the clergy plays a big role in custody situations. If the family court approves, a clergyman will review the decision. He may not rule out Maxim getting custody of Tavoos. But I have some connections in the family court. That always helps."

Knowing that I had no say in what the rules were, I just nodded.

"I will set up an appointment for you with someone in the family court for an interview." She gave me the court's address and said she would let me know as soon as she found out who would see me and at what time. She handed me a card with her name and phone number on it. "Call me if you have any questions."

I thanked her and left, filled with anxiety. Her telling me the clergy had a lot of power in family matters lingered with me. I wandered the streets for a while, sat in a café, ate lunch, and went back to the house.

I had just arrived at the house when Parvaneh called me. "Cyrus Tabatabi can see you tomorrow morning at 10:00. I managed to get a quick appointment, explaining the urgency of the situation."

"I am really grateful."

"I do anything for my clients," she said. Then she asked me some questions about Reza and myself.

I told her my husband was a high school teacher and I worked at home, making children's clothing on consignment.

She got off the phone quickly to take another call.

After a restless night, I woke up early, had breakfast, and got ready to go to the court, which wasn't far from Parvaneh's office. Again, I gave myself a lot of time to get there.

I waited for a bus, but one wasn't coming, and time was ticking away.

A taxi stopped by me. "Need a ride?" It was a woman driver, all covered up with only her eyes showing.

I got into the taxi to make sure I wouldn't be late for my appointment.

"I take someone to the courthouse every day," she said when I told her where I wanted to go. Suddenly, a policeman stopped her and asked for her license.

After she showed it to him, he said, "Move on."

"They don't like to see a woman driving," she said.

Finally, we were at the court, and she dropped me off, saying, "Good luck."

The courthouse's reception room was crowded. A clerk sitting behind a desk was giving out numbers. I took mine and sat on a bench next to several other women. One was complaining bitterly to another about her husband beating her. She was there to file for divorce. The other woman said she was trying to gain custody of her child who had automatically gone to her husband because she initiated their divorce. Yes, that would have been Tala's situation.

Two men were sitting on a bench next to ours and talking heatedly. The younger man was complaining that he was cheated by someone at his shop. "He stole the money from the cash box so slowly that it wasn't obvious at first," he said.

The other man, a little older, said, "My own cousin cheated me . . ."

My number was called, and I got up.

Entering the office, I was weak with anxiety.

Cyrus Tabatabi was sitting behind his wide Formica desk, looking over a document. The framed poem, written in calligraphy, hanging on the wall behind him put me at ease. It was a poem that Baba had also framed and kept on his home desk.

> *Children of Adam are each other's organs,*
> *Since in creation, they are from one seed.*
> *If the world causes pain in one organ,*

*The others will not rest.*
*If you are carefree while others suffer,*
*You do not deserve to be called human.*

He looked up and said, "I've studied your case and am in favor of granting you custody of Tavoos. But I still need approval from several others in charge of this matter," he said.

"I really appreciate your help and kindness."

# Chapter 33

Outside, before turning to go home, an idea came to me. Mostafa, the landlord of the house where Reza and I rented an apartment before we moved to Abyaneh, had strong connections to the clergy through his mosque. He was a compassionate man. He might be willing to use his connections to influence the mullah in charge. Hoping for that, and also wanting to visit his wife, Golnar, who was exceptionally supportive and kind after I lost the baby, I took the metro to the house.

When I entered the alley, I found that some of the uneven cobblestones were replaced by bricks; it seemed the mayor was making the alleys safer. The door to the house was open, and I walked into the courtyard. The morning-glory vine I once planted was still alive, its blue flowers climbing the wall. Long-stemmed daisies in the flower bed swayed gently in the breeze. Butterflies were circling around the sunflowers that Golnar had planted.

I noticed their daughter, now older and even prettier, sitting with another girl on a rug spread on the ground next to the pool. The other girl had bright henna-red hair and henna-tattooed red spots all over her arms. The two girls were poring over the contents of a thick book, probably Hafiz's poetry. The girls would pause on a page, trying to see their future in words written six hundred years ago. I quietly slipped past them and went up the steps to the porch that extended from the row of rooms where the landlord and his family lived.

The living room door was open, and I saw Golnar sitting on a carpet, polishing a silver tray. The red flowers woven into the carpet made it seem as if she was sitting outdoors in nature. The tapestry on the wall behind her, featuring a lake with two swans floating on it and a vast blue sky above, only enhanced that impression.

"Roya *joon*," she exclaimed. "I'm so happy to see you. When did you come back? Is Reza *agha* with you?"

I shook my head no. She invited me inside and served me *sharbat* in a gold-rimmed glass matching the one she was half-finished drinking from. The silver tray she had been engaged in polishing revealed little bird designs scattered on its surface. She was as striking as before with her long black hair, full of ringlets, and she was wearing a yellow dress with black poppy designs. She hadn't finished high school, but she read magazines and newspapers and books by classical Iranian writers and poets.

"Tell me, where are you living now?" she asked. "You left in a rush . . ."

I sank into myself for a moment, trying to think of what to say. Finally, I said, "We're living in Kashan, near Reza's family. He has cousins and nieces there. And he found a good job teaching."

Then, quickly, I changed the subject to Tala's condition, the car accident that killed her husband and landed her in a sanatorium, suffering from shock, and then dying there, Tavoos being in Mercy Home.

"Oh, how devastating," she exclaimed. "I'm really sorry. It all must be so hard to take."

I nodded and filled her in on the custody situation. "Golnar *joon*, can I ask you a favor?"

"Of course."

I told her the clergy had the final word on the situation and asked, "Do you think Mostafa *agha* can use his connections at the mosque if the custody issue becomes a battle in court?"

"Sure. I will ask him. I want to help."

The muezzin began to call people to prayers. Golnar prayed regularly, so I thanked her and stood up. "I'm so grateful to you," I said. I gave her the phone number at the house.

As I went through the porch and down the steps into the courtyard, the two girls were still reading Hafiz. I wished I could believe in the ancient poet's prophecies and reach out to him for guidance. In the alley, a young man riding a bicycle and whistling took my mind back to Reza riding his bicycle to work when we lived there. I felt an ache being separated from him.

At the mouth of the alley, I looked for Gholam, the one-eyed vendor who had told me about Reza being taken away in a Mercedes. The public baths for women, the mosque, and the stationery store were all the same, but Gholam's spot was empty. Was he arrested for one reason or another? Then I noticed a man resembling Abbas, Reza's friend. It was him, I realized, as he said, "Roya, nice to see you. Are you and Reza back in Tehran?"

"No, just me. I came here to take care of . . ." Before I could finish, a car stopped at the curb of the street and the driver called to Abbas to get in. Abbas whispered to me quickly, "Tell Reza to be careful. A few journalists were just arrested. And Hossein . . ."

The man in the car honked loudly. Abbas said goodbye to me and rushed to the car before he finished his sentence. I wished I could ask him questions about the journalists who were arrested and what he was going to tell me about Hossein, but the car sped away and disappeared from my sight.

Oh, Reza, I thought, I hope you aren't going to get into trouble. I turned onto a narrow street lined by peach trees. It was on this street that I took walks with Reza before we were married. I remembered one of the days vividly. The trees were full of buds. It was near dusk, but the sky was still luminous. The trees and houses all had assumed an ethereal quality in that light. The voices of doves, perching on copulas, were audible, in spite of the murmur of traffic from the wider avenues. A mysterious excitement had enveloped me as I walked with him. I loved Reza, no matter the risk he was putting us at.

The family court's reception room was crowded again with men and women. Some paced, looking agitated and anxious. A few sat on a bench and chairs. A young bearded man was sitting behind a desk in a corner. I went over to him and told him about my appointment. He disappeared into one of the offices and returned quickly. "Mr. Jamshid Sepahzadeh will see you."

"My appointment is with Haji Saiid Mohamaddi," I said.

"I'm sorry but he had to leave—family emergency."

Entering Mr. Jamshid Sepahzadeh's office, I was weak with anxiety.

"Sit down," he said in a polite tone, keeping his eyes averted. He was middle-aged, with a pile of white hair and a shaggy beard. On the wall behind him hung portraits of different prominent mullahs, all with long beards and turbans. He didn't ask me any questions. Obviously, he had whatever information he needed about me.

He got to the point quickly. "Considering Maxim Alexandrov's criminal activities, you have a good chance of gaining custody of your nephew," he said. "Parvaneh Jahanbani's urgency prompted us to move your case to the beginning of the waitlist. A child's well-being is of great importance in our court."

"I appreciate your concern and help."

I was lucky, I thought, that Maxim was caught and established to be a criminal, or else the custody would definitely go to him. My mind traveled to years ago when I had imagined holding Tavoos in my arms and running away with him to our apartment, taking care of him.

"Can you come here on Thursday to meet with Haji Saiid Mohammadi, in charge of final decisions?"

"Yes, any time on Thursday."

Again, he explained, "We are putting priority on this case otherwise would take weeks, months, sometimes years. The child having been taken away by a man with shady records makes the situation urgent." His manner and his tone were dry, and he kept his eyes averted. But he didn't seem unkind.

Thursday was just three days away, but it felt like an eternity. "Is it possible for me to see Tavoos before that?"

"Not until Haji Saiid Mohammadi allows it. Be here at ten in the morning and the clerk will lead you to the right office."

On Thursday, I was back in the court again. Haji Saiid Mohammadi was sitting behind his wide Formica desk, looking over a document.

He looked up and greeted me and said, "Sit down."

As soon as I sat on a chair, he said, "I've studied your case and we'll make a decision by the end of this week. You know that you have to stay in Tehran if you get custody of the child."

"Yes," I said.

"Your previous landlord has said good words about you. That is going to be taken into consideration. I'll send my recommendation to the Child Welfare Office and then you'll get a call or a letter from them with their decision." He added, "We take our children's safety very seriously."

I wanted to ask how long it would be before the decision was finalized but restrained myself.

He volunteered the information. "It shouldn't take too long, by the end of this week."

Four more days, I thought; it seemed like an eternity.

Without adding anything else he turned his gaze to the documents on the desk.

I got up, thanked him, and left. He didn't look up at me, as if he had forgotten my presence. Still, my head was reeling with optimism.

In the house, I called Reza and now with the hope that I would get custody of Tavoos, I told him that I would need to stay in Tehran with him. That was one of the rules in custody laws, that the child adopted had to stay where his hometown was.

He was silent for a moment, and when he started talking, he sounded reserved.

"You want me to get custody of him, right?"

"Of course," he said, his voice gathering warmth. "We always wanted a baby. You loved Tavoos from the beginning. We will welcome him as our own. But I don't want to keep our hopes up until you have the final answer."

"You are right," I said.

We talked a little longer about the situation and about what he was working on. Finally, we said goodbye and got off the phone. Stirred up, I went out and took a long walk to calm myself.

## Chapter 34

A few days went by, and I was full of ups and downs about how realistic it was that I would be awarded custody of Tavoos. I tried to look up some of my old friends, but I couldn't reach any of them—either their phone numbers had changed or they moved away from Tehran. Afsaneh's mother answered the phone and said she was away in Paris. Uncle took me out for lunch again and we talked and talked about what we could hope for.

Then one morning, I woke to the doorbell's sound. I put on my *manteau* and went to the hallway, where the mailman always dropped in the mail after ringing the bell.

I found two envelopes—one was from the family affairs court. Still standing in the hallway, I opened that first, with trepidation, and saw at a quick glance that the custody was official, with the restriction that I would need to live in Tehran until Tavoos was ten years old. Then I was allowed to change cities.

It had a signature and a seal. My happiness was so integrated with my grief for losing Tala that I burst into tears. I sat down on the step near the door until I calmed down and then opened the second envelope. It was from Mercy Home. My eyes quickly ran over the words.

*Dear Roya Toorani,*

*I am writing to inform you that we have approval from the family affairs court for you to go to Mercy Home on 15 Mohammadi Street. You can meet Tavoos and interact with him before you take him out. Except for Fridays, any time from 1:00–5:00 p.m. is fine. Someone will lead you inside to the appropriate person.*

*Karman Legabi, Associate Director, Mercy Home.*

It was Wednesday. Feeling urgent to get there as soon as possible, I had a quick breakfast, took a shower, and got dressed. Then I looked at myself in the mirror. How much did I resemble Tala, now older and having had vastly different experiences from hers? Would Tavoos take me to be her, or would he notice the differences? The thoughts going around my mind left me both excited and anxious.

I still had a few hours before I could go to Mercy Home. I quickly made up what once was Tala's bed with sheets and a blanket I found in a closet for Tavoos until I could buy a bed appropriate for him. Then I went to the toy store on Jamaly Avenue and bought a few things, and to the children's clothing shop and bought immediate necessities—pajamas, a sweater, T-shirts, pants. I would be able to make some of his clothes myself. Next to the store was a shop that had freshly prepared meals. I bought *kuku* and meatballs, good for children and adults, so that we could have them together when I brought him home.

Back in the house, I put the food in the refrigerator and the toys on a shelf against the wall in the room, adding to them the red ball I had brought in from the courtyard on the way back to the storage room. Engaging in these activities uplifted me and at the same time made me apprehensive that something still could go wrong, and I would have to wait to remove more obstacles before I could take Tavoos home.

Mercy Home was a sprawling two-story yellow brick building that covered a whole block. I rang the bell, and a young man with a full beard opened the door. He introduced himself as Jamal, an assistant to Delaram Jobrani, the director, and led me inside.

A row of rooms lined one side of the courtyard. Jamal pointed to one of them and said, "Tavoos lives in that room with two other boys. Some of the boys have their residence in the building across the street." He paused by a room on the other side of the children's rooms. He went inside and came out in a moment. "Delaram Jobrani will see you."

A woman, about fifty years old, wearing a navy-blue *manteau* and a headscarf almost the same shade of blue, was sitting behind a desk. She greeted me and I sat on a chair across from her. A framed photograph of a group of boys and a small vase holding flowers stood on the desk.

"As a formality, can you show me the letter you received from the family court?" she asked.

"Yes," I said, and I took it out of my pocketbook.

She looked at it and gave it back to me. "You're lucky that everything lined up in your favor." She slid a newspaper cutting across the desk toward me. I picked it up and read it, my heartbeat accelerating.

Prior to the car accident, the Strategic Research Center, the organization affiliated with the Expediency Council, revealed that Anton Alexandrov had been conveying confidential information to Russia. He was under surveillance by the Intelligence Ministry. His first cousin, Maxim Alexandrov, at one time worked as a clerk for the Natanz branch of the Iranian National Petrochemical Company and was under suspicion for stealing money from the company. He was fired, but not arrested since there was no definitive proof of wrongdoing at the time. He subsequently began to work for Anton Alexandrov, and finally, it was established that the two cousins were stealing from the company's different branches and depositing most of the money in banks in Russia . . .

Though Tala had prepared me for something like this, I was still stunned to see it in writing.

"Maxim was arrested in Natanz and is in the local jail there," she said after I read the article. "Now that it's all settled, I can tell you certain things went in your favor. The Welfare Organization found other incriminating evidence against Maxim. He had tried to reverse Tavoos's trust fund so that instead of being available when he turns eighteen, it would be available soon. He actually forged the document, but he got caught."

"I never felt comfortable with either Anton or Maxim. I was concerned for Tala," I said.

"We don't get to know the man we marry beforehand. That's a cultural dilemma."

I wondered if she was married. She didn't have a wedding ring on, but some people didn't like to wear it. Reading my thoughts, she said, "I never got married. My parents were unhappy in their marriage and that made me wary of it."

"Tala was regretful about her quick decision to accept Anton's proposal."

Delaram jumped to another subject. "There's a place like Mercy Home for girls too. Here we teach the boys practical skills. They teach what they consider useful skills for girls."

She lowered her eyes as if she could not bear seeing my reaction to what she was about to tell me. "There were bruises on Tavoos's face and arms when the welfare workers brought him here. It wasn't clear if they were left over from the car accident or if Maxim abused him."

"Oh, so sad!" was all I could bring out, feeling weak hearing the heart-wrenching details.

"The wounds are healed now, I'm happy to say." After a pause, she added, "Still, you have some legal battles ahead of you in regard to Tavoos's inheritance. But the Welfare Office and Parvaneh Jahanbani, Tala's lawyer, will sort things out. I was informed about your situation, marital status, and your willingness to stay in Tehran. They believe you are the perfect person to take care of Tavoos."

We were interrupted by Morteza, another employee, knocking and then coming in, holding a suitcase in one hand and Tavoos's hand in the other.

Tavoos was wearing blue pants and a pinstriped lemon-green and white shirt. He looked old for a four-year-old boy. He stared at me, perhaps trying to assess if I was his mother.

Then he dropped his gaze. His shoulders were shaking a little, making my heart ache for him.

"This is your Aunt Roya," Morteza said to him gently. "I told you she would be coming for you."

Tavoos was silent. Then he burst into tears.

I picked him up, held him to my chest, and kissed him. I wiped his tears with tissues I took from a box on Delaram's desk.

Delaram got up and kissed Tavoos and kissed my cheek too.

Morteza, a heavy-set young man, accompanied me and Tavoos outside and hailed a taxi for us. He gave the suitcase to the driver to put in the trunk, kissed Tavoos, and said, "We are going to miss you."

Tavoos smiled with a shy expression on his face.

As the taxi drove to the house, Tavoos was quiet. He looked out of the window at the pedestrians and cars rushing by. Having him with me, taking him home, felt like going to sleep on a rainy night and waking to a clear sky full of sunshine.

# Chapter 35

In the room I had quickly prepared for Tavoos, he began to play quietly with the toys and the red ball, throwing it at the wall and catching it. He stared at the ball as if trying to refresh his memory. He hadn't asked me any questions since I took him out of Mercy Home. He was quiet now too, probably trying to absorb what was happening to him. He didn't seem upset, just contemplative. Perhaps the accident destroyed some of his memories connected to his parents. In his hazy state, he could be thinking I was his mother, not his aunt as they told him.

Away from him, in the living room, I rang Reza at our home number, and he picked up. I told him the good news about bringing Tavoos home, that he was playing in what once was Tala's room. We talked for a while about the fact that I had to stay in Tehran.

He said again, "The newspaper may be shutting down, and I will join you. You know it would be risky for me to quit because of Hossein . . ."

We got off the phone when his cell phone rang.

As it began to grow dark, I ate with Tavoos, sharing the food I had bought. I tried to talk to him, and he answered in monosyllables, mixing Farsi and Russian words, which I didn't understand. Then I gave him a shower, put on the pajamas, and tucked him into bed. The bed was large for a child, but comfortable. As soon as I had money I could spend, I would buy furniture appropriate for his age and make the room calm and appealing at the same time. I sang what Mum used to sing to Tala and me when she put us to bed.

> Go to sleep now, close your eyes, and dream this night
> The moon and stars watch over you
> Close your eyes and peaceful dreams are soon to come
> Stars bathe you in soft white light
> Moonbeams whisper goodnight

*The moon is on the rise. The sleepy sun has closed her eyes*
*Sail away on waves of the sea and oceans*
*Realize all your dreams.*

He listened, closed his eyes, and drifted to sleep.

How natural being a mother to Tavoos felt to me!

I went to bed too and was awakened by Tavoos screaming. I rushed to his room, picked him up, and held him to myself. His body was stiff, his face taut. I rocked him until he calmed down. He put his head on my shoulder, perhaps thinking it was his mother's, or at least a reminder of his mother's.

Once he fell asleep again, I went back to bed. Sounds from the courtyard had quieted, and the moonlight and the stars were dimmed by dark clouds. As I drifted to sleep, I had strange dreams. In the dreams, there had never been a Tala separate from me, I was both Tala and Roya. There was only one pregnant woman, Roya-Tala, going to Rey, and it was Roya-Tala giving birth to a baby.

After I woke, I lay awake for a long time. Is Tavoos going to become more aware and upset that his parents died and I took his mother's place, or will he come to accept me as his mother and Reza as his father? Maybe when he was older and strong enough, I would tell him what happened to Tala and Anton.

I began to organize our lives. The money that Tala had deposited in a private account in a bank near Uncle was enough to take care of Tavoos's and my expenses until Tavoos's inheritance issues were resolved. His inheritance was the house and what was left in the bank for him to access when he was older. The house was locked up until Parvaneh Jahanbani got permission from the court and family affairs for me to open it. Uncle transferred the money that Tala left for me to the bank near me in Tehran. I was grateful for Tala's generosity, something that I had refused to accept at different times when she offered to buy me expensive dresses like her own, or give me money if I needed it. Was Reza right that Tala was always trying to buy my love? Did she have a feeling she would die before me and wanted me to forgive her for the periods that she abandoned me? Of course, I would never know now.

Tavoos still didn't mention or ask about his father or mother. It could be that he had seen his parents' bloody faces, broken bodies, and his mind blocked them out completely. Whatever sorrows weighed on his heart, he only expressed in sudden bursts of tears.

Once, when we were eating a plate of rice and white fish and then ice cream with pieces of vanilla embedded in it, he said something in Russian.

"Honey, can you tell me in Farsi?"

He just shook his head.

After he finished eating, I gave him a shower, put on his pajamas, and tucked him in bed. I sat at the edge of the bed and read to him from a book I found at the children's store near the house.

> *Once upon a time, a little red fish lived with its mother in a stream that rose out of the rocky walls of a mountain and flowed into a valley. Their home was behind a black, moss-covered rock, under which both of them slept at night. From morning till evening, the mother and child swam together. Sometimes they joined other fish and rapidly darted in and out of the water. Early one morning before the sun rose, the fish woke the mother and said, "Mother, I want to talk to you." Half-asleep, the mother responded, "My dear child, this isn't the time to talk. Save your words for later. Wouldn't it be better to go swimming?" "No, Mother! I can't go swimming anymore. I must leave here." "Do you really have to leave?" "Yes, Mother, I must go." "Just a minute! Where do you want to go at this hour of the morning?" "I want to go to see where the stream ends. You know, Mother, I've been wondering where the end of the stream is . . . I haven't been able to think about anything else . . .*

He listened with attention, though I wasn't sure of how much of it he understood.

In the morning, at breakfast, I watched a TV program with him that he liked: *Agha Bache* (*Mr. Child*). Children danced with puppets, sang with them, sat with one who acted as a teacher, and they drew pictures together on pads and the best one was given a prize.

A little later I took him to Mellat Park and let him float paper boats on the lake and then to the zoo across from the park.

Gradually, I furnished his room with items appropriate for his age.

But most of the money I was able to take out was absorbed in providing professional care for him. He was often upset and burst into tears, still suffering from the trauma. Did he remember the car swaying, his mother screaming, "Stop, stop," and then the car crashing into something? Waking up in an unfamiliar room with a nurse standing next to him. Him saying, "I want Mother." Did he also ask for his father? What did he remember most clearly from his time with Maxim?

Once a week, I took him to a child psychologist affiliated with Azadi Hospital where Tala was taken to after the accident.

Once a week, I also took him to a physical therapist as he had a limp.

Perhaps due to the trauma and being bilingual, his speech was sometimes jumbled, incoherent, and I took him to a speech therapist a few times a week.

In the fall, I would register him at the private nursery school on Jamaly Avenue, a few blocks from the house.

Sometimes he would lie on his bed, silent, just looking at the ceiling. Is he trying to recall his life with Tala and Anton, wondering what happened to them? Since he never talked about them, I had no way of knowing. But after I told her about Tavoos's past, the pediatrician I took him to said, "He seems to have some amnesia, which often happens after trauma."

Once, looking pensive, Tavoos asked me in articulate Farsi, "Are you going to give me away?"

"No, my darling Tavoos, you will always be with me."

I felt I had found a baby I had lost. Once, when Mum and Baba took me and Tala to Ramsar for vacation, I lost my watch on the beach. It was a birthday present from our parents, one for me and one for Tala. Tala, who was wearing an identical watch, looked with me to find mine. We searched for it everywhere, under rocks and shells, but there was no sign of it. The following day we returned to the beach with Mum, and miraculously, there was the watch at the edge of a pile of sand, its blue band glistening in the sunlight.

"It must have been in the water and a wave brought it back," Mum said. It was still working, as it was waterproof. Even finding a small belonging I had lost was exhilarating.

Thinking of that brought back my loss of Mum. Had she been alive when Tala and I were older, our choices would have been different, I was sure. She would have encouraged us to study hard so that we could get scholarships to good schools abroad. Then we would have the freedom that girls in those countries did, and perhaps Tala wouldn't have fallen into Anton's trap.

Sometimes, I wished I had something I could take refuge in that would envelop me in peace. It was helpful that, gradually, Tavoos was coming out of himself, showing open affection for me. He put his head on my chest and his arms around me and asked me for things with less hesitation.

Once as I was walking him back home from his school, he looked pensive. He suddenly asked, "Am I going back to that place?"

"No, my darling Tavoos, you never have to go there again."

A touch of a smile came over his face.

I wondered if his reference to "that place" was Mercy Home or wherever Maxim had taken him. I decided not to ask him, not to delve into what could only upset him more.

At night, after Tavoos went to sleep, I sat in bed and, in the light of Grandmother's burgundy-colored lamps, wrote in the notebook I had kept for a long time. I hoped all of the conflicts and unanswered questions in my life would find shape and meaning if I wrote about them.

# Chapter 36

D ays went by, and Reza was still waiting for the newspaper to close down so that he could join us without threat from Hossein. I talked to him only on the phone.

Finally, what I hoped for happened. The postman in Abyaneh had noticed the four men working in the isolated house, heard the sound of the printer, and became suspicious. He reported them to the *Basij*. They were lucky the *Basij* let them go, but they were forbidden to stay and work there. Then Hossein decided to stop publishing the newspaper and gave up his office in Tehran.

When Reza arrived, I introduced him to Tavoos, just by his name, thinking later I would tell him he is in place of his father now, that he would love him like a son. Reza picked him up and held him to his chest and kissed him. A faint smile came over Tavoos's face.

After Reza put him down, he ran into his room and began to look through a book I recently bought for him. It was called *Moonlight*, and the words were filled with hopeful ideas. He liked me to read it to him, and he had already memorized some of the passages.

Now, more cautious because of Tavoos being in our care, Reza went back to his teaching in the private boys' high school in Tehran, was hired to work full-time, and stopped trying to publish articles in other radical underground newspapers that would be receptive to them. I resumed doing some knitting for Best Baby Clothes and made some outfits and sweaters for Tavoos.

Reza and I made an agreement that we would set aside Tavoos's inheritance, once it was resolved, for his own expenses—schools, college, and perhaps a higher degree beyond college.

Tavoos's room, which I furnished with appropriate items, stood between Reza's and my bedroom and the living room. The other rooms were left for guests staying overnight, some of them Tavoos's friends, some Reza's friends, mainly Abbas when he visited Tehran. Reza and

Abbas resumed their old conversations about the injustice all around us. Reza also sometimes sheltered journalists in hiding. I felt anxious about this but approved of it at the same time.

I often thought about what profession Tavoos would have when he grew up. I hoped one that wouldn't put him at risk.

I was able to resume my friendships, mainly with Afsaneh, who was back in Tehran. The aching loneliness I felt in Abyaneh was lifted, but still, at times I felt pangs of loss, and at moments felt diminished that Tala was no longer a part of me.

I didn't see Simin. She left with her husband and son to Khazvin for her husband's job. She wasn't there during the adoption process I went through. I was not eager to strike up a friendship with her, to take Tavoos and her son for walks in the park. It would be more than I could bear to take Tala's place, even in friendship with Simin.

I was now trying to turn the notes I scribbled into a novel. I had no hope that it would get published, just as Tala's paintings may never be exhibited in a gallery. I had taken some of them out of the storage room and hung them on the walls. That is one advantage that a painter has over a writer—at least I could exhibit the paintings in our own home.

Weeks and months went by, and Tavoos was in the first grade in the school just five blocks from our house. I always made sure to come home on time for his return. He walked back with a classmate who lived a few doors from our house. He came in, flushed and excited about all sorts of things that had happened—what one teacher said, what one friend had done. Then he flung his school bag into his room and ran out to join his friends playing in the dead-end street nearby. The signs of trauma he went through had gradually faded. Only occasionally he became pensive and withdrawn.

One morning, I had dropped him off at his school, something I still liked to do though it was safe for him to go there by himself. I was turning to go back home when I saw Afsaneh walking in my direction.

After greeting me with her usual warmth, she said, "Why don't we sit in a café and talk? Have you been to Ivan Café? It was just opened. It isn't far from here. We can walk to it. I'm off from work today." Since she had returned home after getting her architecture degree, she had been working in the city planning office.

At the café, we asked for a table overlooking the courtyard, which had a bed of flowers at its center and potted plants set in different spots. A record was playing violin music.

As in most newly opened cafés, the customers were young, dressed in Western styles, boys wearing jeans, girls barely covering their hair. After we ordered tea and pastries, I told her about Tala's death and me getting custody of Tavoos.

Her expression was intense, a combination of sadness and happiness for me. "I know how hard it must be for you to have lost your sister—whatever resentment you had toward her must have receded."

I nodded in agreement and told her that was why I wasn't interested in doing a DNA test. It wouldn't be easy to go to another country to get it. But it was mainly because I didn't want to know; if I knew with certainty, my memories of Tala would be tainted.

"I am not curious to know who my biological parents were. Remember, we talked about it."

"Yes, I remember."

I asked her to tell me about herself now. She was living alone in the same apartment building I did after Grandmother died and before I met Reza and we moved in together. She said she had no desire to marry or have children. She valued her independence and was happy to have full control of her daily life. She had a boyfriend she secretly dated, and that was enough for her.

We talked and talked until I had to go home and wait for Tavoos to return at his lunch break. We promised to see each other often.

After we parted, our conversation lingered with me. I admired her for her independence. I was still not a whole person standing on my own feet. I was tied to Tala by memories; I couldn't imagine how I would survive without that connection to her, even though I had Reza and Tavoos now. I knew I had to get on with my life, without feelings of loss and free-floating, unfocused guilt.

One morning an urgency came over me to look through the last few boxes in the storage room. I went to the rooms on the other side of the courtyard. There was one box I hadn't noticed last time. I mainly found childhood items we didn't want to discard—two pink-and-white blankets our grandmother knitted for us and a few large rag dolls. Another box was filled with different old documents. I took that to the dining room and spread the contents on the table. One was a note that she might have wanted me to see one day. There was no mention of Dr. Semnani in it.

*I can't stop thinking that I did take the baby next to you and moved mine toward you. It haunts me. Then rescue workers arrived and they assumed the alive boy was mine and the dead one yours. I rationalized that your marriage would survive the blow of losing a child, whereas mine would only grow more nightmarish. I want you to get custody of Tavoos if something happens to me. I welcome dying.*

A sickening sensation overwhelmed all my thoughts and emotions. I wished I could make the words disappear like the ones written on a toy, where by removing the top plastic layer, they wouldn't be there anymore.

After a moment I managed to read on.

*"Oh, a dead child here."*
*"It must belong to my sister; my poor sister lost her child."*

How could she possibly have had the presence of mind, under the shock of the earthquake, half buried in debris, to know which baby belonged to her and which to me? It was a dark poisonous flower, sprouting from the bed of her guilt.

On one of my walks a few days before, passing the Pahlavan Mental Clinic, I saw a patient standing behind the fence and screaming, "Look at the rain, you're going to get wet," while bright sunlight was shining. Maybe I too was imagining things. I never lost my baby. Tavoos was my baby, and Reza his father.

I looked at the words in the letter again. I was struck by the handwriting being uncannily similar to mine, as if I wrote the letter myself. I took a pen and a piece of paper from the desk and began to write, to see if I remembered my handwriting correctly. It was identical to the one in the letter. Had she practiced my handwriting, or did it gradually become like mine? Then I wondered: does Tavoos have any of Anton in him? No, none of his looks or mannerisms.

I took the letter to Reza, who was at his desk. I told him about what was in it. He said, "Let me look at it."

He read it; his face contorted even though I already had told him what was in it. He tossed the letter on the table without making a comment.

"Isn't that written in my handwriting?" I asked.

"What are you talking about?"

"It's like I wrote the letter myself."

He picked up the letter and looked at it again. "No, there are differences, small but still there."

So Tala must have written it.

On a Friday, when schools and many offices were closed, Reza took Tavoos out to the nearby Ferdowsi Park, and they returned with Tavoos holding a bright yellow kite in the shape of a butterfly.

"Roya, look what I have." He addressed me as Roya, not Mum or Mother. Whether he fully accepted me as a mother, I didn't want to ask.

"How nice." I leaned over and kissed him.

Looking at Tavoos and Reza together, again I marveled at how similar they looked. He not only had Reza's curly brown hair, but also his high forehead and some of his expressions. There was nothing of Anton in his looks and manner.

"We flew it together in the park," Tavoos said.

"We'll do it again if the weather permits. Would you like that?" Reza asked him.

Tavoos nodded and then wandered away to his room, carrying the kite with him.

That night in bed with Reza, I asked him, "Will you tell me something honestly?"

"Of course, my dear," he said, putting his arm around me.

"Did something ever happen between you and Tala?"

"You are still thinking that way?"

"I still feel it's odd that she called you at your office number without telling me."

He more or less repeated what he said before. "She was distraught. Wanted to ask forgiveness for talking you into going to Rey with her."

Not fully believing that, I asked, "I still wonder if she was trying to start up something with you."

"Haven't we talked about this already?"

"Tavoos looks so much like you."

"That doesn't mean anything. You suspected that Tala might have taken your baby instead of her own, who was dead. We could find out with a DNA test. But we would have to take a trip out of Iran, go to Turkey or another country."

"I guess there's no point to it." My speculations and doubts needed to remain unanswered or else I would have no peace with my memories of Tala.

Secrecy continues to be a part of Reza's and my life. True, he has stopped working for the newspaper, but I am not sure that he isn't involved in other kinds of activities, like distributing pamphlets or getting help from the journalists loyal to him. I have seen articles in *Emrooz* magazine that remind me of Reza's ideas and words.

In my writing, I have tried to make sense of what happened to Tala and me, two girls so identical that people couldn't tell us apart, and yet we ended with different destinies. Again, I fall back to Grandmother's belief that we were created alike so that one could carry on for the other if she happened to die. Yes, I am carrying on for Tala, as a mother to Tavoos.

I feel comfort that the sights and sounds of the house have remained the same as in Tala's and my childhood days. Daily, the voices of vendors flow into the house. There is the jingling coming from the vendor on the back of a donkey, carrying merchandise in a sack with bells sewn onto it. Birds carry on their songs, and the nightingales perch on the courtyard's rafters. I hear voices and sounds of activities from the street or the adjacent houses—a child crying over a lost doll, a boy bouncing a ball against a wall, the alley cat mewing.

Uncle visits whenever he can get away from work. His presence, his warmth, compensates somewhat for my losses. I have reached out to neighbors, and they often drop in with their children when Tavoos is home. I serve tea in my favorite china cups, left by Grandmother, the ones with gold rims and red pomegranate designs on their sides.

As I write this in my notebook, the living room is filled with the pale glow of the autumn afternoon sunlight coming in through the tall French window. A few dry leaves dance in the air with the breeze; some drift against the window and then float downward.

It is Friday and Tavoos is off from school. As we eat breakfast, we watch the daily morning program, *Hello, Iranian People*, that for some reason Tavoos likes. Different people ranging from nutritionists to artists and even one mullah talk in a group setting. When that program ends, we switch to IRNN, a news channel that has world news in English running at the bottom of the screen. I am trying to teach Tavoos English in case, when he is older, he wants to go to college in America.

After I turn off the TV, Reza suggests taking Tavoos to Soheila's house to fly kites with his cousins. Reza doesn't seem unhappy that we've adopted Tavoos. His family's former disapproval of me is now buried in the love they feel for their only brother. Monir, who never shared their unhappiness that Reza wasn't able to have children because of me, has become a friend. She chose a different path from her sisters, never marrying. Now she is going to Efteghar University, majoring in sociology. She wants to teach high school. She shares the house that went to her after her mother died with two other older single students. She has developed a self-assured aura and dresses mainly in jeans and T-shirts under her *manteau*. She is attractive and talks in a knowledgeable way. At her university, a professor is interested in marrying her. But she says, "I've gotten used to leading my own life." She is similar to my friend Afsaneh in many ways.

So often memories of Tala, us falling into the cavity, and miscarriages all come to me like a nightmare. What is real is Tavoos, and Reza and me taking care of Tavoos as our own child. When I wake in the morning and hear Tavoos carrying on activities in his room, I know I am not dreaming. I have come to a state of mind where I prefer not knowing everything, believing and not believing everything that happened since that day when Tala and I went to Rey Castle. Everything comes to me like a mirage, changing shape as if reflecting in running water.

I look at the thick windowpane and I see an image reflected in it; it is of me. But then, maybe it is of Tala. Our images merge and become the same.

I imagine Tala and I in Mum's womb, one embryo, before it split, identical but in two bodies. What Grandmother told me comes to me often.

"Why are there two of us, instead of one? What if one of us dies?"

"Then the one who is alive will carry on what the other can't anymore."

## Biographical Note

Nahid Rachlin went to Columbia University Writing Program on a Doubleday-Columbia Fellowship and then went on to Stanford University's writing program on a Wallace Stegner Fellowship. Her publications include a memoir, *Persian Girls* (Penguin); four novels, *Jumping Over Fire* (City Lights), *Foreigner* (W.W. Norton), *Married to a Stranger* (E.P.Dutton); a novella, *Crowd of Sorrows* (Kindle Singles); and a short story collection, *Veils* (City Lights). Her individual short stories have appeared in many individual magazines, including *Solstice Literary Magazine*, *The Virginia Quarterly Review*, *Prairie Schooner*, *Southern Humanities Review*, *Redbook*, and *Shenandoah*. One of her stories was adopted by Symphony Space, "Selected Shorts," and was aired on NPR around the country, and three stories were nominated for the Pushcart Prize. Her work has received favorable reviews in major magazines and newspapers and translated into Portuguese, Polish, Italian, Dutch, German, Czech, Arabic, and Persian. She has been interviewed on NPR stations such as *Fresh Air* (Terry Gross), for *Poets and Writers* magazine, and AWP's *Writer's Chronicle*. She has written reviews and essays for the *New York Times*, *Newsday*, the *Washington Post,* and the *Los Angeles Times*. Other grants and awards she has received include the Bennet Cerf Award, PEN Syndicated Fiction Project Award, and a National Endowment for the Arts grant. She has taught creative writing at Barnard College, Yale University, and at a wide variety of writer's conferences, including the Paris Writers Conference, Geneva Writers Conference, and Yale Writers Conference. She has been a judge for several fiction awards and competitions, among them the Grace Paley Prize in Short Fiction, the Maureen Egen Writers Exchange Award, the Katherine Anne Porter Fiction Prize, and the Teichmann Fiction Prize. She gives readings and talks at a wide variety of places, including bookstores, high schools, colleges, MFA programs, and libraries. For more please visit her website www.nahidrachlin.com.